In
Search
Of a Soul

Other books by
Dannie C Hill

Tyler Hill's Decision

Coming soon

Outer World- Prairie

In
Search
Of
A
Soul

By

Dannie C Hill

Small Mountain Publishing

ISBN-13:
978-0-9826924-2-4
ISBN-10
0-9826924-2-0

Published by Small
Mountain Publishing
Houston, Texas
http://smallmountainpub.com

Cover and interior design
by
Small Mountain Publishing

Cover photograph by
Robert Ranson
**Robert Ranson
Photography**

Edited by
Sherry Ruschell

First printing in the United
States of America

This is a work of fiction

About the Author:

Dannie was born in Mooresville, North Carolina. He served in the U.S. Army in a warzone. Dannie has traveled around the world and lived in the Marshall Islands for two years. He now lives in Thailand and Texas. Most of his writing is done in Thailand where the sounds of English are quieted and his daydreams can come to life.

For more about the author and his other books go to

http://smallmountainpub.com

This book is dedicated to my wife, Julee, and my three children, Jason, Suginda and Daniel, for helping to make my life happy and good. Thank you for love and companionship through the years.

And to my mother, Dorothy. She has been my strength and guiding light all through my years!
I love you all!

Return

Search the ocean
for a soul not found.
Green the color,
of a forgotten life.
A child to take,
a child to give.
Dark pools to hold;
a promise of hope.
A ship carries
an empty husk.
Until dark pools and child,
return a soul.

dch

In Search of a Soul
By Dannie C Hill

Chapter 1

#

I could hear the soft crunch of rocky sand beneath my black combat boots and feel the weight of the pack on my back. I looked over and in the moonlight could see Moe five feet away and moving with me. Looking ahead I saw a cluster of dwellings about one hundred yards away. Moe signaled a stop and moved to my right ear.

He said, "Be alert. There are five targets but there may be others with them. We take the five out and then bug out."

I gave him thumbs up and we moved out, while lowering my night vision monocular eyepiece. I double-checked my weapon. It was set on single-fire and Moe would be set on three-round burst. If we got into it, this would stagger our reloading. I had three small M67 round grenades clipped to my vest and a Kay-bar strapped to my upper left thigh. When we were within thirty yards of the buildings we clicked on our comm gear but remained silent.

Suddenly arrows of light streaked out of the night towards us. There were at least four gunmen using red tracer rounds. I was behind a small boulder and followed the trail of fire back to its source. I aimed, heard the spurt of my silenced weapon and saw an opponent drop. I moved to the next and could hear Moe's weapon spurting out three at a time. The ambush was poorly designed. They must have had some kind of motion detector but only moments to move into a position. No planning in this or Moe and I would have been dead or wounded at once.

Four were down when I heard the distinct thud of bullets striking flesh and then heard Moe say in my earpiece, "I'm hit but still moving."

As he continued to fire, I moved closer to the houses and around to the left to stay out of Moe's line. There was a stone outcrop near the wall of one of the houses. I moved between it and the wall, bounced up for a quick look and saw the last man stooping under a window. I pulled the pins on two grenades and lobbed them towards the enemy, then raised my weapon, flicked the lever to fully automatic and depressed the trigger. There was a low, long blurb and a tongue of fire and the enemy spouted blood like a fountain in an Italian piazza. Then the grenades blew the wall out of the house. I reloaded and listened. Dead silence.

I moved along the wall and just as I passed the outcrop a body fell on me from behind, taking me to the ground and knocking my weapon from my grip. It was still attached to me by a lanyard but my hand went to my knife and I pulled, twisted, blocked a knife stabbing in at me and plunged my blade into the enemy. I twisted the blade out and rolled over, listening for anyone else. Over my earpiece Moe said in a strained voice that he didn't see anyone moving and we needed to be on our horse.

I could hear small breathing coming from my opponent and felt for movement. The man was very small and his breathing was high pitched with fear. I pulled out my flashlight and shielded the beam.

The face of a child lit up before my eyes. It was a girl, maybe ten years old. Her startling green eyes stared at me in terror. I checked her wound and saw there was no hope, so I tried to calm her with words she would understand.

Her green-eyed stare turned to hate and she whispered in her dialect, "You killed my father." She died and her eyes remained wide as they stared back at me.

I started to lose it but over my earpiece Moe said, "Dougy, I'm hit pretty bad and I hear a vehicle coming. We've got to get out of here now! Help me, please."

I broke my gaze with the child but knew those eyes were burned into my brain. I moved over to Moe, quickly tied off his upper right thigh and left shoulder wounds. He was bleeding but I had staunched the flow and I could now hear the truck approaching. I lifted him up on my shoulder and moved out. We had six hours of normal moving to our extract point but with Moe injured it would take much longer.

It took two days to reach the extract point and as soon as I knew Moe was safe— the green eyes consumed my mind... And then there was nothing...

#

The boat moved through the deep, crystal blue water; its bow leaped as if anticipating a cool drink of iced lemonade after a long run in the burning noonday sun. I sat in the cockpit under the shade of the mainsail and a constant breeze thick with salt. I was cooled by the thin sheen of perspiration the tropics required for comfort. We were on a southwesterly heading, going to nowhere in particular. I had four or five days to contemplate my next tack. Somewhere about six hundred miles ahead I would have to choose, but that was at least two more days of idle thought before I would bring out my dartboard and then another two days before I would put my plan into effect.

When I say "we" I include my boat, *Tirak*, in all my decisions. She — yes, she was most assuredly a *she* and was my lifeline. She had ingrained her sleek, boyish figure into me from the start. She sparkled and moaned like a new-found lover and made me cling to her like a mate of the soul.

In light to medium winds she would chitter or clang and speak to me through sensitive zones such as her wheel and rudder or even a halyard or stay to make her demands known. In strong winds her standing rigging would sing to me of her needs or joy or of her demand to redirect my manipulations. Her halyards and sheets would thrum in ecstasy or consternation, depending on the mood of her world. Her demands were simple— "Take care of me or I will leave you and you will perish without me."

For the past ten years I had traveled through life's stream looking with anticipation for the end. I can't explain why I had this desire, or perhaps lack of desire, except to say that I had found no lasting enjoyment or, to a greater extent, no purpose for my existence.

The past five years I had been aboard *Tirak* almost full time, never stopping in any one place for more than a few months but

~ 3 ~

generally for only a few weeks. I felt no pity for myself. In fact, I felt very little. Over the years I had trained my mind to forego the undulations of life. I had watched others continue down life's road, shuffling their feet until forced to lift them a little higher to pass over a bump. My road now had no bumps or dips to cause course corrections.

In my solitude I had nothing but time for review and can't see where it all started, which leads to the conclusion that it must have happened at birth. It's a dismal thought but solitude had taught me to lay my emotions aside, except for brief interludes, and keep them packed away in the recesses of my mind. Ten years ago my emotions were so erratic they left me with two choices; live or die, with dying being the preferred of the two. At that time I understood why there was a suicide hotline.

Because of what faith I had, I couldn't choose the easy option but instead began to shut down those urges that raced through me, good and bad, and chose solitude as a means to drift rudderless on the stream. The end holds no fear for me and it would come in its own time. I didn't have any pity for myself... It was just the way it was. I did often look forward to the next step and hoped, maybe beyond hope, that there would be more.

I had on a few occasions sat down to make a list of the good and bad of my life, but my pencil never touched paper in fear of what I would see. I had memories of interesting men who I would have liked to have called friends but, as with women, I had an inordinate fear or knowledge that I would expose my failures to the light of day and those I came close to would see through the haze of my facade and turn their heads to hide their smiles.

With men there was no sexual desire, only friendship, but I knew it would come down to a contest of testosterone and I would fail miserably, not knowing when to turn it off. I was not a big man but from past work and sailing single-handed I was strong and balanced. One of my many fears was I would hurt, physically, someone intent in only playing a game of who had the biggest set. Something in my past told me to back away from those situations because I was capable of causing serious harm without thinking of the consequences. I really didn't know where that came from because, as far as I knew, I had never caused that kind of pain before. It lay there like a golden-eyed wolf deciding if it was hungry. I had kept it fed on solitude and it was satisfied.

Another of my fears was a block of five years of my past that was gone. When I tried to approach it, I came to a locked steel door. The face of the lock was imprinted with crossed scimitars above a skull. I had made no attempt to see beyond, afraid of what might be there. I had learned to curb my curiosity and it no longer disturbed my thoughts.

I think my final fear was women. I knew within me at least one held the key to unlock the chains that bound me. As much as I needed their comfort and touch, I could never, even growing up, get within a few feet of them without stumbling over my feet and blurting out something that would always prove how incapable I was of giving them what they sought. Women lived in my daydreams, not as toys but as companions. I knew there was one who would be the answer I sought but I had no confidence to seek her out or even make the attempt. Like many people, I sat by the door and waited for her to knock. I sometimes thought she had come and gone.

Tirak was the only thing I had been able to put my incomplete soul into and she took me in without questions and only demanded my love and care. It was hard for me to believe but she provided me with soft, warm, silky smooth females in need of solace. On those rare occasions I was able to lift myself out of the morass of mediocrity which my life had become and approach my daydreams. Women make this world go round and the sad part was that I was not a part of that world.

Tirak also provided male companionship as well. Often sailors of like mind but also interesting men from other walks of life were drawn to her. They too raised me from my level floor with warmth and friendship that lasted for a few days, until I slipped our mooring and moved out into the blue.

Of all the people or things I had clung to in my life, my darling boat came the closest to satisfying my needs, other than the sexual drive built into my male genes. Even then she had proven a wonderful stimulant and forgiving lover by providing for my needs when in port.

Occasionally, before I even felt the desire to indulge in the one service my darling couldn't provide, I would hear the soft footsteps of a rare flower tapping along the dock and stop with a sigh. This sweet Rose or fragrant Jasmine or even beautiful weed would look down the hatch and softly hail to the man who owned such a beauty. They were always sure it was a man and not a woman because *Tirak* had the aroma and presence of a female that was caressed by the kind hands of a man. How they knew I was alone or even if they cared was a mystery between them and *Tirak*.

When at last I presented myself topside, I could see my looks, age and style had only a small part to play in the meeting. My boat seemed to pick out the one that needed to be touched, held and comforted, as they would offer the same to me. The mystery was her secret and all I could do was fulfill my obligations to her.

Mind you— this wasn't an everyday occurrence and often my short stays in one place or another were met with the near solitude of the sea. When *Tirak* did choose a delicate flower for me I was under great obligation to provide what comfort as I was able.

I am, each and every time, surprised by this undeserved attention. I cherish each encounter until the sea beckoned me.

My mindset and that of most single-handed blue-water sailors was not so much the desire for solitude but from a fear of others. Of course, there were a few who set out to prove their manhood or womanhood by— and I say this with a smile— defeating and defying the great oceans. I say it with a smile because it can't be done. As in a good boat, you were merely allowed their pleasures for as long as they liked, and like the evening lilies of this desperate world, their services were never free.

As I was saying, I had enjoyed the company of a few women and even spent long, laughing days and nights in their warm company. It always took me a few days to get my land-legs and if the lady wished to prowl the hinterlands of wherever I was, she must wait until my head and stomach agree to cohabitate under a temporary truce.

At sea the dashing about or the undulating or even the dead calm was forever in sync with all my body parts, but stepping on land or even mooring dashed one of the ingredients of my stability to the deck and it refused to rise, except in a froth, until I allowed it several days of rest.

Now, if the lady could wait the allotted period for my full attention, then life was good. *Tirak* had a rare ability to choose almost unerringly the one person that would give and receive benefits of a temporary union. Age didn't seem to play a part in the choice, nor beauty, but I had yet to be disappointed.

I would like to tell you that I had an ability to love and did love anyone I was with. The problem with this ability or incapacity, if you will, was that it flows just as my need to sail away ingratiated *Tirak's* need to be gone. When at last I felt the pull of the sea and the needs of my boat I took the woman with us on a few days of sailing and we anchored in the afternoons in a secluded bay to say our farewells. Some few who could draw words from me were often surprised at my ability to articulate my feelings of life. After we parted I would most often suffer for a day or two but the sea could carry any of the castings of my mind into its dark reaches.

I would like to call it love but in truth it was not love but fulfillment and desire. I treated each one I had the honor to receive as the one and only who had captured my attention. I left each one with some small feeling of regret, on both our parts. I knew this to be true on my part. My search for true love had atrophied in the knowledge that I didn't deserve it and was frightened of it. I had met one who would have completed my daydreams, but she was called away.

In the arms of a woman I was not the same being that houses my soul. Without *Tirak*, I would rarely have had the courage to pursue the interaction of a relationship; once again, not from lack of need but from fear of intercourse, in which I would be the bumbling fool with no words to maintain my charade. *Tirak* brought them to me but after the first touch, smile and pleasure, I was off and running, until the fear rose up from the depths of me and drove me back to sea again and again.

I knew I was not the only male of my species to live in the clef of depression and seek the clef of redemption but that alone brought no comfort. We who were the hunters and gatherers were put asunder by this modern world in which only mindless words spring forth, or in my case choked, to impress the objects of our need and success.

I turned off my mindset, if only for a moment, to check my heading and see to the needs of my *Tirak*. We were in a following sea with the wind astern and I watched the waves come forth to caress her backside with a smooth firm stroke as they go forth to find another delicious bottom to entice. The waves, made up of hundreds of its reflections, sprinkled the sparkling light of day across the clear, depthless blue as the sun sought its resting place to the west. The clouds captured and then released the light and reflections into a spectrum from rose at their forefront to medium gray at their stern. Their march did not match the airfoil of the gleaming sails of *Tirak* and fell slowly behind. There would be days in which they raced past and others when they hid completely and the clear azure sky was the only apex of that day's canvas.

A thousand miles from land there was little chance of encounter, but woe to the sailor that lets the ocean be his protector for she would abide you but only to her whims. *Tirak* had radar and the unsightly radar reflector ball attached to her spreaders that took the stealth out of her travels. She wanted to be noticed and painted an eerie green to the behemoths and even others of her kind. She neither wanted nor required contact and by putting on a bright face she kept her solitude safe. Along with the search of my eyes and feelings, we avoided contact.

The sun touched the horizon and started its capitulation to the night. On this day, as if to give a final thrust, the green flair popped to signal surrender. The stars, slowly at first but then with a mobs reaction, jumped upon the stage to celebrate the conquest. With weather clear and reports from satellites good, I did not reduce her sail area but let her drive on in delight to touches of her lover and slice her way in pursuit of the horizon.

I scanned the sea once more and descended into my home and prepared a meal and enjoyed a glass of brandy. Later, I would again take up station on deck to enjoy the delights of the Milky Way and the comfort of a good cigar. It was not yet time for my mind to stray to my daydreams.

My meals were simple, without effort. I didn't set my flying-fish net last evening so a can of beans, day-old steamed rice and hot sauce would adorn my table. For dessert, a strong cheddar cheese with vacuum-packed crackers was the finish. A meal set for a man in search of nourishment and not epicurean delight.

I checked my charts and navigational equipment and saw that the sea had not interposed her will upon *Tirak* and we were heading to the place intended. I switched on the radar, made a long-range search for impediments and found I was alone for at least fifty miles. I switched the range to ten miles, set the system to automatic alert and the timer for a check every thirty minutes. This conserved my power and allowed my GPS system to keep track of my position, address the heading and provide steering information to the autopilot. I did enjoy hand steering, especially at night, but an autopilot or self-steering gear was a must when sailing alone.

When hand steering I glance at the compass from time to time but use the stars as reference, giving me a surreal sense of ancient times. There my imagination could allow my soul to live in the time I knew I was meant to live. Even with my ancient soul I was dependent upon the modern equipment that truly kept me informed. One might think that sailing a thousand miles from any landfall I could forgo worry about where I was, if even for a little while. In the blue, currents, prevailing winds and wave motion were not things you could leave to chance. In the days of old, many ships' crews were lost to the quirks of the world.

Trapped in the wrong current, with no wind or wrong wind and waves, a crew could find themselves learning the hard way that the sea only tolerates us landlings for a short burst in infinity, especially if we know not where we go. Ships were found, back then and even in modern times, devoid of crew but in perfect condition, except for lack of food and water. I thought about this on occasion and know I would prefer being cradled in the cold arms of the sea rather than bloated and cooked on deck after an agonizing death by dehydration. This was not something I thought of often, as I had complete trust in *Tirak* to carry me out of harm's way, even when my ignorance fought her to do as I demanded. I tried to mediate my ignorance by watching her closely and feeling her needs. She had always served me as I served her.

I enjoyed the night at sea. Visibility was limited to hundreds of light years, if one looked to the stars, and a few miles of moonlight if looking upon the incessant waters. In a following sea with a brisk wind the rollers marched in rows high above the sight line, only to lift you for a look at your next massive visitor and then gently lower you along its backside as it slipped past.

After I checked my darling for the night passage she whispered that all was well. I then lit my cigar to fill my lungs with the stimulating poison and retard my night vision. It was a routine and, as any blue-water sailor knew, life was a routine with the occasional moments of stark terror or ethereal mysteries or even acute beauty of the sea. Routines repeated day after day enhanced and hustled time. Once started the only conclusion was another day had passed and one hundred fifty or more miles had crept by. As long as *Tirak* hums or sighs, all was well and she would contently go on for days with only mild caresses. There was joy in routine for me as it required no hasty decisions or conversations that might catch me in the truth of my existence.

So my days and nights carried me on my way to a decision. Upon its arrival, I pulled my charts out to check the options before me. I could turn north and run with the wind abeam on my port side or I could turn more southerly and run with the wind abaft the starboard beam or even continue on this heading and make landfall in only two weeks. I was not ready for such a short passage so I looked to the possibilities and distances. I could run to the Marshalls or abeam reach to Palau.

I enjoyed the Marshall Islands. The people were far from pretty but their hearts were open and they allowed one to be one's own self in silence or laughter. I had never been to Palau but had read of the beauty of the islands and the openness of the people. In my reading I found that many of the smaller islands were made up of one or two family groups and peace was a way of life.

That was a common lifestyle in this region of the Pacific. Islands were often only a few miles long and basically circular in shape. Living on a piece of land that small to you and me had a way of taking aggression out of the gene pool. If one was filled with the need to progress and enhance, then one would soon find one's mind muddled into oblivion, casted into the sea and swimming until death overtook one. A small-islander might move to a place that would allow one to be drowned in progress.

Of all the islanders I had met living in another place, each and every one spoke of going back home to live the good, easy life but very few meant it and they digressed into society to become a part of the mob.

On the bigger islands people were more motivated and able to succeed in becoming almost continental. Many of these big island people reminded me of me, living in a world far too advanced and fast paced to satisfy the soul of the ancient that lived inside.

My decision was to turn north and make for the Marshalls. They were made up of many small islands of which a number were atolls. An atoll is a coral reef built on the ancient rim of an extinct volcano and its caldron a protected lagoon. One of the Marshalls was noted for having the world's largest lagoon. The atoll of Kwajalein had a lagoon that was more than seventy-five miles long at its widest point with a number of deep water entrances through the surrounding reef. I had worked there for a year several years before, and it was a very low-lying group of islands. It was a U.S. military test range for the missiles that could destroy the world.

That was not my destination. Five thousand people living on an island three and half miles long, half mile wide, and five and a half feet above sea level shrunk my soul. The next island in the atoll was Ebi, with some three thousand Marshallese crammed on the four hundred yard long piece of sandy reef. They were there to work the good life and dream of going home.

Other islands in the chain were more to my liking but were not meant for long stays. I would find one with a few families, fill my water tank and live with them for a week or two. I would visit several islands, until the blue called me back.

I continued my routine in anticipation of our new tack in two days. It was near dawn so I set my flying fish net on the windward side of the two forward sails in expectation of enjoying a breakfast meal of fresh winged fish. Lightly fried flying fish brings out the oils and the tangy taste of the meat. Add a chunk of Gouda cheese and strong coffee and it becomes a meal fit for a king. In truth, it was a good meal but few would classify it as a gourmet's delight.

I took my place in the stern and watched the curtain rise to the east; no clouds to obscure the main character as he peeked from behind the dark curtain of night. With his brightest smile, he throws forth the red spectrum as if he were a magician releasing fire from his fingertips. Reds matured to gold and then with nature and God's infinite touch, the day had begun and *Tirak* seems pleased with her part in the show. She gurgled at her stern, lapped at her bow and even nodded to her passing fans. A sudden burst of water and a flapping of wings on the foredeck announced breakfast had arrived. I hurried forward to the squeals and cheeps of the ocean's acrobats and I clapped to the dolphins that had herded this new flock to my deck. Today was a bountiful day as I gathered up twenty multicolored beauties, selected five for my pan, ten for the hunters and five to be freed for another chance at survival. The dolphins broke off long enough to gather the offerings and swooped back to ride the bow wave. At the stern, out of sight of the voracious mammals, I released the freed captives and headed down to the galley to sacrifice five to the plate.

After the wonderful meal I continued my routine of checking the running and fixed rigging. Next, adjustments were the sheets, sails, winches and the mass of other gear that was required to harness the power of the wind to propel my *Tirak* onward. At noon I went below and checked my position and recorded our day's run, one hundred eighty-seven miles of a straight line run. If we were close-hauled in the same conditions, *Tirak* would have made a similar run but perhaps only moving seventy miles closer to our destination.

In the heat of the afternoon I took my position in the cockpit to open my mind to the woes of my life. Depression was a learned way of life but in some families it was passed down like a legacy. I used to fight it with therapy but found for all the good that some doctors did the remission came from the tried and true method of finding the right drug that lifted you but not too much, negated the society one immersed one's self in and dulled the *give-a-damn* from life's trials and tribulations. Drugs were the key; all the talking, just a mere expensive pep talk. The drugs I kept under lock and key for the occasional lift; the talks of old I cast into the briny deep. I had found that depression is not such a bad thing taken in moderation.

It was the fertile ground of inspiration to the classic writers and revolutionaries. Even today hordes of writers, who had the answers to follies of the world, spilled forth their feelings on countless pages to which eager readers went in search of life that sinks below their own. They came away with a saddened joy and optimism that in the heap of life they stood not in the ooze of the foundation of society but somewhere within the mass.

I joined the former to inspire the latter by writing several books on how life should really be...A romantic adventure. I wrote in a simple, easy to read, too good to be true, no dictionary, style. My books became the *Jonathan Livingston Seagull* of the new century. That was how I came to my beloved *Tirak* and we had moved forward on our undulating world ever since. The depths of depression and my daydreams made me rich but *Tirak* saved my life or at the very least prolonged it.

I knew there was someone out there waiting to snatch me up as I sailed by or as I sat aboard waiting for my senses to learn to cohabitate when docked at some future port of call. She would come to me because I was not brave enough to seek her out on my own. *Tirak* had been given a task and she never shrank from her duty. I, like so many others, waited for the door to open which was never locked but slightly askew in its jamb. I had no idea how I would proceed when that day arrived or even if I would recognize what I was seeing but in my heart I knew *Tirak* would not let the tribute pass me by. I did believe that my chance had come and gone, but it was not to be.

Chapter 2

The hour had arrived for me to adjust our path and seek a new trail to the destination selected two days before. I took command of the wheel and made several long, sweeping turns of twenty degrees to either side of my heading just to feel the tightness of the steering gear and then eased *Tirak* over to a northerly beams reach. I winched the sheets on the jib and stay sail to take out the luff and then winched in the main to start the final trim. I heard a distinctive metallic ping and then another. I set the autopilot and went forward on the port side to examine the standing rigging. Standing rigging or stays were the steel cables that hold the mast in place. I saw several broken steel strains of the mast cable standing out and free. I had double steel cables for each run because of all the things you could lose on a sailboat and continue on, the mast was not one of them.

I listened to *Tirak* and heard mild distress. The rudder knocked twice. The mainsail snapped in displeasure and the anchor banged in its seat. I checked the anchor and found nothing amiss so I returned to the cockpit and continued to trim and balance her. An errant wave slapped the hull, sending water into my eyes, and as I cleared my sight I heard the steel *ping* again. I sat down to reconsider my actions. *Tirak* was complaining but her reasons were not clear. Because I had no specific reason to make for the Marshalls and to take the strain off the weakened mainstay, I decided to alter course for Palau.

As I swung her stern through the wind, jibed the main and foresails, I could feel *Tirak* sigh and become her old confident self, no knocks, pings or bumps in the night, only the swish of the sea and the hum of her rigging as she sings of her love for me.

This was the first time she had rebuffed my selection of ports. After I got to know her I could sense something special in her flow. At first I thought maybe my imagination was overcoming my reality but then when one was far from land and totally dependent on a machine, no matter how beautiful, one has two choices to make; treat the machine as an object or allow it to be heard as a being. I chose to listen and, to my joy and expectations, she became a *she*.

I had no idea of what was to come my way on this voyage but I was confident it was to my betterment. After satisfying her with a few tweaks to her firm, lithe body, I went below to change out the charts and pick up my secondary waypoints and change them to primary. I viewed a large chart of the empty sea ahead and could see no impediments. The natural currents and winds would allow me to stay on this tack for more than a week before I had to bring the wind a few points to starboard. The sat-weather charts showed no localized disturbances and I was in a seaway not normally high in traffic. My routine would change slightly but, as it always does, it would settle in by tomorrow evening. I took out my gourmet's delight for this evening's meal, macaroni and cheese with an infusion of hot sauce. Sous-chefs would gape in revulsion and show their fangs if asked to complete the entrée.

Now my routine was thrown asunder by anticipation; to what I know not, but it was coming and by our tack it had some 28 days to come to fruition. The number of days seemed significant. It was the cycle of the moon and the cycle of a woman. The moon seemed more likely in the middle of the ocean, sailing within the Trade winds, but my guesses and questions to *Tirak* were only met with a coquettish hum and no enlightenment was forthcoming. Still I looked to the sea, by eye and electronics.

I ran the diesel an extra two hours to bring my batteries to full power. Water tanks were three-quarters full but my seawater conversion tank was nearly empty. I decided to use an extravagant amount of power to press the salt, minerals and whatever through the filters to extract enough usable water to fill the small twenty-gallon tank. This water was for survival only as there was no pleasure in its taste. Tomorrow I would recharge the batteries and begin conservation. I would only operate nav equipment, radar and running lights, also perhaps navigation lights high on the mast, which would extend *Tirak*'s visual contact another ten miles at night. I tried to set my routine to maintain some semblance of normalcy but to no avail. I found my eyes scanning the sea, my ears listening for nuances in *Tirak*'s behavior and quelling the dreams that knocked insistently on my needs.

As I seemed to rush through my scattered routine, I could feel the flutters of panic hum within me. I considered unlocking the box where I hide or horde my chemical self in but resisted. I let the ultra-awareness come forth in measure to enhance and tune my frenzy.

By the next day, lack of sleep had dulled the electric highway and I began to settle into resonance and once more put my trust in *Tirak*. Her mood was joyous as she leapt and swished her tail on a heading of her choosing. I had passed her test of devotion but what was her reward for me? I began to anticipate Palau and its mountainous peaks and lagoons of its group. A new adventure awaited, with fresh sights and possibly a guide to the island's nature and sensuality that only a woman could give me, which I suddenly had a craving for.

A woman of the islands with her laid-back love and sense of living could very well put my mind in order and prepare me for my next bout of solitude. I was beginning to think I had put too much into this unexpected intervention. Perhaps it was *Tirak* applying her will just for the sake of reminding me of our symbiotic relationship. If anything, it has been most interesting and given me a lesson in self-control.

I finally gave in to the need for sleep and lay down on a cushioned bench in the cockpit and fell into a deep dream-filled sleep that expunged the tensions that I created in an effort to foresee the future.

#

It was the Northern Marianas on a small island called Rota; I had moored for two days. I set a wind scoop in the fore hatch and enjoyed the pleasing breeze flowing through the main salon. My body was almost in harmony as I spent more and more time ashore but returned, alone, each night to her, my boat.

I had met a lovely woman or, more precisely, she met me while I walked the shoreline. She seemed very shy but determined. She had seen *Tirak* and wondered if I might allow her to visit my boat. Somewhere in my mumbling I must have agreed but all I could remember were her eyes. There was a trilling of anxiety in her voice and I took it to mean she had no real interest in me. She kept her body covered and would look at me for only small moments. She wanted, or at least it seemed to me, to say something more but her nerves were at their limits. We spent a total of one hour together and three different times she began to say something but she would blush furiously and stop. Her eyes would glisten in fear and I had no idea how to handle this but tried to speak without losing myself in those dark, liquid eyes. We parted in a rush of heated embarrassment and I expected never to see her again but the next evening while I took my recovering senses for a walk through the night market I saw her watching me from afar. I tried to go to her but by the time I arrived at the spot where I saw her, she was gone. Was this some kind of game in which I didn't know the rules?

The next morning I was moving *Tirak* to the dock to take on fresh water and supplies I had ordered. I would spend the day replacing a circuit board in the radar electronics and then checking the mechanics of the radar sweep. A noise had caught my attention and I needed to find its source.

The tap-tap-tap of small feet approached with a confidence that was not the normal precursor of a lady in need.

The shoes stopped and "Permission to come aboard?" came forth from a tiny but sultry voice.

I answered with a, "Come ahead with shoes off," and returned to my work on the innards of the radar electronics. I was curious but electrical pursuits were not something I could put aside unfinished if I hoped to have a working piece in the end.

Without turning I told the woman who *Tirak* had encouraged to visit, to make herself comfortable and make a drink or just have a look around until I was finished with my work. I heard the rustle of clothing against smooth skin as she moved about the cabin. She went to the galley, opened the reefer and poured a glass of juice and continued her tour. As she brushed past me on her way aft to the *stateroom* I briefly turned my head and saw long, sun-lightened black hair, a smooth bare back, long brown legs and beautiful buttocks entering my sleeping area. I looked up at the ceiling and wondered what I had done to please

Tirak. My curiosity was trying to overcome my less-than-perfect electronic skills but *Tirak* came first and I was her number two so I continued.

I heard the delivery of my supplies and took a moment to go on deck, check the supplies and send the boy away with a nice tip. I stowed the boxes below, briefly glanced at my cabin and turned back to the internals of the transceiver. The sound of a body rustling upon sheets was the only indication that my visitor was still aboard.

I finished my work, tested the system and gazed at the forward cabin bulkhead wondering what my next move would be. *Tirak* bumped the dock, caused by the wave of a passing boat, with a force that surely flattened the fenders and brought her glossy skin within a few microns of contact. That decision settled, I untied her and motored back to the mooring and then went below to view this woman snared by my *Tirak*.

From the short companionway I looked into my small portside cabin and filled my eyes with a remarkable beauty. She lay on top of the sheets, which were in need of cleaning, in her natural wrap. Her golden brown, smooth, shining skin was flawless and breasts of a proportion that fit her long equine body were a rare delight to my eyes. I looked at her face last, not because of unimportance but because I had yet to see a truly unattractive woman. Her eyebrows were thick, at least for the standards of the day, her forehead smooth and free, eyelashes long and dark, nose thin on the ridge and flared softly at the nostrils, chin firm and lips pursed full, and overall a mysterious look to her closed-eyed features completed her beauty.

Her lips widened and turned up slightly at the edges and her eyes smoothly opened to reveal large, coal black liquid orbs looking at me in a curious, undemanding, nervous glisten. It was her, the woman who I had spoken to briefly and had watched me in the market. My heart hammered in a way it had never done in the past. She did not attempt to speak but slid her feet up the sheets and opened herself to my eyes. Her flower sealed but also glistened and the dark trimmed hair completed the canvas. I removed my trunks and joined her. We introduced ourselves with lips, touches and murmurs. Our first joining was physical but I knew there was more.

Afterwards, her nervousness gone with her decision, she began to talk in an American accent I could not place. It was a second language but her first was never revealed. We spoke of the world and she drew forth from me secrets of my soul as she revealed some truths that she had given to no one else. It was one of her many gifts to me.

She had seen me enter the harbor and, of course, *Tirak* was the first thing she gazed upon. She looked through binoculars, saw me and made her decision to talk to me. She said it was not done lightly, because she had never done anything like this before, but as her time grew short, so did her need. She came to *Tirak* with no thought of failure and claimed me as her prize.

We sailed the islands for three days and on the fourth I set *Tirak* to cruise straight away into the blue. On the evening of the fifth day she commanded me to return to Rota. I say commanded because that was what was required for me to turn in my course. This was the woman I had searched for.

Tirak spun like a ballerina and that was the only time in our life together that I hated her. The voyage back was spent making love under the sails with the wind gusting to cool my fever. We talked as two who knew each other for an age. She told me more of her life and what she was to return to and the absolute of what was required.

She was to be given to an older man of her family's choosing and she had agreed but she begged to be set free for two weeks. The time was coming to an end and I was slowly building to a panic. I told her we, *Tirak* and I, would carry her away and hide her in the sea. I would make her happy and she could forget obligations. She laughed and the sound resonated in harmony with *Tirak*'s rigging. She kissed and held me and let her soul comfort me in my time of need. She looked into my eyes and I was mesmerized by her eyes and words. She told me I was one of the many that went through life adrift unless we had clear instructions from another. She could see right away that I was a good man who needed help but that one day I would be the one providing help to another. She told me if not for her commitment to duty she would be my guide but only until I tired of the lead.

It was not to be and she told me that one day the guide would come and take my painter, a small boat's rope, and move me along the stream to a fulfilling purpose my unconscious and ethereal soul sought. It might not be a woman to calm and direct me with her soothing voice and loins but the one person I needed to put my heart and soul into sync and give all my trust to.

She smiled at my dilemma and again her laughter coursed through me like a spark to light the flame of hope. She never told me she loved me but showed it through tactile actions and looks. Glances of truth stole from her liquid eyes and her firm fingertips caressed me back from the depths in which I tried to plunge. Her body was ancillary but necessary to leave me with tastes and scents that would sooth my waking and sleeping dreams.

We sailed into the harbor and I lowered the main, furled the staysail and finally let fly the jib as I ghosted to the dock. She secured the bow and stern lines with the deftness of a proven sailor. She asked me to retrieve her small bag from the cabin and I knew that when I reappeared she would be gone. I pulled her aboard for a final kiss and as I moved through the cabin I felt the tilt of *Tirak*'s deck as she released me.

I left port that very hour for a destination I had no time to consider or give care. Over the next two weeks I slowly released the garments she left behind to the deep, certain in the knowledge that in doing so I completed our passage. Her aroma was locked in a compartment that would only open in its own time. I realized that my depressed life had been put on hold for the six days she had entered my world. Afterwards, on a pilgrimage that only time would fulfill, I used her interlude in the dark times to give me buoyancy.

#

I awoke with ascension of my spirit that Jamila always brings to me. As I looked, my world was dark and *Tirak* was continuing her diagonal leaps across the waves. My cares tucked away with the closing of my dream, I caressed her wheel and felt

~ 20 ~

her vibrations in tune with her world. I don't often smile but tonight I felt the command of the sultry woman I once knew.

On occasion I had tried to find her but even in that I knew it was hopeless because I doubted the name she let me speak, which means desert flower or beautiful one, was her true name. She had the look of the desert but could have come from any number of places Muslims inhabit. I knew from her obligation and unwavering call that she was from among those who accepted their tier as changeless. If one were to delve into that society with questions about a woman who belonged to another it could bring death to one's door in the blink of an eye. I left her to her calling and only enjoyed the gifts she bestowed as gifts of living.

I went below, checked my position, made a long-range sweep of the radar and made a meal fit for a sailor of old. I had a water-conserving shower, changed to a *Paakowma*, a short sarong wrap many men from Thailand wear, and went on deck to try and restart my routine by lighting a cigar. Cloud cover had moved in but it was the cotton balls of the sea and no harbinger of change. The moon highlighted their tops and reflections from the sea muted their bottoms.

I heard the chattering of the dolphins and took comfort that my vanguard was on watch. I walked to the bowsprit and leaned against *Tirak*'s forward engine as she transferred the power of the wind into near silent motion. I watched the ever-changing sameness of the sea as the waves marched in formation, off to continue their never-ending war with dry land wherever it could be found.

In the times of old the native islanders navigated by stars and wave action. Exploring the unknown, they used wave direction as their path to land. Even in modern times, if one found time to release one's education and gather about one the elements of the earth, one could begin to differentiate the strength, direction and discourse of waves deflected by islands out in the watery desert of the sea. It would be another few days before I could again move backwards in time to try and plot my position using this method but it was something I looked to in anticipation.

Tirak hummed and sang to me and drew me back to the cockpit to relax and enjoy her as she danced. This was one of her few demands and I relished in obeying. I took the wheel from the autopilot and wrapped her in my arms and let *Tirak* lead me. Not unlike a woman, the right woman held in my arms, she transmitted her feelings, her need and desire to my hands and on into my body where I let the feeling soothe the aches and uncertainties of my soul. I often wonder how women can do these things when they too are as fragile of heart and soul as men are.

I had known men who looked upon women as a tool or service which was expected to render unto him that which was owed. I sometimes envied them their confidence, but I was grateful that my expectations were replete with fear of contact and yet the thing I strive for. For me, interaction with men was a consuming need that only required the occasional treatment. Talking as an aggressive sport, bolstered by numerous cans of loudmouth, can be spirited and enjoyable but always, for me, the next day brings a feeling of embarrassment, even when the time spent was as pleasant as a walk along the beach.

Talking with other sailors, I was always on guard that my ignorance would spring forth. I recall once in my early years when with a group of likeminded men who obviously outclassed me I asked a somewhat simple question. We were looking over a beautiful sloop that had just gone through refit with a new teakwood deck installed and glowing dully in the sunshine. I asked what I thought at the time was a reasonable question— when would the finish be put on the wood? I was met with a benevolent silence and, because I was among friends, no answer was given.

My inexperience was quickly overlooked by the one man I wanted so much to be my friend and never a mention of my unseamanlike ignorance was to come forth. He went on to be a true friend and my knowledge of seamanship grew by leaps under his tutelage. I envied the way in which he would ignore my advice on life without seeming to. He was younger than me but a sage in my eyes.

My mind jumps in straight lines but not always forward. The modern women of today were not required to hide their confidence but, as in bygone eras, too much was a detriment to the mating game. Women fill this world with laughter, passion, rivalry, compassion, need and fragrance. The list goes on but it would take a lexicographer to continue.

I find pleasure and color being around women, but if I had to choose only one word, it would have to be fear. As a stumble-tongued male who had never learned to mature past the age of around sixteen when in their presence, I walked on eggshells with hobnail boots as I made my way through the interactions of their world.

But for *Tirak*, I had no doubt I would be holed up in some high-rise or mountaintop or perhaps deep, dark jungle, awaiting the woman of my dreams to saunter up, take me in her arms and proceed to sweep me off my feet. The only one who has, left me after six days to perform the duties demanded of her. She did not leave me crushed to the floor but with a renewed hope of life to come.

My long-distance routine was slowly returning and after a few hours of navigational inputs to the GPS system and a visual chart search of the realm in which our passage would take us, I went back on deck to enjoy the night watch. I rarely listen to music while riding the blue but let my mind entertain or drag me through the passing miles.

On sporadic moments when my melancholy dipped into unwanted waters I would crank up the tunes and call forth to the creatures of the deep. On one occasion I attracted the attention of three Great Whites which, if in orchestrated consensus, could have consumed *Tirak* and her foolhardy pilot. They consented to merely observe the jester which I appeared to be, then turned and left the stage.

Whales had visited sporadically while I traversed the upper and lower latitudes, and although they were gentle behemoths and a sight to behold, they were not the preferred companions of a small sailing vessel. I doubt the intelligence that people place upon them but as mammals go, they were extraordinary.

Dolphins, on the other hand, either from knowledge or exhibitionist tendencies, were a true delight to my senses. When they roll to their sides and look me in the eye, there can be no doubt they were achievers in the animal kingdom. I may be mere amusement to them, being some life form attached to the hard shell of a top-water creature that moves with grace, if not speed, across the limitless deep. They take pleasure being the herdsmen and receiving a share of the bounty when providing me with a breakfast of winged fish. Their acrobatic nature was one of the few actions guaranteed to put a smile on my face and in my soul.

As I sat and watched the sparkling darkness give over to the muted grays, pastels and finally hard brightness of day, I scanned the horizon for intruders. We were nearing one of the busier shipping lanes and I decided to continue the intermittent sweeps of the radar throughout the day.

The sea suddenly erupted in a froth of a square mile, with the savagery of tuna feeding on the bounty of a huge school of lesser fish. I grabbed a fishing rod, which I kept just inside the passageway, and threw a lure into the battle zone and quickly had a small yellowfin hooked-up. I used a heavy line to haul the tuna in as quickly as I could before I was left with only a head. It was always a race between equipment and shark to provide a bounty to my table. Today I vanquished the predator of the predators.

It takes skill and dexterity to subdue a quivering, jumping twenty pound tuna with a belaying pin. One's mind must turn to the animal inside to submerse one's full attention to a task such as this. Injury at sea was an unwanted danger so diligence and concentration were required skills.

Once subdued, I now had a pleasure to the palate for several meals to come. I cleaned and stowed most of the beautiful flesh but hurried with the soy and wasabi to delight in the taste of a fresh kill. Sashimi was not a delicacy I could undertake on a daily basis but in episodic events, with an infusion of the volcanic adjuvant wasabi, it can be an experience of delightful agony.

Throughout the day I continued my routine as my sinuses returned to normal. All the gear was in good working order and the errant mainstay, which turned my fate to Palau, showed no sign of weakness. I walked along the safety rail of my beauty, listening for complaints or needs, but heard only satisfaction in her rhythm. I returned to my station in the cockpit and relaxed for an interlude with my daydreams.

Chapter 3

On a visit to Thailand I subscribed my living to the land for a few months while I awaited a new sprocket and chain for *Tirak*'s autopilot. *Tirak*, by the way, is a Thai word which means *sweetheart*. I had on several occasions traveled to the interior of the Land of Smiles and had always come away wanting more, but the proximity of the multitudes has always driven me back to the sea.

The inner lands of Thailand, away from the tourist spots and sex trade, were nothing like what I had imagined. Nearly every inch or centimeter of usable land was in use by family farmers and corporate agriculturist alike. Rice, bananas and numerous succulents in the lower lands and corn, tapioca, sugarcane and a plethora of fruit-bearing trees, vines and bushes in the upper drier lands were manipulated with an unstrained effort of living in the heat. The people were seemingly unconcerned with the need to reach above oneself and satisfied to maintain their life of easy poverty.

My delight in being there was the children. I must admit I love children, when taken in moderation and with the ability to abscond without responsibility. Thai's start at birth to enjoy life as it comes. When I go into a small village away from the hustle of the large cities and speak in their language I become an instant item of curiosity and enjoyment. The children, at first shy, soon take me on as a spectacle in which they're permitted to wring the secrets of my makeup through squeals and laughter. There was no fear of abuse or harm and the mothers go about their business leaving the cherubs to fend for themselves.

If I spend a few days with a family, I am forever surrounded by the little ones. When I leave them, it is always with a feeling of self-importance and joy at being in their company. I often wonder what kind of father I would be but fear of failure always triumphs.

Would I want to watch a child grow with my phobic fears or could they overcome the neglected joy I could provide?

#

I return to my world, noting that the sun has hidden itself from an evening viewing of its departure. I go below and check the weather and see a front moving in about a day's travel ahead of us. It carries some added wind and probable rain but nothing that would create a need to redirect *Tirak*, even if I had somewhere to go, several hundred miles from the nearest landfall. I take the precaution of furling the staysail and taking a single reef in the main. Our speed would drop, but in the event of a quick squall, there should be no reason for forward deck work. *Tirak* takes the reduced sail in stride and hums her secret songs and remains smug in her knowledge. I give her a questioning caress but to no avail. She holds our future in her closed lips, like a beautiful woman with a missing tooth.

At midnight I went below, checked for intruders on the radar and read the progress of the front. I sat in the salon for a moment, picked up a book I had been trying to read for days and drifted off to the land of nod.

#

I dreamed of my childhood and my parents trying to pry my insecurities from my small grasp. I succumbed to the ministration but only for a moment, learning how to live a life within another life.

As I grew and girls moved to the forefront, I learned to love from afar. The fear of ridicule and rejection was strong and could not be vanquished by a weakling such as me. I took every opportunity to avail myself to them from behind the façade of friendship. They were soft to the touch and smelled of flowers in the field, but I knew for certain their fangs were dipped in fatal venom, just waiting for the chance to strike at a moment of weakness on my part. Oh, but I needed one to escort me to the land of fulfillment.

I infused myself in their proximity while maintaining a shield of normalcy to deflect any questions of my humanity. Later in life I reasoned the fault to be of my own making but in youth

~ 26 ~

there was only the underlying fear of failed destiny. I loved women from an early age but like fish in an aquarium, they remained an unreachable treasure that would wither and die if brought within my realm.

In school a few did attempt the impossible and I love them to this day, but in the end my pubescent nature forced them to acquiesce to another's confident charms. After testosterone infusions forced my needs past my inhibitions, I was successful in snaring one of the fair sex and found that I had missed a lifetime of solace.

Once upon the road, I learned to turn off my insecurities for the companionship and warmth of a woman's embrace. I could not hold this semblance of normalcy for an extended period but tried to trade my short periods of contentment in barter of kindness and caring. The knowledge that fear would drive me onward to an unfulfilled life was a constant companion. As the pain and panic grew in me, in later years the world of solitude took me further afield from life's superfluous game.

Of all the currents in the stream that I could have ever envisioned, becoming a writer was not a foreseen outcome. Out of boredom or desperate need I put pen to paper, as it were, writing of a life that would have been my ultimate dream. The stories had always lived within my daydreams but no understanding of potential allowed them to come forth. On a whim I sent one off to an agent and to my amazement it became a success. Two more followed and then *Tirak* bound into my life. I finally had the opportunity to escape in the fashion of which I dreamed.

#

Chapter 4

I awoke with a start. Dreams of childhood did that to me and usually left me trembling but something else had brought me back to reality. My love, *Tirak*, was trembling and moving in an odd way. I quickly checked the compass and saw we were far off our heading and then I extended the range of the radar and saw a mass in our intended direction. There was also a curious squeaking noise that had a familiar enunciation but I could not extract it from my memory. A feathery bump also radiated with the acoustic sensation.

I went up to the cockpit to see our world standing still. The sails hung like wet towels on a clothesline. The wind had dropped to nothing, the cloud cover complete, and the ocean had taken on the appearance of viscous oil. I scanned the horizon and looked upon a black, lightning-filled squall line perhaps five miles away.

The squeak and bump touched me again and emanated from the port bow area. After another hurried check of the sea I turned on the spreader lights, floodlights mounted high on the main mast, and I looked over my silent *Tirak*. No clinking, slating or creaking was heard. I moved forward, peering over the side and found, to my amazement, a large square of Styrofoam nesting alongside the hull. It was about twenty-five square feet in area and at least several feet thick. I had grabbed my flashlight, which put out nearly one million candlepower, and pressed the button.

Night vision became a thing of the past as my world shrunk to the circle of the beam. Something dark and spindly with a froth of a darker hue at one end blurred my perception. As it began to take focus in the reality of the moment, I looked down at a human form. I applied the tremendous beam of light toward the head and it moved slightly. The hair atop its head moved of its own accord. The hair made small thrashes in the oily water as it flowed over the side of this impediment to navigation. The body moved again and an ethereal sound emanated from within its core like the sound of a specter.

I ran back to the cockpit, took up my boat hook and ran forward again. I probed the body lightly to convince myself that this was not an apparition. The touch transmitted through the pole was solid and worldly. I hooked the ungainly piece of flotsam, not the body but the flotation, and maneuvered it towards the stern of *Tirak*. All this time *Tirak* made not a sound of protest at being becalmed before an incoming squall. I reached through the mainstays as I continued to motivate the flotsam toward my boarding ladder. I refused to think of the responsibility I was investing us in. There would be time for retrospect in the coming hours.

I raised my gaze to the approaching squall line and approximated time to impact to be about fifteen minutes. While making the precarious maneuver I looked more closely at the device which the body lay upon. I could see cracks in its structure, opening and closing as I propelled it aft. There were also a number of small white curved objects springing from its surface.

The hair on the body continued its eerie dance below the water line and as my beam raked the surface I could see small fish clinging to the hair in an apparent attempt to pull their victim onto their plate. I thought of the tenacity of the miniature predators and smiled, even while thinking, in revulsion, of the potential outcome. Animal life would turn any situation into opportunity without regard.

I attempted to imbed my boat hook into the substance of the Styrofoam but the raft quickly began to disintegrate. I lowered the boarding ladder, unhooked the safety rail and just had time to grasp a limb of the person before he slipped into the waiting school of obviously hungry fish. He was light, near childlike, and I lifted him onto my shoulder as the raft broke into numerous segments. With a hurried glance at the approaching weather, I secured the ladder, safety rail, and then hauled person, lamp and hook below.

I dropped my gear and moved to my quarters with the person and four fish still attached to his tresses. I laid him upon my bed, used my knife to free the victim of his unwanted guests and moved to the galley for a glass of water. I threw the fish through the hatchway, noticing they were not the perpetrators but the acquisitions of the man by way of hooks tied to his hair. I quickly entered my quarters, knowing I must hurry because of the approaching squall, flipped on the light and stood in fascination and near horror.

The man was covered in sores, caused by prolonged exposure to saltwater and sun, but what froze my being was the cleft where a penis should have been attached. This was a girl! My mind began to spin towards the panic that was always lurking and waiting for the opportunity to leap upon my back.

I, through a massive effort of will and, more to the point, fear for my *Tirak* at the approaching storm, cast my devil down and temporally smote it. I lifted the head of this female and touched her lips with the rim of the glass. Her swollen lips parted and she hungrily took in half a tumbler of life-giving liquid. I told her to lie still as I must attend to my boat and raised the lee net to keep her from rolling off the bed when the weather worsened.

I moved to the forward locker, closed the deck hatch, went on deck, closed the passageway and prepared us for hard weather. *Tirak* bobbed, began to clink and clatter, almost in delight, as the wind gave us steerage. I changed our heading to angle into the wind and waves on a port tack, trimmed the jib, winched in the boom and loosened the outhaul a bit to ease the mainsail. We were not close-hauled but with the wind forward the beam I could tack, head up or fall off as necessary. I wanted to keep the strain off the port side mainstays.

Once her point of sailing was to her approval she leaped to do battle with the elements. She scoffed at the inadequate attempts by the wind and rain to dissuade her from her course. The sea builds up quickly but with *Tirak*'s nimble lines she plunges and surges in concert with the sea. Herein lies the thrill of the sea; hand steering through a strong squall in the dead of night on a vessel made to perform with glee in such conditions. It also detached any thoughts of what lay below deck from my mind.

If it had been a calm night, the smell of fear would have been pervasive. A responsibility, not of my making, awaited the quietening of the blue. As for now, my mind came to life in the exhilaration of placing my fate and faith in *Tirak* and my own abilities. We plowed through the storm for three hours and then met the steadiness of the trade winds. The sea slowly dropped and now I could no longer avoid the fearful object that waited below deck to dash my sensibilities.

I returned to our correct heading, trimmed the sails, leaving main reefed and furled staysail until daylight. I steeled my resolve and went below. I rechecked my navigational equipment and radar then went to the medical supplies and drew a large pot of water. I entered my compartment to find the female in much the same position as I had left her. I hurriedly grabbed a towel, covered her nether region, lowered the lee netting and lifted the frail stick form and then carried her into the main salon.

Lowering her to the cushioned bench, I looked at the pixie in my arms. She was thin, with ribs and inner structure showing below the cankers that covered her body. Her skin was burnt dark but her face still retained an Asian bearing and potential beauty. I guessed that she had been on the water for at least a month but how she survived was a mystery that was about to be partially revealed.

Her hair was shattered by breaks, snags, and to my consternation some of the tips had embedded into my left arm and lower back. As I removed the adhesive strands I found more hooks tied to her locks. A closer examination revealed small fish bones that served as hooks. My admiration for her tenacity to survive grew. This child had wanted to live and she had a quick mind, even in extreme conditions.

I pressed more water to her lips and she drank greedily but her eyes never opened. I used a soft cotton towel to rinse and swab her upper body and back and then washed her legs, ankles and feet. My reluctance to expose my fears and insecurities as well as her flowered region was something I had to quell if I was to serve her medical needs properly. I looked around as if there might be a hidden camera in the cabin, blushed at my frailty and removed her only covering. Her flower had only a light dusting of fine golden brown pubescent down along with dried, caked salt deposits and lesions.

This was a child but a girl-child like the ones I had entertained with my wit and meager language skills in the interior of Thailand. She was nothing to fear, at least not for several more years. I almost smiled but not quite. I cleaned her front and back and then applied a medicated ointment to all the raw sores. I only covered her hips with a light towel, knowing dry air would aid in her recovery. I also administered an antibiotic by mouth, gave her more water and allowed her to rest while I changed the sheets on my, now her bed.

I sat and looked at this emaciated creature for a long time, trying not to think of what I would do with her when we reached port. I could change our heading to make landfall within a few weeks or continue on for another month to Palau. I had read that Palau had a good hospital and, if needed, an airport to transport this waif to better treatment. Physically she appeared to need only tender care, nourishment and light medications, but until she woke and spoke of her needs, I was only surmising. I made the decision to continue on to my intended port.

I could only hazard her age to be between eight and fourteen, hoping for the former. Her body was long, and I imagine when healthy she would fill her adolescent form to be a lithesome sprite. I lifted her and carried her to the bed and on impulse kissed her forehead and smiled with a cleansing lift to my spirit. I still had no idea what to do with her but my decision to nurture this child back to health was resolved and I would put my efforts into that task.

I ate a quick bite, took a brandy and cigar up on deck and watched the final act of the night bring on the finale to this most unusual day.

By sunrise the sea was steady, rolling its way to collision leagues behind us. The cotton-ball clouds had taken station as foreground to the bright azure of the sky and the day had a lift to it that I left to others to decipher. I felt the need to sleep but was reluctant to enter the lower world below deck. My fears of responsibility and failure followed me like a shadow as I inspected my one true companion.

Tirak hummed contently and commanded caresses as I passed her fittings. Even the tender/dingy strapped forward of the mast made pretended demands of my time and attention. All was well in the bright world of my *Tirak*. The dim light of the cabin whispered its needs, and thoughts of the medical care I must attend to finally coaxed my presence.

As I descended, my eyes strayed to the compartment that held obligation and fear. I took a glass of water as alms to gain audience with my guest. Her condition had visibly improved but still needed close attention. Her eyes remained closed and that caused me an anxious moment until I gazed upon one of my cooking pots resting beside the bed. I lifted her head and back up slightly and pressed the glass to her lips and once again she greedily consumed its contents. Her eyes remained closed but she was either in REM or refusing to view her caregiver. I laid her back and removed the errant pot.

In the galley I examined the contents and found the aroma of urine. There were things to teach as her health progressed but for now I took this as a good sign. I cleaned the container and returned it to the bedside. I applied more ointment, administered another antibiotic, wiped her forehead and smoothed her hair. I must wash the still salt-laden tangles but that ordeal would come later. I left without placing demands of sight on her. I lay down on the salon bench and plunged into a deep, peaceful sleep.

I awoke to an unexpected scurrying that touched my ears and periphery. I turned my head in time to see her compartment door ease closed. I sat up and saw minor confusion in the galley; cupboard hatches not fully secured and items not in their designated spots. As a man of solitude, I know my localized world, haphazard as it might seem to an intruder. Each item had a place, if not a reason.

I went to the galley and followed the trail of someone in search of food but not yet of sufficient height to reach the repository in the overhead compartments. I smiled with worry at my guest's self-reliance but wondered at her reluctance to expose her eyes to me. I put a pot— not the one used in her voiding— of water on the stove to heat, removed a tuna steak and several broth cubes of chicken and added them to the soup. I gave it a dash of soy to add a slight Asian flavor and waited for it to boil. I would administer the light broth to begin her reentry to nutrition.

As I waited I went to look in on her and found her in very much the same position as I had left her several hours before. I went to the nav-station and checked the radar and GPS to find all was well and on course. I climbed to the cockpit for a momentary view of *Tirak*'s set and the condition of the sea.

I returned to the galley. I turned the heat down to let the concoction simmer. I put on my medic's attitude and took up my equipment and went to my patient. As I sat beside her on the bed I felt a slight trembling of the sheets. I thought now was the time to sooth her with my soft southern accent. Up to this point I had uttered only a few words in her presence and hoped the sound of another voice would reassure this young lassie.

I spoke of my need to view her wounds and apply the ointment. No response. I asked for her name. No response. I assured her I meant her no harm. A slight movement of her right leg was all I received. I began to apply the salve to the non-intimate areas of her arms, face, neck, lower legs and feet. I rolled her over, being sure to keep the towel over her posterior, and dedicated my hands to her back and legs. I slowly removed the towel and felt the tremble again. I assured her of my wish to return her to health, with as little embarrassment as possible, but no reaction was forthcoming.

I had to open her buttocks slightly but I first wiped the nervous fear from my face and hands. Once completed, I turned her for the final test of my panicky condition. As I moved her legs apart I felt the tremors of fear run through us both. I quickly applied myself to the uncomfortable task and took a deep breath. I covered her female identity. As before, I wiped her face with a cool cloth and lightly kissed her forehead. Her eyes, as before, never opened.

I left her, to the relief of us both, and made my way to the galley, removed the pot to let the ingredients steep. I leaned on my forearms over the sink and moistened the cloth I held and wiped my face. I caught a whiff of day-old male sweat with a tinge of fear and went to the head and sponged my body clean, adding a bit of scented corn powder to recondition my psyche.

#

There was one girl I dated for a short time in school with soft blonde hair, blue eyes and an angelic face that stole my heart

~ 34 ~

with little effort on her part. Her family and mine had always been close friends and one day she smiled at me during one of my pubescent surges and I was lost in her. She even kissed me at our first contact as more than child-friends. Now I'm not so sure but at the time I knew she did it out of duty to the families and charity towards a poor imbecile whose deformed tongue failed him at the most inopportune times when in her presence.

Growing up with her made our conversations easy and fun, until the day I realized she was a beautiful potential woman. She put a great effort into my introduction to the world of touching and kisses but soon tired of the unpredictable responses coming from the idiot of the grove. She always wore a corn scented body powder and to this day the smell triggers a euphoric discharge within my brain.

#

I went to the compartment to prepare her for the meal to come by elevating her upper torso with a pillow. As I entered the tiny space I saw her nostrils flare and her face soften. Ah, another victim of remembered smells. I smiled and filed the knowledge away as a treasure to present on occasions of distress.

I gathered the meal onto a tray, adding a small slice of lightly buttered soft bread, and sat down on the edge of the bed next to her. Her nostrils flared, not in remembrance but in need, and as I placed the spoon to her lips she allowed her chapped lips to part and the broth to flow into her mouth. She savored the taste and a slow smile worked at the corners of her lips. I increased the input and she at no time indicated she was replete.

I lifted her small hand and felt resistance at first and then capitulation as I placed the bread in her weak grasp. She consumed the buttered piece of manna and waited for more. Only twice was there a fluttering of her eyelids as they remained closed. I must admit my curiosity was overcoming my fear of the required interaction with this sea sprite.

I removed the dinnerware to the galley and upon returning to the confines of her lair found her reaching for my best soup pot— nightjar. I sat down and explained what the proper way to attend to one's needs was. I took her hand and lightly pulled her from the bed until she stood. I guided her from behind, with small touches to her shoulders, to the head, toilet. I opened the door and continued to stand behind her in hopes she would open her eyes out of curiosity, and she did but only for a moment until she glimpsed me in the mirror.

I introduced her to the components of a sea-going bathroom. I spoke in hopes that our languages were in concert and guided her hands to touch the apparatus that would complete the course of duty required. When I levered the vacuum flush she jumped back into my legs in fright and then sprang away from the inadvertent touch.

The noise of the motor-driven vacuum flush always gives me a start and I smiled again, for perhaps the fourth time since her arrival. This child was making me into a humanist. I'm not sure I liked the turmoil smiling and even, God forbid, laughing could cause in my life.

I pushed her further into the tiny compartment, shut the door and left her to her own devices. I soon felt my ears pop from the pressure drop the vacuum causes and damn— another smile strolled across my unyielding face.

In consternation I sat at the nav-table and began my noonday records for the ship's log. I heard the door to the head open and then light touches of bare feet moved past me. I glanced to see her eyes open but not wavering in my direction. I continued my routine throughout the day and rest of that night. I administered her medication and ointment once more but determined that on the next application to her female regions she could self-medicate.

As I sat in the cockpit enjoying a brandy and cigar I heard her moving about the cabin, investigating her new abode. At one point she even came up on deck, and since it was quite dark, she was able to enjoy the sights of the undulating rhythm of sea by moonlight and the spectacle of the upper sea of stars. Several shooting stars streaked through the heavens and she clapped in delight but quickly subdued her display.

After a while she lay down on the padded bench and I could see her slow, even breathing. *Tirak*'s hum seemed quieter in an effort to cradle this child which rested in her arms. I watched this wonder for a long moment and then took her in my arms and carried her to her chamber. She was soft and warm in my arms and I felt her giving rather than drawing strength from me. I kissed her healing forehead and closed her door.

What was I going to do with her? I could not allow an attachment to form; that was not my life, nor an option I felt I could contemplate.

Chapter 5

I returned to my night watch to spend time alone with *Tirak*. On a beams reach she heeled nicely and the lean supported me snugly in position. I reached out to caress her wheel and then I decided to take command of her progress for a while. I chose Betelgeuse as my reference. Betelgeuse was a first magnitude red star and the second brightest in the constellation Orion. Rigel was the brightest but tonight it was not the closest to my present heading.

#

Orion, a mythical Boeotian hunter, has always been in my life. As a child I heard the story of his pursuit of the seven daughters of Atlas and at the time wondered what he would do with seven women. He was a hunter and I was raised in the South and taught to hunt and fish at an early age. This was part of my makeup and I think the main reason why I feel I was born in the wrong age.

I had lived in the Marshall Islands for a year and met a young Hawaiian woman who, as they all did, stole my heart but returned only a part of it. We would sit in the sand by the reef and look at the stars and Orion became our marker as I told her of how he came to be placed in the sky.

She was not a willowy Polynesian woman books were written about but slightly heavy. Her face, dark eyes, golden skin and long traces made up for any imperfection in her figure. She could speak in her slight accent and hold me enthralled. I think my odd, to her, southern accent held her in the same manner. She introduced me to the novels of fantasy and allegory as well as her beautiful golden brown skin, taste and aromas. I met her once afterwards in Hawaii and the feelings were there but a barrier held us apart, knowing it could never be more than it was.

There were parts of my life that were cloaked in a misty shroud and even a few dark spots that should remain closed. Other parts spring forth through smells, sights and sounds: not all good but with a clarity that hurls them to the present. This maiden of the sea was a pleasant remembrance of my past.

Orion has followed me everywhere except the far north and I didn't dwell in those regions for long. The Hunter provides a small anchor in my wayward life. I used to tell my parents about Orion and the others cast into the night sky and they seemed proud of my knowledge and hoped I could take my intelligence and make a life that would provide me security and joy. Neither of those two elements has been a part of my psyche but rays of hope burn through in meteoric moments and then leaves a darker dark behind its sparkling trail.

My parents tried to keep the confident child alive and in some ways they were successful. Events of my making had provided monetary security but joy did not follow. I was not meant to live outside of my solitude.

#

I engaged the autopilot and reclined on the bench to sleep for an hour or so. I woke to a face, hidden by the backlight of the cabin below, staring at me. I started for an instant but then released the tension and looked back at the little face watching me. I said hello and gave her a smile but she only closed her eyes as she turned and returned below deck. I wanted her to see the glory of the sunrise and the start of a new day so I called to her. Not knowing her name, I called her Little Bit, but she refused to respond.

I had set my deck net before the event and was rewarded with a small school of the winged fish. I offered my thanks to the dolphins and carried my bounty below deck. I quickly cooked the fish and divided them into two portions. Her door was closed so I placed her meal on a tray and knocked before entering. She appeared to be asleep but I saw the tension in her body. I placed the tray on the stand beside the bed and left, closing the door behind me. Even before I reached the galley, three steps away, I heard the clinking of plate and glass. I was worried about this condition and decided to insert a cause to extract an effect, after I had eaten and started my routine.

I went about my routine checking *Tirak* and finding her in need of nothing. She felt a little tight in her handling but otherwise flying in the joy of freedom. In the cabin I checked all of the navigational gear, looked for intruders with the radar and looked around for the book I'd been making meager attempts at completing. I couldn't get through one page so I put it aside and looked at the closed door. I had no real plan but it was time.

I opened the door without knocking and caught her looking out the porthole. She jerked around, closed her eyes and lay down. She was wearing a clean tee-shirt I gave her and I could see that the sores on her legs had responded to treatment and were neatly scabbed over and much reduced in size.

I sat at the foot of the bed and took her foot in my hands. On impulse I lightly raked my finger down the sole of her left foot and she wiggled strongly, trying to escape my manipulations. I did it again and she sat up, eyes closed, and slapped viciously at my hand. I released her but took her shoulders in my extended arms. I did not try to draw her in but held her until she stopped struggling. I could feel her body trembling at my touch and it hurt me to cause her such distress but there had to be cessation in our mutual solitude, at least long enough for me to ascertain some information about her origin. I couldn't just drop her off at my next port of call and expect her to fend for herself.

I spoke calmly but with what authority I could muster and asked her to open her eyes. She refused to move or indicate she heard me. I told her I meant her no harm, and she let out a minuscule huff. Progress, I think. I continued to ask her and even used minor pleas to extract any kind of information, to no avail. This situation continued for an hour and my resolve became stronger at her rudeness. After all, I rescued her, had nursed her and placated to her wishes, up to now. I again told her I only wanted to help find her family and would not harm her or allow anyone else to harm her.

By now she had bolstered herself and with a loud huff lashed out at me and raked her fingernail down my left cheek. When she felt the contact with me, her eyes sprang open, for an instant, and she tried to cower from me. Her whole body was shaking in apparent fear.

Chapter 6

The shock of her fear and the surprise of the pain to my face caused me to shout, "Open your eyes right now!"

At the command her eyes sprang open and looked directly at me. Her eyes, which seemed too big for her face, were a beautiful brown surrounded by red-veined white and filled with tears and fear. The fear in them caused me to release my grip and withdraw my hands. She backed up to the bulkhead but the eyes never left me. The stark terror in them was more than I could bear and my eyes filled with tears as well. There was a questioning look on her face but the terror remained. I told her again I meant her no harm and would let no one hurt her. Her expression blanked but the stare never left me.

I got up to get her a glass of water and after I poured water from the cooler unit I turned and nearly dropped the tumbler. She was there, not two feet away, staring at me with defiance and terror. I gave her the glass and she drank it down without losing eye contact with me.

Now I started to feel the terror creeping into my soul. What had I awakened in this poor child? I went up to the cockpit and walked to the stern and turned. She was there, just outside the hatch, with those eyes. I sat down and she did likewise but at the forward end of the cockpit and diagonal from me. I asked her why she was afraid of me but only the eyes gave an answer I could not translate. I asked her if she spoke English and again it was the eyes that answered.

I felt the beginnings of panic start to hum through my body and fought it as I had trained myself to do. I had minor success in keeping it at a level that I could endure. I asked her why she was looking at me like that and only the eyes answered. I tried to ignore her.

After about forty minutes I got up and went below but she was there following me. My panic, not from fear of her but from frustration, built and I searched for an answer. I saw the head and sprang to it, flung the door open and rushed in, closing the door behind me.

Safety at last! The head was the smallest compartment on *Tirak*, with only room to stand and shower or sit on the head. You could easily shower while sitting. I looked in the mirror and saw the stranger that always looks back at me but this time I saw a grown man locked in the confines of a tiny room, afraid to enter the world of those eyes.

I sat and looked at my new world and wondered if it was possible to sleep while sitting on the head. I had thoughts of nodding off and hitting the lever to activate the vacuum toilet. This was the thing nightmares were made of. I was a grown man, locked in my bathroom in near total fear of a child's eyes. Why did I tell her to open them? It was much more pleasant before she opened her portals to hell. This was crazy, I thought, while an insane cackle tried to escape my lips.

I checked the heading. I had repeater compasses in every compartment of *Tirak*. We were on course and I had confidence that *Tirak* would arrive in Palau at eight to ten knots and plow into whatever reef was available, while the deranged man in the head waited to drown.

After the longest hour I had ever spent in the head, I steeled myself to enter the other world— the world where the eyes live. I thought of drawing my knife that I always keep close for emergencies at sea but squashed that as overboard. I splashed water in my face, raked my hair and tried to remove the tension from my face. I opened the door and, with a weak artistic smile, stepped out. She was there with the same terror locked in her eyes.

I screamed, "Stop looking at me!"

She immediately turned her head and stared at the bulkhead. Success. I had vanquished the beast! I moved around the salon, watching her, and she only stared at the forward bulkhead. I moved into her field of vision and the eyes moved away from me. I could see the terror in them but at least they were aimed elsewhere. I went up on deck and collapsed on the bench and, as if passing out, fell into a grateful stupor.

I awakened at sunset and saw the child sitting across from me. I asked if she was all right and she nodded her head in the affirmative but refused to look at me. I went below and made us a hearty meal of macaroni and cheese, hot sauce and crackers. I offered her a sip of my wine and she downed it in one gulp. I filed that away so I would remember to lock the liquor cabinet.

After eating, I went to the chart table and was amazed to find noonday readings of location and distance travel recorded on a piece of paper. I added the calculations to the log and asked if she did that, and she nodded without looking at me. She must have paid attention to my every action since arriving. I was impressed and still a little terrified.

I went on deck to watch the sunset and she took station forward and away from me. Her eyes were turned to the west and I hoped she enjoyed the spectacle that included a large green flare. We stayed on deck for several more hours and *Tirak* made not a pip, hum or clink.

I went below and she followed, taking station against the forward bulkhead. She appeared to want to keep to the weather gage in case there was a need to flee. I could see her trembling as I became sleepy but she showed no indication of wanting to retire. I closed my eyes as I lay on the salon bench but perceived the tendrils of an outsider in my psyche, opened my eyes and saw her look snap away from me. I went back to the cockpit along with my escort but in the dim red glow of the instruments I was able to journey to Nod.

As I awoke, I opened my eyes slowly and could see her slumped against the cabin bulkhead and the side of the cockpit in what would have been a most uncomfortable position for me. In repose she looked angelic. I moved slightly and the noise of the cushion snapped her eyes open and her knees clamped together. The terror took only an instant to return as she focused and her head snapped away from me. It was still dark so by starlight I made my rounds forward to look over my *Tirak* and perhaps garner respite from my discomfort.

To my delight, she did not follow. *Tirak* whispered and with soft hums cast off chips of my depression. How could I wallow in my unworthy life if this hob gave me no peace? Why hadn't she continued her voyage to oblivion without attaching her raft to *Tirak*?

At that moment *Tirak*'s halyards slapped the mast resoundingly as an errant wave passed her by. It was enough to make me in my state of quandary jump in shame. I would devise a routine to take that evil line from my thoughts. My life required the stability of routine and Miss Little Bit was ingratiating her fear of me... Of me! What had I done to deserve her attitude? No, that was an unsound train because if somehow she knew more of me than was possible in our short time together, she could claim the fear with conviction. Things in my life hidden from my memory in a locked room within me must be kept from the light of day. What if she somehow had the key? No; that key was destroyed in a war of the past.

I looked aft and could see the top of her head leaning against the combing. She was so frail and in need of care but even in her state of distress she frightened me. I almost smiled at the thought of a big man hiding from a child. I must find a way to prove my trust so she would relent and offer me a portion of assuage, even if not totally deserved.

I moved back to the cabin to check the charts and look for alternative drop-off ports. I made a study of isolated islands with lagoons, fresh water and few inhabitants. This was another quirk I had developed, for an unknown reason, so that I could always possess the location of solitude.

She was in terrible need of sleep but fought like a storm trooper against the onslaught of repose. I could see it was affecting her medically. Her tremors were becoming constant but even my slightest movement toward her brought her guard to full and her eyes stayed away. I asked her to look at me, if only for a moment, but no response came. I spoke again of my promise to bring her no harm and there was no response.

I finally said, "Look at me."

Her eyes snapped to and the terror leaped into my chest. She sat for a few hours with her eyes locked on me while I tried to think of some way to respond to her fear.

In the end and at my wits' end, I unlocked my cabinet of medicated normalcy and removed a sleep-inducing tablet. I explained to my charge that I was going to clean her wounds, apply the salve and give her a needed antibiotic. She deferred to my request but continued to tremble at my touch. I couldn't think of any worse hurt than causing a child's terror, even if it was undeserved, except perhaps to falsely drug one into sleep. At this point her physical recovery was paramount and deceit would be the lesser of my guilts. I administered the pill, gave her a drink of cool water and returned to my chart work and let my senses watch and wait for the known result.

She was asleep within minutes and as I lifted her into my arms I felt the pleasure of her tiny form without the terror exposing its self. I carried her to her compartment, gathered a bowl of water, towel, and washed her parts and then put a clean tee-shirt on her. I turned on the small wall fan, nightlight, and closed the door. I stumbled to the salon and fell once again into a peaceful stupor of peace-laden sleep.

I awoke with the dawn, started my routine and moved on deck to enjoy the triumph of light and smoked an unscheduled cigar. The sound of the wind, waves, *Tirak* and solitude almost brought tears to my eyes. A sudden thought thrashed my world and I raced to her compartment and quietly opened the door. I saw her breathing slowly and peacefully. Contentment and something akin to love flowed through me. I closed the door and returned to the cockpit to resurrect the feelings of the dawn. What a wonderful being she was in repose. I hoped that the long sleep would restore her to normal, whatever that would be. Anything would be better than the goblin of fear.

Sometime in the afternoon while I remained on deck I heard a door open and slam, the tap of feet and then the door to the head repeat the sounds of her compartment door. I actually smiled and awaited the true child to emerge into the light. My wait was interminable but about twenty minutes later I heard her enter the salon area. Expectation gripped me. I watched her hair, forehead and then face expose their glow above the deck floor but expectation sprinted to shock as I looked into the hate-filled eyes of my own personal tormentor.

She stormed on deck and stood within striking distance of me and in a dialect unknown to me shouted what I could only conclude to be expletives of the unkind variety. I recognized only a few possible words. She changed to some form of English because of my blank stare.

"Whaa you do me?"

My first reaction was glee at hearing her voice but then turned to wonder at what she said. Her words had the tonal quality of a Chinese dialect but it was a broken form of English.

"What...?" was my reply.

"Whaa you do me?"

I thought of all the possible translations and finally responded by telling her I had done nothing to her.

She responded in kind, "Yoou lie!"

She held her position like Lord Nelson at Trafalgar and lashed out with her hate-filled eyes. I hurriedly explained everything that took place the previous evening and opened my arms, palms out, to show... I had no idea what it meant but something in my past caused the reaction. There was an immediate reduction of hate emanating from her and she took her station, sitting at the forward corner of the cockpit with a thoughtful expression on her face.

After a moment she turned to me and said, "Ok."

After an obvious think-tank session she once again turned her attention to me and said in a commanding voice, "You give me bottle pill. I keep for my very own self! You never do that again, hey ya!"

I compiled the unintelligible sequence of semi-English and garnered her meaning and then thought of a proper response.

I wanted and needed to curry favor to expel the obvious hate from her being so I said, "Ok."

"Ok...? Ok, wha?"

I responded with an affirmation, "I will not do that again. I will give you the bottle of pills. I will not harm you or let anyone else harm you, little one!"

She looked at me for a long time and I could see the wheels of a well-oiled machine turning in her thought process. She slid from station closer to me and a miniscule smile touched the corners of her lips. "Ok."

I went below and returned with the main object of her concern and dutifully handed the bottle of sedatives over to her care. She disappeared but returned quickly, empty-handed, and took up her new station closer to my proximity. No more words were spoken on her part. I asked for her name but only a negative shake of the head was forthcoming.

Over the next two days I valiantly tried to return to my routine and on occasion, if I missed a step, she would point to the obvious flaw and I would correct my undertaking. As if words were above her status, she uttered them not but maintained a careful watch of my every move. She seemed prepared to spring away at any awkward movement I made in her direction but at least the hate was gone. Although I was relieved at this vast improvement, I was still concerned at our lack of communication.

During the early evening of our second day of the cessation of terror and hate she indicated that she would retire to her chambers. I bolted to the cockpit with brandy and cigar to enjoy an interlude with *Tirak*. She was responsive and drove on into the night in a show of reliable trust. I walked to the bowsprit and flew across the turbulent blue with the oblique trail of the moon sparkling in reflection from the troops of waves passing abeam— releasing my worries, if only for a moment.

I turned to return to the lower cabin and *Tirak* shook slightly as if giving me a warning of things to come. I went below and before retiring I decided to look in upon my charge. I crept to the door and eased it open. The open bottle of pills with a few tablets scattered on the nightstand were the first thing that my eyes locked on.

Fear raced headlong and I threw on the light. I looked to her and froze. She was lying naked on her back with her feet pulled up and her spindly thighs spread in an adolescent invitation. The sight of her vulnerability nearly stopped my heart, not in any form of desire but raw fear.

I looked to her chest with the small buds of promised womanhood and saw them rise and fall in an easy rhythm. I was stunned at her openness but relieved beyond measure to see her calmly sleeping, with a smile on her face. I touched her feet and pulled them down to lower her legs and then took the sheet that was thrown to the side and covered her maiden form. I turned off the light and returned to the salon and hoped, for the love of God, never to witness that scene again.

As my heart's rhythm returned to normal I thought of the pills. I rushed back in to find her as I had left her and gathered the contents and receptacle and locked them away. I lay down with my mind in turmoil but fell into a deep, dream-filled sleep.

Chapter 7

I awoke to the smell of fish frying and looked around to see the smiling face of little Venus beaming at me. I sat up, looked around and found everything neat and orderly. The small table was set and waiting for my waking. A tall glass of orange juice, fried eggs and buttered toast had been placed at my usual spot. I turned back to look at the small stove and the smile was still focused on me. I returned the smile and asked if she had slept well.

Her smile turned coquettish and she said, "I sleep good and happy see you."

I hoped that I had seen all of her moods and that this one would last. I sat at my place and the plate of freshly fried flying fish was placed nearby. She sat across from me and waited with a smile. I took a drink of juice and a minor frown crossed her face for a moment and quickly disappeared. She had her own plate and water. She served me two of the neatly cooked fish and then added two to her plate. She paused for a brief second and began to eat with feeling. The fish were prepared in a style I didn't recognize but they were delicious. Even the eggs had a savory flavor of some unaccustomed ingredient. After we consumed the meal I commented on its quality and she responded with an even wider smile.

I started my routine as she cleaned the table and washed the dishes, using water sparingly. This too impressed me with her knowledge that fresh water was a precious substance on a long distance passage. I went on deck and could feel and hear the hum of delight in *Tirak*.

As I completed the morning routine, she came up with a sliced apple and offered me several pieces. I accepted, sat back and looked at her for almost the first time without fear or trepidation. Her face was angelic, in an Asian form, but still gaunt from her ordeal.

Those eyes that had regarded me in terror, hate and distrust were now soft and beautiful. The rich brown surrounded by the clear white gazed back at me undisturbed. They were almond shaped and rose in a modest slant. They would smile, except in times of fright or anger. Her burnt brown nose turned up at the tip slightly and her cheeks were high and forward on her face. Her long black hair was jagged, frayed and in places bleached reddish by the sun but still retained a little of its former silkiness.

I wanted to ask her many things but I let the moment pass in the silence that I craved. She offered no explanation or recrimination, only a quiet contentment. She did not stare only at me but looked over *Tirak*, the sea and clouds.

Her hand strayed to the fittings and glossy surface of *Tirak* and I could see a bond forming that few people understood. I couldn't decide if I wanted that bond to extend to me. What was I to do with a girl child on the road to puberty?

#

I had thought of raising a family on several occasions but each time I could only see the damage I would do to a child's psyche.

I did not fit in the plucking society that continually tried to snare my inadequate skills in all its forms and expose me to the ridicule I constantly strived against. In some of the labors I had undertaken I had been placed in charge of people and I could feel the scorn they threw at leadership given to a dullard. I was not meant, in this day and age, to take on the responsibilities of leadership. My skills of guidance were only a spurted phrase away as words leaped with good intentions from my lips to turn the mob against me. I was a modern day follower, not a leader.

Later, some ten years ago, as panic became my companion, I faded into solitude. I could not vanquish the hum of panic but I did come to recognize its onset and learned to begin a routine of acceptance, first with the aid of pharmaceuticals and then in mind-numbing routines to cover the panic in dull activity. Imparting this on a child would be a great disservice.

#

As the day progressed, she moved about *Tirak* with surefooted confidence, exploring her intricate system to synchronize her transfer of wind to forward motion. Little Bit's lithe form was spindly but time and nourishment would add to her child qualities. She spent time at the stern looking at *Tirak*'s name painted on the transom, but no questions came from the child.

She now wore one of my green tee-shirts and red swimming trunks. The tee was tucked in and the drawstring on the trunks was wrapped twice around her waist with the long ends tucked into a pocket. I would try, with my meager skills, to adjust a small wardrobe for her later. Her exposed skin still showed some of the ravages of saltwater but her healing was progressing nicely.

I began to make a game of guessing her name, origin, background and, most importantly, why I found her alone in the middle of the ocean. I would hazard her intended destination and what brought about a journey of epic proportion as I went along. I wanted her to open her life to me but I knew it would be in her own time.

I could only conclude that she was ethnic Chinese because of the lilt of her voice and the words she used in her incomplete command of English. I would not put a name to her, except Little Bit, and how she came to be so far from land was a mystery that only she could explicate. The dialect of her first words to me gave me pause. It was unintelligible to me but had a quality that was most definitely Chinese.

I had only one gift given to me but I fear it was misplaced. It was the ability to learn and retain new languages quickly. I don't mean I could in a few weeks step up to a podium and explain the meaning of life, but I could speak and understand enough to make myself understood in most cases.

The Chinese dialects were ones that I did not retain except for a few polite phrases. I found that once it was thought that one might understand what was being said the Chinese would quickly change to a dialect of the village they come from or one of the other major dialects to ensure you do not insult them in their business dealings by speaking their language. They were good people but, as in many societies, regarded themselves as the top of the rung and refused to lower their standards for an outsider.

At the evening meal she concocted a repast of the last of the tuna, noodles and vegetables that were still in an edible condition from the cooler. She served it as a servant would their employer or master, with deference and silence. I thanked her for her efforts but told her it was not a requirement and if she intended to continue I required her to do it as a friend, not a house servant. Those big brown eyes regarded me intensely for a moment and then she nodded and took her seat. I could almost hear the wheels turning and watched as she began to relax in my company.

I went to the chart table and pulled the charts needed for the remainder of our passage. She moved close to me but not touching and observed my every move.

She asked, "Where we go?"

I turned to her and told her to sit. She complied by moving to the nearby bench. I began in a soft southern drawl and told her I wanted to help her with her English. Her eyes flared but then blanked. This threw me for a moment but I continued on by telling her I meant no offense but did wish to aid her. I told her each time she incorrectly phrased a sentence I would correct it, if that met with her approval. The blank stare switched to one of near adoration that I assumed came from my giving her the ability to make the final decision in the matter.

Her thoughts came to fruition with a simple, "Ok."

I motioned her back to the table and began to plot our passage. I showed her on the electronic plotter as well as the paper charts and her eyes never wavered as I manipulated the equipment. I pointed to an island and asked if she knew the name. It was labeled in English just below the spot indicating the island. She looked at it for a moment and shook her head. I told her its name and continued with my plot to our destination, naming the way points, other islands, reefs and shoals.

She asked, "How long?"

I corrected her phrase but she did not repeat my words. I measured the distance in miles and explained that it depended on how we progressed day to day but then gave her an approximation of three more weeks. She seemed relieved at my answer. I did not press her for anything except her name.

She gave the question some serious thought and finally said, "Little Bit."

That ended our verbal interlude for the evening.

I went to the cockpit and I enjoyed a cigar. To my surprise, Little Bit joined me, bringing a small glass of brandy and water. She offered my libation without deference and sat away from the fumes of my cigar but made no complaint. She offered to help trim the sails as the wind moved a few degrees and impressed me with her retention. I escorted her to the bowsprit and stood behind her small frame as we flew the wind. She retired a short time later and I was alone in my solitude until the wee hours.

The next day I spent my time on deck and Little Bit below. I could hear her exploring but made no effort to interfere. In the afternoon she came to the hatchway and smiled, enticed me below. As I entered the cabin I could see things neat and tidy.

She opened the door to the port side forward cabin and she looked expectantly at me. I looked in and found the compartment clean and clear of all the items I had stowed. I had a system in which I hopefully had access to all equipment in case of an emergency.

My system was in shambles but I forced my face to remain calm while my internals raged with apprehension.

She said, "No worry! I make place sleep for me. I show where other at."

I knew what she meant. To my surprise, I was becoming accustomed to her speech but I still made the corrective response and waited. She opened the starboard compartment and I could see neat, orderly and at a glance coherently arranged items from both compartments. I continued my calm expression but a small smile did escape. I asked her to confer with me before moving things of importance to the safety of ourselves and *Tirak* in the future.

She replied, "Ok."

I told her that her work was neat and precise and I thanked her. She beamed in relief.

She spent the rest of the day in *her* cabin and I sat in the cockpit with my thoughts. There was a protective need beginning to envelop me. It was something I had tried to avoid, successfully, for some time. I wanted no responsibilities that would test or require my decision-making abilities. Other than *Tirak*, I had dedicated my life to detachment. This alien sentiment had qualities that unnerved me by its familiarity. There was a knock on a locked door in my mind.

In the fog between childhood and my solitude something stirred like a giant wrath awaking with esurient hunger for my blood alone. It moved, more felt than seen, and as its piercing gaze turned toward me the red orbs of past actions paralyzed me. As the gaze passed me by, I jumped to my feet with a shout that brought her from below.

She could see the terror that had enveloped me and she moved slowly to me and took my hand. She led me to the cushioned bench seat, sat me down and stood for a moment, letting me look into her deep, liquid, brown eyes. She sat beside me and then placed her head in my lap, took my right hand and placed it upon her head. When I looked down a few minutes later she was asleep. It was as if she was telling me her trust in me was complete. Tears rolled down my face and fell to her hair but she never stirred. I had not cried for a long time.

In my first years of panic and depression tears would betray my weaknesses at any given moment. Movies, books, conversations, sporadic memories or a variety of triggers would bring a foolish flood of tears, much to my embarrassment. I finally sought medical help and was treated for depression. This began my sojourn into prescribed drugs. I hadn't cried for a long time but often felt the tension that brought it about. I let the memory that had brought this episode on fade, closed my eyes and fell into a soulful sleep.

I awoke only a few minutes later to find her still asleep with her head in my lap. I stroked her hair and wondered at her insight. She was a young girl and again I wondered of her background. I imagined her parents frantic with worry or even in acceptance of her probable fate.

I would not let her ingratiate herself into my life. I couldn't do that. What life could I offer a smart child with the intuitiveness she has shown? I would not let her be dragged into the dark hole of solitude that I chose to make of my life. There was room for me alone. *Tirak* was my guide in an attempt to come forth, but with the addition of another being, I knew I would slide headlong back to where I belonged.

Throughout the next day she attended me in the manner of a friend. In my routine I tried to remove the memories of my waking dream and the brown eyes that soothed me.

I would have to get the information from her so I could alert the people who must be desperately searching for her.

Before I could formulate a plan of action the weather changed. A front was moving in and at its van was a sizable storm system. I explained that we would have to alter course for a few days in order to ride the weather to *Tirak's* best advantage. She seemed unconcerned but listened to all my instructions and helped me secure the loose gear aboard.

While I was on deck checking for deficiencies, she prepared simple fare for several days and stored them in the cooler. I charged the storage batteries, checked the engine and went again to view the charts. My foul weather gear was laid out, along with a second set. I took two safety harnesses with leads and had her put on one of the waterproof coats, fitted her into a harness and adjusted it as I explained its use.

She asked no questions nor showed the slightest fear as she smiled at my manipulations. I wrote down course information and explained the preferred wind direction. I told her that I intended to hand steer *Tirak* and use the autopilot only when fatigued.

She stood tall as she said, "I help drive boat too!"

I only responded with a "We'll see, and its *steer* the boat not drive."

I didn't expect the storm to last more than a few days at the most so I was confident I could deal with it as I had many others. From all the weather information I gathered, this storm didn't appear to be particularly strong, but I had learned from past experience not to take anything the ocean presents you with lightly. A bag of emergency gear was clipped to the salon table stanchion for quick access. We were ready.

With hundreds of miles of sea room and no particular hurry, I had chosen to take a point of sail that would produce the least strain on *Tirak's* port side standing rigging. The weakness that changed my destination and brought the little one to me had not progressed, but if the blow turned angry, I didn't want to rely on a suspect piece of equipment. On deck I watched the squall line and turned *Tirak* to meet it and the sea at an oblique angle on a port tack.

She was with me and I showed her how to clip into a safety ring and had her stand before the wheel. I went through trimming the main and jib, having furled the staysail and reefed the mainsail earlier. She handled the winch with a strong back and I could see the gleam in her eyes as she looked to the coming encounter.

I gave her the helm but stayed close to her in an ancillary capacity for the moment. She got behind the first few waves and our course strayed but she fought the rudder to bring *Tirak* back to the correct heading. I placed my hands next to hers so she could feel my actions through the wheel.

After a few more waves I returned the helm to her and I could see her anticipating the bow swing and soon the compass needle moved only a few degrees before the correction took it back to course. She was an apt pupil and she was quickly learning to use her lesser strength to caress *Tirak* rather than fight her. *Tirak* sang and leaped in her Beguine with the sea. I could feel *Tirak*'s satisfaction at having Little Bit's help and the child's smile was infectious. I leaned down and told her that we had about thirty seconds before the rain and heavy wind would be upon us. She looked up at me and in a balanced moment when the wheel was at ease she waved me down to speak to me. I put my face near hers and looked upon her siren's joy and she kissed my cheek and then laughed in an ecstatic elation.

The initial clash took her by surprise at its strength and I helped her maintain course. She shrugged me off and soon had taken full command of the helm. I let her go for twenty minutes as I watched the wave sets build and kept a careful watch on *Tirak*'s movements.

I leaned down and spoke into her ear, telling her I would take over now but we would share the watch. She looked in my eyes to see the truth of my words and nodded. She sat down behind me and after a few moments I felt her arms wrap around one of my planted legs. I glanced down and saw that she wanted to feel my strength so I allowed the contact that would normally cause me concern. Her touch warmed me and for a time I cast my attention only to the battle forward of us. After a while she released me and made her way below but soon returned with a closed mug of coffee.

She put the cup in a lock holder and moved between me and the wheel. She took her stance, grasped the wheel and pushed me off with her backside. I couldn't help but smile at her determination and authority. I released the helm and stood ready for a minute or two but then sat down to drink the coffee she had provided. One particularly large wave crashed across the foredeck but she maintained the heading like an old salt.

As the massive roller passed beneath us she let out a cry of glee and looked at me and yelled, "Arr."

I nearly choked as the laughter erupted from me. It spilled forth with an abandonment I had not had in... Well, I don't think I had ever laughed like that.

The danger of this weather brought out a sustained joy in her, *Tirak* and me. I knew that I would pay dearly for this outburst in the future but for now it was worth it. This child was doing something to me and I could only hope it would not haunt me as a mistake.

I unclipped and moved forward to go below. As I turned to look I expected to see fright or at least concern in her eyes but what I saw was pride. I continued into the cabin, letting my senses stay attuned for a dash to the wheel. I made her a drink of hot cocoa with a little coffee. I waited for five minutes, letting her have total command, and then casually made my way to the cockpit. I insinuated myself into position and bumped her with my backside as I took over. I heard her giggle as she sat down and took a well-earned break.

We continued our intertwined watches for five more hours, and even though I knew her fatigue must be bringing her to near exhaustion, she refused to succumb. I sent her below for two hours and she glared at me but complied. This was a small victory on my part. I engaged the autopilot and, once confident it would hold, I moved to the hatch and opened it slightly to peer in. She was asleep, still in her foul weather gear. I returned to the wheel but settled into a watchful repose and allowed the autopilot to steer.

Two hours later the wind started to veer and I adjusted our course. This was a tropical storm but not one seeking death. Thrashing us about seemed to satisfy it. She returned to her post but seemed disappointed that her job as helmsman had been taken over by a mechanical system.

After a few more hours, with the dawn approaching, the sea became confused and the wind and rain abated. By dawn the rain had stopped and the wind was down to around forty knots. An hour later it dropped to thirty knots and I could see she wanted to steer so I gave her the helm and told her to come up into the wind. She obeyed without question and I removed the reef in the main and unfurled the staysail.

I looked to her and pointed out our course. She turned *Tirak* and as I trimmed the sails we were close-hauled and *Tirak* began to stretch her legs and heel over nicely. For a cutter-rigged sloop, this was her best point of sail and *Tirak* leaped at the chance to show what she was capable of to this new guide at her helm.

All the fatigue fell away for us both as *Tirak* took us across the confused sea in leaps and bounds. The child screamed, giggled and danced in abandonment as she felt the hum of *Tirak*'s rudder reaching hull speed. I offered to take over but was shunned in my efforts. I sat close to her in enjoyment of the flat-out run and stole some of her pleasure for myself.

I let her steer for an hour and then as the wind dropped more I gave her another course to steer. I trimmed the sails and the wind came more from the beam. I set the autopilot and forced her below. I was stiff, wet and had need of rest. As I began to remove my gear she was there to aid me. She quickly sloughed off her gear and took a towel to dry me.

I started to protest but she said, "I know what to do. You relax, please."

Her first please. I allowed her to dry me and she told me to put on dry shorts but no shirt and come back. I did as she asked and then she led me to the salon bench and I lay down on my stomach. Her tiny hands began to massage my neck, shoulders and back.

Her hands were strong and experienced and I was soon relaxing to her touch. I fell into a deep sleep, filled with lost opportunities and failed promises. My dreams slowly changed to a pastel of sailing on calm seas and lightness as *Tirak* skimmed the water, her keel barely touching and making only a slight ripple. The dolphins had wings and performed aerial acrobatics. One was ridden by a tiny dark-haired girl and when she looked at me I could feel her eyes penetrating my soul, drawing a piece of black sludge from my chest.

I awoke in a sweat. I touched my chest but nothing was there. I looked around but she was gone. I went on deck and found her asleep by the wheel. I returned to the cabin and went over the charts to see what corrections must be made to return us to our course. For all our dashing about, we only needed a minor correction to join our original course. I set the new heading and intersect into the GPS. We were ten days from Palau. I paused to think about my dream.

I went on deck and sat next to her and she reached out and pulled her head into my lap and continued to sleep. I looked at the little sprite and feelings warmed my heart. What would I do when we reached port? I must know what brought her to me.

I sensed danger for the first time. It was no accident she was on that raft alone. She was escaping from someone or somewhere, but if she refused to tell me, what could I do?

My hand strayed to her hair as I scanned the ocean. She had changed so much since that first night. Her little body had filled out and she was no longer the skeletal wraith that appeared more dead than alive. Her face was rounder and her eyes, still large for her face, no longer gave her a starved look. I leaned my head back and slowly drifted off.

#

As a young man it seemed I was always on the verge of failure. I had this deceiver in me that tried at every opportunity to trip me in front of the people I wanted to impress. I used to think that if I could somehow reach inside my body and grasp its wiggling tail I could pull it from me and I would be free and confident, but I could never hold on to its slippery body. I felt that the people I met were just waiting for the fool to emerge.

I remember finally finding something that took that all away and I became a man of action and swelled in the life I had, but what was it I did? That part of my life has always been veiled and I couldn't seem to break through the curtain, but now as I look the veil starts to part and I saw green eyes looking at me in confusion and my heart began to die. I could feel my mind trying to slam shut but a child's arm was in the doorway. It was covered in blood and I tried to run but my legs were frozen. I felt the scream build in me trying to burst forth but suddenly the arm was gone; the doorway was gone; the eyes were gone and warmth covered me and my sleep was broken.

#

I opened my eyes and looked into her dark eyes and she held my face in her hands.

There were tears in her eyes and she was murmuring, "It's okay. I am here."

She laid her head on my shoulder and the tears flowed from me again. Tears of embarrassment, pain and, in a miniscule measure, relief came forth but I felt her grip tighten around me as if to tell me she wouldn't leave. My arms wrapped around this tiny creature and held on for my life, but I didn't understand what was happening. I tried to disengage but she refused to release me. Her strength was that of Colossus and I succumbed to her wishes and continued to hold her to me, knowing I had nothing to give but could only take from her.

After a long while she leaned back to look at me again and smiled wanly and said, "You have many problems but I help you because I see your heart. You think too much!"

She said she was hungry and jumped down and headed to the cabin. What was I going to do with this child?

That night I went to my bed for some much needed rest. My dreams were mild and not haunting. I awoke to whimpering and found her lying next to me, crying in her sleep. I lay for a moment and listened to her. She was muttering in the language she first used in her anger but now it came in frightened utterances.

I put my arm around her and drew her close and she molded her body to me. I could feel the fear and tension within her. I thought I had done this to her, giving my dreads to her, but her nightmare was different from what I experienced. This was a product of her making. I wondered what could grip a young girl in so much fear that she strangled as it came forth.

I cooed to her and tried to take some of it from her because this was my world and I could deal with the ghouls that resided in the dark hole of the soul. She relaxed but still clung to me as if one wrong move would plunge her into the depths. I must know more about her, because I knew that she sought my protection and I could not turn away now. She had woven her short life to mine and come-what-may; I would do what I must to keep her path clear of terror. I thought of the times in my life I begged to be held in this manner but was shunned by my own inadequacies.

This girl child was slowly seeping into my brittle being. Only one other had that innate knowledge of me and she was taken by duty. I would learn her secrets. A small smile crossed my face at the knowledge that I didn't even know her name. We would not enter port without sharing some of our enigmas. A lance of panic pierced me at what this might unlock within me. I closed my eyes and descended into sleep with this girl child in my arms.

I woke to find her gone and then I rose and went to the salon and saw her with a meal prepared for us. She smiled brightly and after I sat she kissed my cheek. No words were spoken that day but her happiness was audible. Even *Tirak* hummed and sang with renewed vigor.

We sailed on for five more days and I had included her in my routine and given her responsibilities beyond what a young child should be expected to complete but she excelled at anything I put before her. I showed her once and she practiced until she needed no guidance.

On several occasions I tried to extract information from her but she would only say, "I thinking."

She allowed me my solitude but was always close by.

Two days before we were to reach our destination I awoke to an uncomfortable pitch in *Tirak*'s movement. I jumped up and ran on deck to find all her sails furled and she was drifting with the current. Her stays, sheets and halyards clattered in the disquieted movement. Her wheel was tied off to keep her rudder amidships but *Tirak* seemed to be enjoying her respite from the wind. She sat near the stern and when I gave her a questioning look she merely patted the cushion beside her. I sat down and waited for what was to come.

"I must talk with you. It is time for you to know why you must help me."

Her English had suddenly become quite good but I held my tongue and only nodded.

"My name is Mei Yue and I am to be concubine to a powerful man who wants the power of my virginity."

Mei Yue... I thought that it meant *beautiful moon* but was not sure. She took my hand and fastened her pretty eyes on me so I could not look away.

"My family famous in China for daughters. Very much uncommon in China. Daughters from my family give great power and long life to man who takes virginity. I read names in family history and see that many daughters die after fourteen and I thinking somebody kill them so man keep power. That was long time ago. Now not so many die that young. I think I will be slave to him forever. My father tell me I bring great honor to family."

I sat stunned as I listened to her and knew that she was speaking a truth that would condemn her if others knew this. Family was important in all societies but it was everything to the Chinese. Any disobedience could remove the name of the transgressor and they would be lost in a society of families.

Mei Yue never broke her gaze as she spilled forth things that had been locked in her for at least several years. She told me that killing a woman was uncommon after taking her virginity but in some lines the power was secured in this fashion in ancient time. Even today a Chinese woman was a lower class person in many parts of China and the death of a woman was not an important matter.

She told me that arrangements were made when she was eight years old because she showed such aptitude for learning. Her family was poor and was very pleased to find such a boon in a girl child. Her father knew of her mother's lineage and negotiated a tremendous price for her. She said this with pride in her voice.

She was taken away at the beginning of her ninth year, with her parents' blessings. After another year she was taken out of China and trained in numerous skills that would add to her power.

As I listened to her I filed away many questions. I would not interrupt her while she spoke. My heart, which had become a withered leathery thing, was softening in the tears of Mei Yue's words.

She told me for the past two years she had lived on an island and people were brought in to tutor her in language, music, art, fighting and many other skills. She was always watched and never allowed to be alone with the tutors. She had women around her to train her in womanly skills. She blushed as she said this but her eyes never lost contact.

As she spoke, I could feel a heat come over me, not a lustful heat but one of anger and need to protect her. It was a sensation I haven't felt in many years. In fact, I couldn't remember the last time I felt it or what had caused it but I knew in my past this anger had been a part of my life. I tried to put my inner feelings away so I could concentrate on this girl that sat before me, but I had lived with repressed emotions for so long, it was impossible to close that part of my mind off.

I began to see the self-pity that I had wrapped my life in and my anger took another branch. Mei Yue in only three years of her short life had become a person of skills it would take others a lifetime to acquire. She spoke several languages, including dialects of Chinese, could play the violin and had other skills for the one purpose of pleasing one man.

This man had purchased her at the age of eight to become an instrument of his pleasure. It did not shock me that this could happen in this world of self-seekers but when confronted with its reality I sat frozen. Like a deer caught in the headlights of an oncoming car, I was locked to her gaze.

She turned her head away and said, "I will not trap you with my power. Your decision must be your own but my decision waits for you." She turned back to me and looked at me with a softer gaze. She continued with details of her training and treatment but never shed a tear.

She finally talked about escaping the island by taking a small boat late one night and rowing around the island to find a current that would carry her away from their searching eyes. She rowed for two days with only a one-gallon bottle of water onboard.

The boat was in poor condition and she had to bail the seawater out every few hours.

When she was far out to sea and the boat was about to swamp she saw a giant white island and made for it. It was a large Styrofoam block and was much more stable than the leaking boat. Once she moved to it she fell into a deep sleep.

She was awakened by something pulling on her hair, which had slipped over the side of her raft. It frightened her, making her sit up quickly, and several small fish flopped onto her raft. They had been trying to nibble at her hair. This was how she survived. She didn't know how long she had been on the raft but she had seen the full moon at least twice. She had struggled with life and fought death until it suited her.

At last she talked about being rescued by me.

"You are first white man I ever see for real. I very much afraid of you and I think if you see my eyes you take my power for your own, but then I see you are special man and I think you are the one I need." She looked at me with an impish smile and said, "You must be very much big fool to save this life. In China when you save a life you are responsible for that life. Now I belong to you and you must protect me! I very much happy my raft find *Tirak* but I very afraid you only want my power."

It took a moment for me to take in her words and when it finally registered that she thought I would... would do that to a little girl, the heat flew to my face and she laughed with a trill that brought the dolphins up to chitter and squeak.

She put her hands on my face to take away the heat and said, "I not worry anymore. You pass all my test. You are to be my protector."

She took on a look of sad concern and she leaned in and kissed my cheek again.

She said, "You are a strange man. You are full of hurt and try to hide. I see you before were a strong and dangerous man but now you are danger only to yourself. You forget much that you must remember if you wish to live. I will be your guide, for now, and open your eyes. It will hurt but I am here and I will stay here."

As she finished she placed her hand over my heart and emotion flooded my brain.

She slapped me and said, "Not now! I not finished and I not say all this things again."

I looked at her with startled eyes and began to laugh. I knew I now had two females to hold me to task. Mei Yue and *Tirak* would throw their expectations at me and see them fulfilled.

I asked, "What test?"

Mei Yue looked at me and said, "Wha?"

I repeated my question by asking her what test I had passed. She told me of a myriad of actions, many of which were unintelligible to me but seemed to make complete sense to her.

She said, "You pass big test. After you drug me, I very much angry you, hey ya! I trick you and make you give me pills. I trick you again and you think I take your drugs and fall deep sleep. I see you come in my room and look at my power."

She gave her coquettish smile and tilted her head down, just enough to cause her eyes to look up at a flirtatious angle and continued, "I feel you touch my power when I sick but you touch like doctor. You look at me that night like a man and I see desire but I also see fear. Most important of all, I see you worry, until you look at my breasts and know I alive! Then I know I must trust you. I tell you this truth. If you give me to police or anyone else, I will die. If you keep me, I will take pain away, and if you desire... I give you my power."

I thought of that night when I looked at her emaciated nude form. There was no desire, only pity and then joy that she lived. I would not tell her my thoughts but I did tell her I did not want her power and would never take it in such a way. I told her she was never to offer or suggest I take it or I might throw her overboard to see what kind of bait she would be.

I said this with a smile but the smile turned to surprise as she sat back and laughed saying, "Too late. My bait already catch a big boat and big man, hey ya! Now I do one thing more and then wait for you to decide."

She nimbly dropped to the deck of the cockpit, bowed with her hands flat and placed her forehead on my feet. It took me by such surprise that before I could react she jumped back to the bench and sat looking at me.

Her gaze was intense and I said, "What?"

She said, "What is your decision?"

I sat thinking about all she had said, and from her look it was clear she would wait as long as it took to receive an answer. I believed most of what she told me and the thought of giving her to the authorities just to watch her handed back to this man was unacceptable, but what was I going to do with a little girl?

I looked at her and said, "I don't have an answer to all you ask but I will not allow you to go back to that man and I will protect you as best I can. I have to think about this and we will talk more."

She dazzled me with another smile, stood and went below.

I sat and watched the sunset and the light never seemed to dim but became more brilliant, casting a complete spectrum, making the sky into one tremendous rainbow and then just as suddenly it was fully dark and the stars were on stage waiting for their audience.

I went below, found a meal set on the table. She was not there so I went to her cabin and looked in to find her soundly sleeping with the look of complete innocence on her face. I returned to the salon, ate and retired to the cockpit with wine and cigar to think about my choices.

It was then that I realized that *Tirak*'s sails were still furled so I went about getting us underway once again. We had drifted twenty miles but it was of no moment. I plotted a course that would extend our time to port by two more days.

As *Tirak* took to her heels and sped across the light seas I could hear her rejoicing in her song. I knew in my factual mind that she was an object made by man for the convenience of man and had no soul, but in my heart I knew also that she had comforted me in the depths of my solitude. Her moods may only be the sounds of my soul but I would take guidance from her as long as I had ears to hear. I would allow her to aid me in this decision I must make.

I think I already knew the answer but making the choice would be life-altering. I thought of Mei Yue's words about me, and maybe it was time for me to live again. I would never fit into the bustling world but I could do much more.

Chapter 8

I went about *Tirak* checking her over and trying to regain my routine. Sometime near dawn I retired to my cabin for an hour or so. I was asleep almost immediately and the woman of my past returned to me. Her liquid eyes locked me in her regard and her lips smiled at my contentment. She stood before me in all her natural beauty but now her skin had taken on an almost translucent glow. Her waist-length, silky hair flowed past her shoulders outlining her womanly form in black. She was almost the same as when we were together. Her breasts were perhaps larger, rounded and softer, her stomach etched in strength, her hips flared a little more and her flower covered in a cloud of short black silk. She gripped my heart with her overall beauty but it was still her eyes that held me fast. She spoke of me finding the guide she had foretold and she was pleased.

As I tried to speak her fingers moved to my lips to hush my utterance. She spoke of my need to unlock the truth within me, no matter how painful, and she assured me that my guide would ease my pain. She spoke of the child with the strength and power of innocence that would protect me until I was strong enough to protect her. She lay down beside me and her words were like a thick, warm blanket on a wintry night and she wrapped me in them and would not let me sleep. She finally rose, leaned over and kissed me for a long moment.

Just before she stood she moved her lips to my ear and whispered, "I love you and I need you, too. Look for me, my love."

I reached for her but she had fled from my dream.

I opened my eyes and looked to find Mei Yue's head resting on my chest and her soulful eyes staring into mine. I tried to sit up but she stayed me with gentle hands on my shoulders.

She said, "Do not worry. I am here as a child, not a woman. I enjoy your comfort and I only share mine with you. No need to worry, please."

I relaxed but still felt uncomfortable with her in my bed.

She stood and said, "Thank you. One day I will ask you who this Jamila is and I hope you will answer."

At the mention of her name an excitement came on me that forced me to turn away from this child and as she walked out of my compartment her giggles flowed in her wake.

Throughout that day as I went about my routine she busied herself with altering shorts and a few tees of mine. Her adept hands worked at taking apart the seams and then sewing them together to fit her small form perfectly.

I talked to her about what would happen when we arrived in Palau and how she must hide until customs and immigration had checked *Tirak* and me. I told her we had to stop for a few days in order to pick up some needed supplies and replace the suspect mast stay. She listened attentively and asked only a few questions.

She told me she had learned to speak and read English, French and Thai, along with a number of Chinese dialects she already knew. I spoke to her in Thai and was greatly impressed with her pronunciation and tones. Thai is called a singing language because many words had completely different meanings according to the tone it was spoken in. My French was poor but passable and Chinese was not a language I chose to put much effort in.

I asked her about the dialect she used when she first spoke to me and I could see her eyes become hooded and thoughtful. I explained that it may help alert me to anyone who could be dangerous to her. When she realized that I was only interested in protecting her, she looked at me in wonder and a new-found love.

Once she made her decision the day before to trust me she wanted to give me that trust completely but it was still fragile. She asked me a few questions and then went into a long explanation of when and where this language could be used. She asked me to only speak it to her on the boat or in whispers if we were ashore and then only if there was danger. I agreed and our lessons began.

The dialect was a variant of Cantonese but even one fluent in Cantonese would not have been able to understand. Mei Yue told me it was from a very small village and had become the working language of the man's organization. His headquarters were in Hong Kong and he was the head of a Tong called the Blue

Dragon. She only knew a few facts but she told me everything she could think of.

Tongs were groups of organized crime operating throughout China and now the world. They were involved in almost every facet of Chinese life from drugs, slavery, prostitution and protection to shipping, building and banking. This was not a group that I wanted to be noticed by.

That night as we relaxed in the cockpit before starting our watch rotation Mei sat close to me and I asked her questions about her young life and how she got to be in this situation. In many ways she spoke as an adult but youthful excitement would spring forth as she described some of her training.

She was twelve years old and would be thirteen next month. Fourteen was the age that girls of her lineage had their power taken from them. Her parents were poor but influential in her village. Her aptitude for learning was noticed at an early age and many took an interest in her and gave what knowledge they had to her.

She was the sixth child but since it was dangerous for her family to have so many children, with the edicts of the government being so stringent, she was treated as a relative and sent to live with her elderly aunt. She was allowed to attend school but only if she attended her aunt and her household as a servant.

This left little time for her to be a child. She was too young to be bitter but instead accepted her life as a preparation for something to come. When she spoke of this she looked at me with a fixed smile and shining eyes. Her eyes trapped me in their quiet pools and I submerged my heart in them, letting it soften and become pliable.

I kept telling myself that I had not completely come over to her but I knew it was too late even if I didn't want it. I was thinking of her as my responsibility. I felt a need growing in me and, with her promise to help bring me out of my solitude, the need was strong. I would make inquiries with my agent and lawyer about a proper way to proceed. She would be my secret until she was safe but I wanted legitimacy to our life. This was what came to me but I realized I hadn't broached the subject with her.

Mei Yue told me of the contract her parents gladly signed. They would become wealthy by the standards of the village and Mei had accepted her fate as one raised on the importance of family. She spoke more of the training and I could see the delight she took from acquiring knowledge. She learned cooking in different styles, new languages, martial arts and ways to please a man. She blushed at the last part but no embarrassment crept into her voice. Before she continued she looked into my eyes for a moment and I saw a sadness envelope her. She spoke of the man's visits, where she had to strip and let him examine every part of her.

After one of these meetings, which she gave no details of, she decided to escape or end her life. She spoke of stepping into that tiny boat as the end of her life. Her name would be removed from her family's history and she would become a non-person to her parents. I knew something of what she was thinking and tried to put my arms around her but she wouldn't allow it.

She had no real plan when she escaped but prayed and put herself in the hands of fate. She did not care if her fate would bring death or salvation.

I asked why she thought the man would take her life if she returned, and she said in a simple child's logic, "He not take my life. I take!"

She would not go back to her previous fate and had no apparent fear of death.

My heart flooded with her and I knew that I would do whatever I could to change her life. My commitment was absolute, if only she would accept me. I took on society's requirements with trepidation and much analyzing and even then only if there was no other recourse, but in that moment the bright light of commitment radiated within me and chased the darkness back into the night. This feeling of freedom that washed over me brought with it an old fear.

I asked what she wanted for the future and I saw the terror return to her but she suppressed it and told me she hadn't thought about it. She would not look me in the eye and I knew I must make a revelation of my feelings and accept her rejection of me. I wanted to do this early so my suffering could have time to conceal itself. I spoke in a soft voice and the fear in its sound made her look at me with glistening eyes.

I said, "Mei Yue, I would like to be more than your temporary protector. I want— no, that's not right— I need you to be a part of my life."

I could see her begin to sink in her seat. She clasped her hands in front of her and then straightened her back and looked out into the night. The red glow of the instruments was the only light that lit her small body and glistening eyes.

I continued, "This may not be what you want but I will ask and let you know how I feel. I would like to become your guardian and would like you to be a part of my family. Would you consider being my child?"

Her tiny body slumped but then as my words moved from her expectations to reality her head snapped up to look at me and she said, "Wha? Wha you say? Wha...?"

I repeated my final question and she looked at me in slight confusion but there was hope in her eyes.

She asked, "You want my power and keep for you only?"

"No! I don't want your power— not in that way. I do need the power of your heart to help make me a better man but I want you... to be like my daughter. You will never have to worry about me trying to do... what others have kept you for. When I touch you it will be like a father touches his daughter and I will let no one hurt you. You will not be a servant or captive but you will be my family. Do you want to be a part of my family? I really should ask would you be my family since I have no one."

Before the question was completed she sprang into my lap and put her face to my chest and began to cry. It was not a cry of fear or even pleasure but of release. I smoothed her hair with my hand and my other wrapped around her. I tried once to pry her away but her strength was incredible so I resigned to let her deal with this in her own way. My ragged mind was still unsure of her answer. Too many expectations in my life had been dashed by disappointment but I prayed that this time would be different.

After ten or more minutes she relaxed her grip and raised her eyes to mine and asked, "You want me to be like your daughter? Is that wha you say?"

"Yes, Mei, that is what I asked."

Her tears flooded back and her face was lost in my chest once again. Her whole body trembled but I could feel her begin to relax. Slowly, she rose up again and kissed my cheek and then turned her cheek to me. I lifted her and kissed her softly.

She spoke in a tiny, quiet voice and said, "Yes, I will be your daughter, and now you ask and I answer, you cannot change mind. I won't let you."

I had opened one of the locked doors of my being and knew it could never be closed again. I started to slump to the bench, not able to support myself, and I felt her hands guide me. I was lost in a deep, dreamless sleep, unfettered by worries.

I awoke with the feeling that a great weight had been lifted from me and I could take a full breath for the first time in years. It was full daylight and the sea was small and the wind brisk. I looked *Tirak* over and could feel her contentment. I went below to fresh fish, toast, juice, jam and stir-fried macaroni and vegetables. It was a meal fit for a king of old and I devoured it all.

I restarted my routine but my buoyancy made everything I did a new experience in touches and sight. I reveled in *Tirak*'s contentment and came to see it was my own contentment that possessed her.

I went below and began to write emails to my literary agent. She was a trusted friend and had never refused any odd request I asked of her. I think she hoped that I would begin to write again and that my peculiar requests were for research. I would let her continue thinking that until I knew more about how to proceed.

I asked her to order several items and have them shipped to the marina at Malakal Island in Palau. My other requests were for information from adoption to Tong activities. I sent my email via Sat-com and then began to write down everything that had happened in the past few weeks. Out of an old habit I didn't really understand, I used an encryption and password that would be difficult to break if anyone other than me gained access to my laptop. I could hear Mei humming in her compartment and another unbidden smile cracked my face.

To my joy, she granted me hours of silence. When we did talk I was adjusting to conversations of happy prattle that would have sent me to sea in the past but she too enjoyed the sounds of silence. I suspected her thoughts were nothing like my own but filled with plans for the future. My thoughts were of getting in and out of Palau without undue attention. I had no idea where we would travel after that but would wait on the information I requested before anything long term arose.

The island of Koror appeared on the horizon. My plan was to enter the boatyard on Malakal Island just before five o'clock in the afternoon, checking in with immigration and customs and moving out to a mooring after refilling my water and fuel tanks.

I printed a copy of the flag of Palau on fibrous paper that would stand up for at least three weeks. I also removed the small American flag and yellow *Q* flag for immigration from their cubby in preparation. I double-checked the hiding place under the forward starboard cabin bunk where Mei Yue would stay until all the officials had come and gone. Once that was over she would blend into the island's population and be able to go about with me as my guide.

Check-in in most small island states was a brief encounter; paying for a visa and allowing them a look at my manifest and looking the vessel over for any unusual items. Unless a real interest was raised, *Tirak* looked like many other visiting vessels, except for the larger amount of stores. When they saw I was alone and *Tirak* was rigged for single-handed sailing they would overlook the extra gear. On rare occasions a gratuity could be expected but Pacific Islanders were for the most part honest. I often offered a nice bottle of wine or whiskey to the official out of courtesy and would receive smiles during my stay.

At four-thirty we entered the small harbor with the yellow Quarantine flag run up on the signal halyard to the starboard spreader. This flag if flown alone lets the officials of the port know that you are free of infectious diseases and says, '*I require free pratique.*' It allows you to enter a foreign port and clear immigration and customs.

Once cleared, a courtesy flag of the country one was visiting was flown in its place. This was done each time you entered a foreign port for the first time. Once you were cleared it was no longer required, as you were flying the courtesy flag of the country.

The small American flag was flown at the port spreader as a courtesy to show the nationality of the captain. The ship's flag was flown on a stern stanchion and raised and lowered at sunrise and sunset.

I motored to the dock, secured *Tirak* and watched as two dark-skinned gentlemen walked onto the dock. I waited onboard until they motioned me ashore. We shook hands and exchanged a few pleasantries and they looked my paperwork over. I invited them both onboard and with all hatches and doorways opened they made a brief walk-through.

The immigration officer looked at my log and asked if I had seen any debris on my passage. I told him there was always some flotsam but nothing of size to cause problems for shipping. He smiled and explained that they had a report of a small child lost at sea and a massive search had just concluded with no results. I expressed sympathy but gave them no help. I offered each a fine bottle of whiskey, which they accepted with a smile, paid my embarkation fees so I would be free to leave from another island in their system without causing a problem, and they were off for home.

I had arrived in the nick of time or I would have had to spend the night tied to the dock. I removed the yellow flag and mounted the flag of Palau and then with the aid of the boatyard crew I fueled *Tirak*, filled her water tanks and then motored out to the assigned mooring buoy.

It was dark when I freed my stowaway from her confinement and she congratulated me on my tact with the officials. She had a light supper and I lay down in the cockpit, with all but the white anchor light out. My senses were beginning to realize that I had forced stability on them and each in its own way began to protest.

Mei found it quite amusing to watch me practice for the Olympic hurling team and she even rigged a small rod and caught several fish I had successfully chummed to the area. After my frothy bout she brought a cool hand-towel and wiped my protesting body down and then softly sang me to sleep. Before sleep took me I mentioned that her voice carried across the water but she said I could claim that the radio was on. Her voice soothed me like no medication could.

I slept until noon the next day and at some point during the night an uneasy truce between my senses must have been agreed upon because I felt much better. I put the tender into the water, using the main halyard to winch it up and over the side.

Mei Yue came on deck to assist me and she looked quite cute in her remade shorts and shirts. Her hair was pulled up, making it look natural and short. As we worked I noticed her salt wounds had completely healed and her skin had lightened considerably. She was still a little gaunt but that may have been her normal look. I told her she was a very pretty young girl. She frowned slightly but then gave me a dazzling smile.

I rigged a wind scoop for the forward hatch that would produce a cooling breeze though the cabin. We discussed how we should act toward each other when on shore and I decided that she would spend the rest of the day below deck. We would look at the city in the evening but first I needed to order food supplies, some extra gear and check on some items I had previously ordered. Mei was happy to stay away from prying eyes for awhile so I was soon off to deal with our needs.

At the chandler I confirmed my order and added several items to the list. It would be delivered to *Tirak*. I also made arrangements with the boatyard to replace the suspect main stay that had turned me to Palau.

I walked to the market and found the town neat and clean. The islanders were friendly and I noticed several other ethnic groups, with a large portion of them having a Chinese look, running many of the shops. I stopped at the produce market and made several big orders of fruits and vegetables, making arrangements for the items to be delivered. I normally didn't resupply so quickly because as a rule I didn't know how long I would be in port but I wanted to be ready to leave quickly if needed.

I circled the plaza where the day-stalls were and became aware of the way I noticed everyone. This was not something typical for me but my senses were sharp. This must be the protective spirit in me and I smiled at the thought.

By the time I returned to *Tirak* Mei Yue had rigged side covers for the cockpit, which added to our privacy. She was busy finding places to stow the supplies I had ordered. Her sense of order was good and I could see we were like-minded in our need of an uncluttered salon.

I still needed some down time as my queasiness returned so while I napped Mei spent the afternoon swimming and enjoying the sights around the small harbor. That evening we enjoyed a meal of fresh stir-fried vegetables and several glasses of juice and then we headed for the dock. Mei desperately wanted to hold my hand but we did not want to draw attention.

As we walked through the night market I bought several items for Mei. When I received a look of interest I explained that I had several nieces nearly the same size of this little girl and I had asked her to walk with me while I purchased items. She examined each item as if it cost a small fortune and spoke to me in French and occasionally in Thai, never in English.

We moved through the market and down the main street. I bought ice cream for the two of us and it was exciting for me to watch Mei Yue's eyes taking in everything. She was trained in many subjects but had never been allowed to leave the island where she was taken to. It was all fresh and new to her. We returned to *Tirak* and I was soon asleep in my cabin as Mei went through her newly purchased treasures.

The next day I sent her off in the dingy to get her away from the docks while I had several repairs done to *Tirak*. I watched with trepidation as she sped off toward shore. She did not wave but kept her eyes and smile on me until she neared the dock.

Tirak slipped her mooring and we headed for the boatyard. It took most of the day to service the engine, replace the stay and make several routine repairs. It was late afternoon when I returned to the mooring. As soon as I came out of the boatyard I saw Mei in the tender making way toward the mooring. My whole body brightened at the sight of her and from the bright smile she wore I could see the feelings were mutual.

I had given her some money but not enough to make any larger purchases and she had several bags piled in the bow. As I tied the tender to the stern, she was secretive about the contents and I allowed her, her mystery. She went below and busied herself with her horde.

I was relaxing on deck reading a book I had had no time to finish and allowed the last of my land sickness to die away. She called me down to the cabin and when I arrived she came out of her cabin wearing a tiny bikini bottom and a very shear cotton shirt. Her smile of expected praise was so that I could do nothing but admire her outfit. She was a beautiful young girl and I could see that as a woman she would be extraordinary.

I wanted to ask her to cover herself but in the tropics she wore a common style when on a boat or at the beach. I would try hard not to repress her with standards that were from my upbringing so I gave homage to her selection of colors. She ran back to her cabin in a giggle and returned with another brief outfit that, when looked at objectively, had a look of one who knew how to dress.

I asked her where she got the money to purchase all these items and she said, "You give me. You think I steal from you, hey ya?"

I laughed, corrected her English, and told her it was only a question, not an accusation. She looked at me for a moment, then smiled and explained how she had bargained for the best price. She ran back to her cabin and returned with a very nice light cotton shirt in an earth tone print and presented it to me. She insisted I try it on and it fit well. She explained that later, when she had time to make me right, she would buy brighter colors but for now this would do. She had brought out a small bag and sat next to me and removed the contents.

One of the items was a book and I recognized it immediately as one of mine. She turned to the inside cover and compared the photograph to the man sitting next to her.

She looked at me and said, "Now I know your name. Why you never tell me your name before? It very nice *Farang* name. What other people call you?"

It surprised me that I had never given her my name before but in my solitude it was enough just to exist.

I said, "People call me DJ."

"Well, I for one not call you DJ. What kind of name DJ anyway?"

I told her it's a nickname and asked if she had a nickname. She told me Chinese had many names but that I must call her Mei or Mei Yue, no other.

She said, "I read this book and tell you if good or not."

I corrected her English and she looked at me for a long time. I felt a reprimand coming but was amused by her thoughtful expression. I also pointed to the bookshelf and told her I had several books that she could read.

She said, "This is mine!" Mei continued, "It important to you I speak much good English?"

I told her it was important to her and I very much liked the way she expressed herself. I explained that I was only trying to help her for a time when it would be important to speak correctly.

She laughed and said, "You want me to talk correct. Wha that you talk? It not sound like correct English. It sound like you come from some other place. I never hear someone speak like you."

At that I had to laugh, and when I saw her anger I began to tell her about where I came from and why I pronounced words differently from others. I told her my accent was Southern American but it was still English. I told her that many people enjoyed my accent but others associated it with uneducated people.

She thought about this and finally stood in front of me, took my hands and said, "You not uneducated but you do sound different. When you talk I feel good inside, like you hold me and tell me I am good girl. So I decide. I will talk good but I will speak like you, not like people from England."

I hugged her and laughed saying, "A Southern Chinese. I would like that!"

She kissed me, opened my book and said she would call me Douglas. That night we walked the streets again, tasting, smelling and enjoying the sights and sounds of Palau.

The next day I rented a car and we drove the short distance over the bridge to Babeldaob Island. I drove around the mountain and stopped at a secluded beach with pure white sand and crystal clear water. There were coconut and tamarind trees all around and we swam and ate our packed lunch in the shade. My enjoyment increased each day this child was near me and she made me laugh at her antics and her attempts at speaking *Southern. Y'all* would take many weeks of work.

As we relaxed by the sea my thoughts went back along my childhood. I remember all the embarrassing times of my life with vivid detail but good times were slowly returning to me. I smiled at the boating, fishing and camping times I had spent with my parents.

#

I drifted off to sleep and suddenly I was in a rocky desert in the predawn hours with a rifle in my hands. I had an unusual uniform on that blended in with the desert. My rifle was long and heavy with a thick covering at the end of the barrel. As dawn broke I heard the sound I had been waiting for.

At a stone house nine hundred yards away people were stirring. I put the scope to my eye and watched men move outside and lay out mats for morning prayers. They went to a well and washed their hands, face and feet. The one I waited for was last to come out of the house and take his position at the end of the group facing a westerly direction. As they bent their heads to their mats I waited. As the man rose from his third bow I pulled the trigger and through the scope watched his head explode.

#

I must have screamed because I felt hands shaking me and I looked into the terror-filled eyes of Mei. When she was sure I was awake she laid her head on my chest and sang softly as she stroked my arm. I could feel the trembling leave me and her soothing voice was like a balm that chased away my scattered thoughts. After a moment she rose up and looked at me. The terror was gone, replaced by dark pools of love.

She only said, "Do not worry, Douglas. I will make it go away."

As we returned to the dock a worker from the chandlery was waiting with a message that my package had arrived. He looked at Mei with curious eyes but said nothing. I left her at the dock and went to pick up my package and a few other items. When I returned she was nowhere to be found. A sense of panic crept into me and I raced back to *Tirak*. Mei was there drying her hair. I asked why she hadn't waited and she told me too many people were looking at her. In the middle of the night we slipped the mooring and headed out to sea.

We sailed northeast for a few days and came to a small island atoll with a passage through the reef to a nearly closed lagoon. The water was brilliantly clear and the white coral sand reflected the light as if there were giant underwater lights illuminated. In a few of the deep holes the water was navy blue and seemed to be depthless. Fish of every hue swam around the coral heads in languid lines and clustered schools. The island was devoid of people and had a large hill at the north end but the rest was covered in coconut and flowering Laburnum trees.

We spent a week there, swimming, fishing and collecting Puka shells on the ocean side of the island. Puka shells were seashells that had been worn down to a small disk by wave action and many people wear them as necklaces. She swam topless but I did not interfere.

Mei spent a long time explaining our relationship in carefully chosen words and elucidated that she was like a daughter to me so it was perfectly natural for me to see part of her power. I could only smile at her seriousness and concur with her conclusion.

Mei saw large spider crabs and became so excited trying to catch them that it became one of the highlights for me of our stay. She was successful in gathering several into a webbed sack and made a delicious meal of them cooked in coconut milk with slivers of coconut meat and hot peppers.

Near the end of our stay we sat at the chart table and I asked her where she would like to go next. She told me she would think about it. She studied the charts, read a travel book describing the different island groups and finally went up on deck while I cleaned up our meal. Several hours later she had me sit down and told me we were going to the Cook Islands. I asked her how she came to that decision and she simply said she asked *Tirak*. That was good enough for me.

While we were still in the lagoon I showed her most of the contents of the package I had received. My agent had sent several books, including some classic tales in English and American literature, two young adult fictions, self-taught math, and a book on navigation. There was also a star chart, a book on sailing and a doll I had asked her to send. Her eyes became as big as saucers as I handed her the doll.

She asked in a small voice, "Is this for me?"

I said yes and she began to cry, causing me some concern until she looked up and I could see the pure joy in her eyes. She threw her arms around me, kissed me and then ran to her room and shut the door.

It was becoming clear to me that her joy in new things had a soulful effect on me. I was finding that emotions I had long overlooked or ignored or simply vanquished were creeping back from a place long hidden. Before Mei Yue, I couldn't remember the last big swing in emotions I had had. For me, life was something to travel through until the next step in my existence came. Joy, anticipation, laughter and full breaths were not a part of my life. Mild sadness, tears, panic and depression were things that visited me from time to time but my life was mainly apathy. My only respite was the brief encounters with the women *Tirak* brought to me and *Tirak* herself.

I had looked at creation and all its beauty and it produced little long-term effect on me but now I could feel my life changing. I was frightened by it and all that might come with this change but I would do whatever was necessary to give this child a chance in life, including sacrificing my solitude and even my life.

The memories of books and movies I had read or seen came back to me. I enjoyed action adventure and as I read or watched I tried to put myself in the main character but always found that I would be the assistant or member that followed the leader and would sacrifice my own life to aid in victory or success. As much as I tried, I could never see myself in the lead. Was this the life I would give to this child? She would lead me and I would see her victorious in the end.

I couldn't remember the last time I had enjoyed life so much as the week spent in that small lagoon. Her joy increased by the day and I watched the fear of being returned to her other life diminish equally. As we sailed through the pass she looked longingly on this tiny speck of land.

She came to me and put her arms around my waist and said, "This is where my life started over. Thank you, Papa."

Her endearment jolted me to my core but I held my emotion in. I never thought to hear that word spoken to me and as *Tirak* took us out I was blinded by its impact. I set a course back to Malakal Island but it took an hour for my mind to register the course change.

Before we entered the harbor I put Mei back into her hiding place, called the man from immigration and asked him to meet me at the dock. As I secured *Tirak* to the dock the officer came strolling down to meet me. I told him I was moving on and wanted to clear now for an early start in the morning. He stamped my passport and signed my declaration of goods and then asked me about the young girl who had been with me.

I explained I had met her family while walking the first day and that she had been my guide while on the island. He asked for her address and I explained I had met her family in the market and didn't know where they lived. I said I hadn't seen them or her for a week as I had been sailing to the outer islands. I told him I had paid her, through her parents, and bought them a few small gifts of appreciation. I told him how much I enjoyed my stay in Palau and would be sure to return.

He gave me a hard look, asked if he could go onboard and look around. I readily complied and he checked every cabin. Finally satisfied, he again mentioned the child who had been lost at sea and asked me to keep a lookout for her. We shook hands and he gave me a pleasant smile and hoped I would return soon. I had several pieces of block ice delivered, topped off the water and returned *Tirak* to her mooring. We agreed that Mei would remain below deck until we were out to sea.

Chapter 9

We left before dawn the next morning and watched the sunrise behind us chasing the night and stars back to their resting place. It was a beautiful day as we turned and beat to the north. I wanted any prying eyes to see me heading off in a direction that would take many days to arrive anywhere.

During the evening I set our course for the Cooks and turned south to run with the wind abeam until we reached the westerly winds and then we could run for days. We began our watches to give me most of the night and get me back into my routine. We sailed for ten days, only having to trim *Tirak* occasionally.

Before we reached our first waypoint I had Mei go on deck and keep watch for flotsam and kept her up on top for several hours. She was becoming irritated and wanted to come below but I wouldn't allow it. When I told her it was important she acquiesced and remained on deck. I finally asked her to come down below, sat her down, and I put a blindfold over her eyes. She tensed for a moment and then began to fidget. I told her not to move and placed the preparation in front of her.

I removed the blindfold and she could only stare at what lay before her. It was a small birthday cake with thirteen lighted candles and a small wrapped gift. She looked at me, unsure of what to do, and I told her to blow out all the candles at once and she would be granted a wish. Her eyes sparkled in the firelight and she concentrated on her objective. She blew and blew until all the candles were out and then she read the writing on the top of the cake.

It simply read, "Happy Birthday Mei Yue."

Her eyes filled with tears but I told her this was not a time to cry.

I said, "That's no way to start a new year, Mei."

She quickly dried her eyes and looked at the gift.

I told her to open it and she jumped at it. She removed the string and wrapping with great care and put them aside. She opened the small box and removed a polished Puka shell necklace strung on a fine chain of gold and now the tears could not be restrained.

She made me sit down on the bench seat and sat in my lap. She wrapped her arms around me and kissed my cheek and then turned her cheek to me. I kissed her softly and wanted to tell her I... but the words would not come so I hugged her to me to enjoy her happiness. She put the necklace on and promised to keep it forever. She took wrapping, string and box to her cabin and then returned.

She started to kneel on the floor but I caught her and made her look me in the eye and then said, "You will not kowtow to me again. You are my equal and we are family. I want you to be happy."

She thought for a moment and then she said in all seriousness, "Thank you for this honor. My wish is for you to be happy, too."

I laughed and told her she shouldn't tell others her wish because it wouldn't come true. She replied that this was not her birthday wish and that this one would come true. Tears sprang to my eyes and I went up on deck to watch the sunset and let the wind dry my eyes. She brought me a piece of cake and one for herself. We sat in the cockpit and watched the day end in brilliant sherbet orange and clear blue. This was a good day.

Over the next ten days Mei Yue would read, spend time going over the charts and navigation gear, and ask me to explain some of the sailing terms from her book. She also would come to the cockpit and read my book and look up at me from time to time.

When she finished it she stood and said, "This is a good book. If only life could be like that." She looked at me with a seriousness I hadn't seen for a while and said, "Someday I will ask you to sign this book for me."

She would have me re-read my book aloud and stop me at points that interested her and make notations, then had me continue reading. She would always return the book to her room and once made certain that I knew where she hid it.

Mei stood her watch with new confidence and often made minor adjustments in *Tirak*'s trim. I would show her how to adjust the travelers, outhaul, Cunningham and all the items needed for best speed, just one time and then she would try it on her own. She was a natural helmsman, keeping her course dead on as the sea moved around us.

At times she would sit beside me with her hand resting lightly on my arm and look at me with a penetrating stare. It was a little unnerving but I remained silent during these sessions. For the most part she allowed me my solitude as she was in a constant state of activity.

She had found a book on how to use the internet and pored over it in fascination. She asked about my laptop and I showed her how to start it and told her to explore it all she wanted. I had not been around children except for brief periods and it amazed me to see one so hungry for knowledge. I noticed once that she had hooked my laptop to my sat phone but refrained from saying anything. An hour later everything was back to its normal place and I thought no more of it.

Cruising on a long tack far from land was the only real relaxing part of sailing. It was hard work, physically and mentally, when close to land or in traffic and especially in a storm. There were many days where sleep was only a catnap so when the opportunity arose to relax I took advantage of it. Mei sensed this and let me enjoy my daydreams.

#

After I had crept through my youth, I suddenly discovered I was an accomplished athlete. To my great surprise, I excelled at team sports but even with my new-found skills I often fell short when pitting myself against a lone opponent. It was not a lack of ability but I knew in my heart I was not good enough to overcome my failures.

There was a man who took a keen interest in me and spent long hours talking and allowing me to finally face my fears head-on. I came away from the experience with a new power within me. I was confident and had no fear of failure. I started training with other likeminded men. I trained in hand fighting, knives, and firearms of all types.

#

I came out of my daydream confused. This was a new track of my life and I had no recollection of ever doing any of those things. It left me shaken, and as I looked around Mei was there. She moved close to me and laid her head on my shoulder. I could feel her soothing aura hug me. She never said a word when she offered me her comfort like this but only smiled and returned to the cabin.

I couldn't believe all children were like her, with a gift of empathy and ability to give solace. She was at times like a cool drink of mountain spring water and other times like a bee preparing for winter. Her activities were always on my periphery, never moving into my space unless she had a question or felt me sliding back into my hole.

With such a mature bearing, she was still a young girl and had no fear of being demonstrative in her pleasures. I shaved some of our precious ice into a cup and added cherry syrup to show appreciation of her hard work. I brought it up to the cockpit and she screamed with joy at the sight of it. She launched herself at it and was soon beaming with her rosy lips. She told me it was one of the few treats she was allowed as a child. I laughed at her discussion of childhood and she gave me a momentary glare but return to her joyful delight of slowly consuming the treat.

After we reached the currents and wind shift I was looking for, we turned to the next waypoint and began another long tack with the wind still abeam. Running with the wind and waves coming at us from the side, abeam, is slower but it gives us a constant breeze and saves wear and tear on the equipment.

Tirak was ready for record runs but gave no protest in our more sedate mode. We could have run with the wind and made better time but running with the wind drops the breeze across the boat to almost nothing and the motion was more a swaying and not as pleasant as being healed over with a good breeze.

On our second day of the new tack Mei came on deck just before sundown. She sat next to me and we watched the glories of prism light that painted the cotton balls above us. The horizon was clear and she seemed to be waiting. Just as the sun dripped below the horizon the green pop effloresced and, as if it were the signal flare she had been waiting for, she turned to me.

She said, "Douglas, it is time to begin. I tell you... I will tell you some things I expect from you and you will do as you're told." I looked at her, astonished at her new-found English and also at her brazen commands.

I started to say something but she snapped, "You no talk, hey ya! I am sorry to speak like this to you but you must know it is because I need you to be strong for me. I need you be strong for you, too."

I could see and hear the effort she was putting into her speak. I could also see the glistening of tears in her eyes so I nodded and remained quiet.

She took a deep breath and then took both my hands in hers.

She said, "I will try to speak correctly but if I make a mistake, then just listen to my words, please. You have become very important to me. You save my life! When I went to sea in that little boat I think I will die, but that was ok. I knew I couldn't go back to the life that was made for me. I give up my family and that hurt very much but not enough to turn back. I live off small fish and little rain for many days and I think that this is better than other life. *Tirak* find me and I know that is true. She find me for you. After you pass my test, I look at you very much and I see a life that needs help. I tell you before, you once very dangerous man but now you only danger to yourself. That must change because you have me now. You become very important to me. You are only one who care about me. You have many people who care about you but you don't see them. You only look to the end of the path and that is a long way and the wrong way, hey... Sorry."

She stopped for a moment, stood, kissed me and sat back down. I had only a vague idea about my life as a dangerous man, but with a clarity brought on by years of apathy, I knew precisely what she meant by looking to the end of the path.

She pulled my hand to bring me back and continued. "You are very important to me, not only because you help me but I see how much I need you! And you need me. You must start to remember now. I know it will hurt you but I will never leave you alone to hurt by yourself. You did something that hurt you inside but I know you could never do something bad like that except in accident. You must face this thing and you must tell me this thing. I promise I never leave you by myself. Even if you tell me to leave, I won't do it! I promise I never tell anyone what you say to me about this."

Now tears were flowing from her and she laid her head on my chest for a long moment. I could feel something in me tearing at the locked doors. I couldn't take the pain I was causing her. She sat up quickly and slapped my face a stinging blow. It froze my thoughts.

"You still try to blame yourself for everything. You have done nothing to me, except care for me and protect me and I even think you have love for me. Stop taking everything. This not your fault! I, Jing Wei- Mei Yue, tell you that you are good man and I won't allow you this blame!" She kissed me again. "Now, I finish for now. You must do what I say to protect me. I need you more than you need me but you no good to me if you don't come back. Last thing I say for now. Douglas John Durian, I love you and you are my family."

She lay down and put her head in my lap and went to sleep. I could feel how much effort and control that it had taken her to unburden herself. My mind was in turmoil as well. She had said words I had longed to hear but I never expected them from a child. As the words she spoke repeated themselves in my mind I could feel the cement that held us together change to steel. I would do whatever I must to earn her trust, even if it meant my sanity, because she loved me!

The next day she hovered about me, seeing to my needs; almost as if she were ashamed of her speech and her rudeness toward me. I stopped her after the noon day recording of our position and distance. I took her in my arms and held her tight for a moment, kissed her cheek and then turned my cheek to her. She kissed me firmly and a smile of relief came to her face. She jumped up and ran on deck.

After I finished my routine with the navigation, I went on deck and saw her at the bowsprit and joined her. We watched as dolphins rode our bow wave and a few even performed acrobatic feats to our delight. After our evening meal she allowed me the solitude of the cockpit as she again turned her attention to my laptop.

I sat with a glass of brandy and cigar and watched the rollers pass under us. They came out of the night and were lit momentarily by the running and cabin lights. Black beasts with sparkling backs moved past as they grazed in a huge herd, lifting and lowering us gently as they moved on in peace.

The wind was at about twenty knots and *Tirak* moved along briskly, only looking ahead. I looked over her trim and took the wheel to feel her. The stars put on their play with the Big Bear low in the northern sky. I chose a first magnitude star to keep station with for an hour or so.

Over the horizon flashes of lightning lit the western sky. The flashes looked like an artillery battle fought from a long distance away. Mei has found my music selection and put on *Andrea Bocelli* and piped him into the cockpit. The great tenor carried us deep into the night. She relieved me for a few hours and I lay down on the starboard cockpit bench and was soon asleep.

Chapter 10

#

The night was cold and crisp as I moved through the bare dead rocks. My only light were the stars and crescent moon. My pack was heavy, filled with the food and equipment I needed for a long journey. My boots were soft and hushed as I moved toward my objective.

Suddenly children were running at me with automatic weapons and their eyes glowed eerie green. As they circled me, more children, this time all small girls ran in at me with long curved blades and slashed at me. My arms refused to bring my weapon up to defend myself against children.

As they came in I could see they all had the same angelic face, with dark hair, cream-colored skin and bright green eyes. They smiled and laughed as they plunged their blades into me. I stumbled and fell hard to the rocks, losing my pack. I lay on my back bleeding but not dying and the girls became only one and she moved on top of me.

I was frozen, unable to turn my head. Her face was only inches from mine as she held me with her gaze. Her look implored me to help as blood came flowing from her hair, across her face and dripped down to mine. Her expression became frightened and as I watched, her eyes began to glaze over. She rose up and showed me the knife sticking from her chest and she then pointed to the hand that held the blade. It was my hand and I tried to move but all my struggles were to no avail and those green eyes never strayed from my face as they turned to terror.

#

I cried out and she was gone, the rocky plain was gone and in their place was a soft voice soothing me and telling me to come back in peace. The voice blanketed me in tranquility and I fell into a deep sleep.

Her voice roused me and I opened my eyes to the beautiful dark brown eyes of Mei Yue. She told me she needed to rest and I sat up ready to take my watch. The dream had faded to only an ethereal touch, except for the voice that took the pain away. I tried to cling to it but it too slipped away. Mei hugged my head to her small chest and her fingers ran through my hair.

She asked, "Tomorrow will you tell me about your dream?"

I told her if I could remember it we would talk. She kissed my forehead and went below. I heard her cabin door close.

I stood up and scanned the dark horizon and then moved forward to put my back against the mast. I felt *Tirak* vibrating through me, adding her own comfort. These were new dreams but I knew they had been in my past also. I didn't like what they were doing to me. My emotions were coming back to life and I wanted to cast them away. I wanted the invariance that had taken so long to develop. I needed my world two shades from bright, not the one of joy and inclusiveness followed by suffering and fright. I knew with an innate sense that there could be no joy, happiness or even pride unless there was suffering, pain and loneliness. My world had been becalmed, with only minor rises and falls like a mild tide. I also knew that world was over now that this child had come into my life.

The thought struck me that if she were gone or even dead... Revulsion and despair swept me to the deck and I was violently ill. As I clung to the mast the voice returned and it flowed over me like a gentle mountain stream washing me clean again. I could feel the soothing touch of *Tirak* aiding the voice as I returned. I went to the cockpit, opened a seat hatch and took a bucket and line out. I moved to the bowsprit and scooped seawater with the bucket and poured it over my head to wash my clothes and soul. I stripped and poured buckets of water over me. I rubbed my body clean and as I touched myself, he sprang to life with an urgent need. I stood and let the wind dry and calm me. I turned my head to see the smiling face of Mei watching me from the cockpit. She gave me a long look and then went below.

In the heat of the day as I sat in the shade of the cockpit she came up on deck in her swimming bottoms and light shirt. She made me move and took the bucket out. She moved to the bowsprit and lowered the bucket into the fast-moving water. She placed the bucket on the deck and removed her clothes, clipping them to the forestay.

I watched, fascinated by her poise and balance as she tipped the bucket over her head. I admired her faerie form. All her wounds had healed and I had helped her cut her hair to give it a less ragged look. It was still long and flowed over her shoulder in the wind. Her body had filled out from the emaciated state I had found her in. Her girl child lines were changing to a promise of the woman she would become. Mei's muscles were strong and smooth from the work and balance required on a sailing vessel. I thought of the boys I would soon have to battle off our boat to protect her and I smiled.

She was desirable to me in a way that gave me no embarrassment or guilt. It was paternal desire. As my gaze cast over her developing chest, I raised my eyes to her face and those dark eyes trapped me. Her smile was not one of allure but of pride; that I looked at her with no thought of the power within her. She dressed and came and stood before me.

She said, "I feel safe when you look at me. You have beautiful body, too."

She laughed as my face blossomed to the pink of sunrise.

I worked on deck the rest of the day. One of the portside winches had developed a click and I disassembled, cleaned and lubricated it. Sailing will harden your body and give it strong, clean lines from the constant balance that was required to stay afoot and all the duties required to keep the boat in Bristol shape. Your endurance would lag due to the confinement, so part of my routine each day was breathing and body exercises.

Mei joined me almost every day as I taught her to breathe, to raise her heart rate and extend her endurance. We made a game of the rapid breathing and isometrics and usually ended by me tickling her into submission. I would always be breathless at the end and she would merely stand and go below smiling, her breathing barely above normal.

I saw a weed line off the port bow and told Mei to bring up two rods and a box of lures. As I shortened *Tirak*'s sail area Mei rigged both rods. She asked what we would fish for and I told her to wait and see. I sailed *Tirak* until we were leeward of the large weed line and then brought her up into the wind, right at its edge. I told Mei to cast along the edge of the weeds and if she hooked anything to bring it to the starboard side, away from the weeds.

As we both cast, her line went taut and danced in the water. I yelled at her not to bring in the fish until I had hooked one and I quickly reeled my line in. Mei dutifully brought the fish to the side but didn't lift it from the water. She was straining and giggling, trying to subdue the strong flash of color below the water. I slapped my lure on the surface and a school of flashing percoidean rainbows filled the water below. I told Mei to bring her fish in and club it and then quickly get her lure back in the water. As she hooked up again I brought my thrashing rainbow onboard and subdued it. I told her to leave her fish in the water and watch the school.

There were hundreds of them swirling around their hooked brother, thinking that he had something they all wanted. Mei squealed with laughter as the ten-pound lightning bolt tried to break free.

As the school disappeared I assisted her in bringing the MahiMahi, dolphinfish, onboard. They were beautiful males with a pronounced flat head rising high above shining eyes. Their colors were striking, from bright yellow, silver and red to vivid blue. As their life left them the colors dulled.

I assembled a cutting table and quickly cleaned them as Mei went below to make a fiery sauce with soy and wasabi. I cut a number of thin slices and then made steaks of the rest. We enjoyed sashimi and laughed as we watched the wasabi attack the other. I packed the steaks into the freezer but left two in the cooler for our dinner that night.

I insisted on cooking the fish in my fashion, with butter and *Old Bay*, sautéed scallions and a few slivers of ginger. Mei Yue looked dubiously at this western style of cooking but I saw the smile reach her eyes as she tasted the flesh. I served it with fried sliced potatoes and blanched frozen broccoli. I allowed her a small glass of watered wine and she took pride in drinking the biting fermented grapes.

We moved to the dark cockpit and I enjoyed a brandy and cigar and she a ripened mango. As I relaxed and watched the silver tail of the crescent moon follow along dutifully, I felt Mei move closer to me. I looked down and saw her watching me closely.

She asked, "You are happy?"

I answered, "Yes, and content as well."

"That make me happy, too. Will you tell me about your dream? It is time for me to help you more."

I sat for a long time thinking if I should answer or not. Why should I bring suffering into this beautiful night? I did not want to relive the darkness but I knew I must if I were to fulfill my promise to this child. I thought about crawling back into my hole of solitude but it was a choice I wouldn't make because I needed this warm thing that waited patiently with her saucer eyes looking up at me.

She saw my turmoil and relented by saying, "First, I want to hear about how you lived when you were a child."

I slowly began to recount my youth and she sat wrapped in my words. I talked for two hours and as I paused, I thought I had never talked for so long in many years. She stood, kissed me and looked at me.

I kissed her and she said, "Enough for tonight. You will learn to trust me completely. I put my life in your hands and you make me proud."

She left me to go below and I couldn't stop the feeling that she was dissatisfied with what I had told her. Could this slip of a girl have the presence to know the voids of my speech? I couldn't get over the feeling of role reversal but in some ways I took solace in it. I knew I must learn to offer the same comfort in her times of strife but it was an action I must learn again. I looked forward to the daylight, when my life... our life could continue without the visits of night terrors. I went to the bowsprit and spent a long moment flying across the water free from my haunts.

The next day I was requested to attend a luncheon prepared by the gourmet from the east; MahiMahi sautéed in oyster sauce and a portion stir fried with mango, onions and sweet peas, served over fragrant steamed rice. I sat back after the succulent meal and applauded the epicurean master. Mei beamed and dipped in a *wai* of appreciation.

She busied herself the rest of the afternoon manipulating the contents of my navigation system. I looked over her shoulder once but she stopped until I moved on. I had no idea what she was doing but I knew she was careful not to program any inputs into the system so I left her to her secrets.

We had a light meal at our evening repast and I went on deck with my usual libation. I sat a little unnerved, waiting for her to continue with her analysis but she delayed until I finished my cigar before venturing forth onto the field. She could tell that this was a difficult position for me and made an effort to ease my anxiety. She sat next to me, took my hand and put it around her shoulders and snuggled close.

She said, "I only do this to help you. Then you will be able to help me. Do you believe me?"

I kissed the top of her head and said, "Yes, I believe you, Mei. I will try but this is not easy for me."

She looked up at me with glistening eyes and said, "I no want to hurt you, Pa... Douglas."

She put her head to my chest and waited. I started over again but this time I left nothing out. She stopped me when I reached my college years and smiled brightly up at me.

She said, "You are good man. Soon you be strong again."

She pushed me down below and took over her watch. I heard her make a few adjustments to *Tirak* and could feel the bow wake passing by a little more swiftly. I finished my book and poked my head above the deck and could not see her. I went up the stairs and looked forward. She was flying in the bowsprit with her hair streaming behind her and her arms opened wide. This was a moment I would not disturb so I returned to the cabin until I heard her moving to the cockpit.

We watched the sun rise above the small seas and the morning brightened, gray above black to azure above royal blue. Later that morning we sat and discussed our port of call. I let her read over the descriptions of the many islands in the Cook chain and explained our first port must be one of three or four to satisfy the local authorities.

I didn't like the idea of having to smuggle her into every country we entered and being furtive in our actions when ashore but for now it was the only choice before me.

I had sent off a detailed email to my agent, entrusting her with the secret of Mei Yue. My faith in her, my literary agent had never been questioned and I needed help in resolving our dilemma. I knew she would go to my other trusted friend, my literary lawyer, but would not disclose her complete knowledge to him. Mei picked out Hondo Island and several small islets so I fine-tuned our last two waypoints and we were ready.

Each day we spent time practicing the Chinese dialect that she had learned while in training for the man who had bought her. She also spent a few minutes most days learning the 'secret' language of the Southern Redneck. She had asked before to learn my dialect but it had fallen by the wayside until she heard me use a few southern expressions, which totally confused her, and she pleaded with me to teach her this strange language. It took many hours of practice for her to say y'all and heea correctly.

I had a good laugh when one morning she came on deck and asked, "Whaat y'all doeing?" And as I was going below she called out, "Y'all come back now ya heea."

It perhaps started when I was working on one of the main winches and had it disassembled and spread all over my work table. I was trying to concentrate but had been thinking about some incident from my past and as I started reassembling the winch my hands were shaking slightly.

I shook them and said out loud to myself, "I'm shakin' like a hound dawg shittin' peach pits."

To my embarrassment Mei was standing behind me.

She stood there for a long moment thinking about what she had heard and finally asked, "Wha? Wha you just say?"

I told her to forget it but she became angry and said if she was going to teach me her secret language then I must teach her my secret language.

I laughed and explained that it was not a secret language but only a colloquial expression from the region I grew up. She wouldn't accept that and refused to talk to me for the rest of the day. Finally, I relented and began to teach her some more gentile phrases after I first explained the hound dog comment. It took a while for her to digest the concept of a hunting dog eating peaches whole and later passing the rock-hard seed pit. I was checking the charts below several hours later when I heard a most un-girl-like guffaw come from above.

She ran down the companionway and burst out, "I understand!" and fell to the bench in laughter.

So began her tutelage into the vulgarities of the Southern American language.

She slowly began to pick up my accent and inflections as well. I had lost much of my accent so she didn't sound like a Southern Belle right off the plantation but she, even with her poor grammar, began to have a decidedly southern sound. My smiles came more often as the days passed and I would hear her talking and turn to see the beautiful Chinese face looking at me and speaking with a southern drawl. I tried to convince her to drop the accent or at least learn how to turn it off and on but she took offense at this and refused to hear any more on the subject.

I made a call to my agent and ordered more books, including southern history, to be sent to our next port. My agent asked several questions and at the end of our conversation told me how much better I sounded. Just before we disconnected she told me that parenting seemed to agree with me. She promised more information soon.

Mei Yue had a natural talent of getting the best speed out of *Tirak*. She could *feel* the wind and learned to observe our surroundings and anticipate slight shifts. *Tirak* responded with leaps and bows as she sliced through the water.

I spent time with her explaining reflective wave patterns and we watched as errant waves occasionally passed us by, with their secret of land in their wake. She took this knowledge in and it amazed me how she never seemed bored or at a loss with nothing to do. The sea was in her blood and would demand her return all through her life.

I recalled even when hiking the rocky plains and mountains of Afghanistan I could feel the ocean's pull. With sudden clarity I knew that I had spent time in Afghanistan and with the memory came a soulful pain that staggered me but the why remained a mystery.

Three days out from our port of call the wind dropped to nothing and it was overcast except for sporadic openings letting the sun through. The sea continued to undulate in orderly wave patterns but it took on an oily thickness.

I called Mei to come on deck and we walked out to the bowsprit to see a phenomenon of rare occurrence. With the overcast and sun streaming through at the correct angle shining into the water ahead, the sea turned a thick molten metal color that had the appearance of liquid mercury. Our sight could not penetrate the surface of the water.

I told Mei that this was called *Silver Sea* and she stood in awed silence. I had only seen this two other times— once in the water off the Bahamas and once near the coast of Chile. This time the water had a decidedly silver-blue tint and shown like a mirror. It held her until the clouds changed the angle of the sun and then the ocean returned to its depthless clear blue. An hour later the wind returned as if it had never left and we continued on.

The weather began to change but the winds held true. Localized storms flirted around us and we had to remain vigilant. Inside the small disturbance the winds would howl and swirl with surprising strength. Mei laid out our foul weather gear and I went over our tactics if a squall line was unavoidable. We practiced shorting sails until she was adroit at the maneuvers. She looked forward to applying her new found skills and was rewarded in the late afternoon when a strong, several mile wide squall rushed at us.

We went through our paces and she took the helm as I stood close behind her. The ferocity of the squall took her by surprise and at first I had to help her hold a course but within a few minutes she pushed me away and took command. Her strength still amazed me and her appreciation of my trust warmed me. The squall lasted only about forty minutes and once in the clear we reset *Tirak*'s sails and drove on toward night.

Once during the very early morning hours a small squall came at us and I prepared *Tirak* to join the battle without Mei's aid. As the storm and winds hit, she rushed on deck with the light of anger in her eyes but said nothing as she stood close and watched me at the wheel. After the storm passed she helped shake out the sails and returned to her bed, without a word.

Chapter 11

We sighted land soon after sunrise and I decided to head straight into the harbor. I had planned on heaving to until near sunset as I did in Palau but with the wind and weather building I made for the safety of the harbor. We entered around two in the afternoon, with Mei secure in her hidden chamber and yellow Q flag flying off the starboard spreader.

With the storm approaching, customs and immigration was quickly concluded and I moved *Tirak* out to a mooring buoy and secured her with double lines and anchor ready in the stern if needed. It was a good harbor, with a well constructed breakwater at the entrance, but the wind had turned the normally placid waters into froth.

Outside the reef I could see the sea was being torn to shreds by the wind, and the waves marched like huge elephants as the current fought a valiant battle with the upper elements. The storm raged for two days and then on the third morning we awoke to a calm, gentle breeze. The waves outside the reef were still in turmoil but by afternoon lowered to their normal magnitude.

I readied the tender and as night fell we headed for shore. Mei stayed hidden in the stern until I was well away from the docks and then she slipped ashore. There was an open market filled with fresh food delights and I made several small purchases. I noticed there were a few Chinese people in the group of stalls. It was not uncommon to see and meet Chinese anywhere in the world. Either descendants from the earlier days of slavery or cheap labor or having moved for a better life, Chinese were everywhere, living and keeping their customs alive.

Mei bumped into me by prearrangement and I soon employed her to carry my burden. She jabbered in pigeon English, wore a big worn coconut frond hat and kept her face hidden from prying eyes. I quickly made more purchases and, at her physical signals, bought several items she wanted. She then escorted me down to the dock carrying my purchases. She lowered the cargo to the dock and walked away. I busied myself arranging my booty, taking my time before leaving the dock. She slithered aboard and slunk down in the bow. I quickly started the outboard engine and leaped away toward *Tirak*.

The next morning I took *Tirak* to the service dock, fueled and replenished the water tanks and then went to check for a post. I stopped by the chandler, bought several items, ordered provisions and moved *Tirak* to a boatyard dock to do some preventive maintenance on the engine. Even on a sailing vessel a small diesel engine was a must for maneuvering in tight harbors and charging banks of batteries to run the electronic equipment necessary for navigation and for the small freezer and chiller units to keep fruits, vegetables and meat in good condition.

While at the dock Mei was forced to keep a low profile and when I saw two uniformed men approaching I whistled softly to signal her. Before the men approached I heard her moving into her hiding area. It dawned on me that my body had forgotten to reject the land, until that moment.

My equilibrium suddenly swept me to the deck and I struggled to maintain a calm attitude as the officials walked up to the dock. One asked if I was all right and I told him it was just land sickness. They both laughed in understanding and the other man began to ask me where I hailed from and how long I would be visiting. I gave him the information while his assistant peered into my boat.

I asked if there was a problem and he told me about a small child that had been lost at sea. I asked where the child had been lost but he only gave a broad general area without any information on the child. I could see that this man who had had Mei had a wide reach. I told them I had passed through that general area but saw no ships or flotsam.

He then questioned me about the child I was seen with at the market. I gave the same answer as I had in Palau and he looked at me quizzically. He asked for her and her parents' names. I gave him a common Chinese name but told him I did not know where the family lived. I then asked if there was a problem with hiring locals to assist me and show me around. He said that it was a little unusual for a young local female to be seen in the company of a tourist. I assured him my intentions were strictly harmless. I explained that the child had approached me and her parents had agreed to her assistance, for pay, of course. I also told him I found that young girls were more trustworthy and less likely to cause problems. He laughed and agreed but then asked if they could go aboard *Tirak* to look around. I quickly allowed them access to *Tirak*'s cabin area without going below myself. I went back to work with my senses heightened and my stomach battling my guts. I suddenly found myself practicing my hurling techniques to the delight of a school of small fish.

The two men returned empty-handed and smiled at my dilemma. As they left, the one in charge suggested that I use one of the local adults as a guide and I waved my hand in agreement. I continued work on the engine and my concentration helped my body relax. It was the first time in several years I could remember not being sick immediately on entering a calm harbor. I surmised that the storm had helped.

My provisions arrived along with several pieces of sealed mail and a package. I motored back to the mooring buoy and lay down in the salon. Mei took a cool cloth and wiped my face and arms and put the food away.

When I awoke it was near sundown and I noticed the curtains were drawn but the hatches opened, allowing the breeze to flow through the cabin.

Mei was eating but when she saw me awake she said, "People watch *Tirak*. I no...don't like this place."

I told her we would have to remain for a day or two to throw off suspicion but we would soon find a quiet spot to anchor away from prying eyes. She handed me a list of things she needed but I rejected several items as being too feminine if my purchases were checked.

I left her onboard and took the tender to the dock to make an appearance onshore. I visited several small pubs and made conversation with a few locals and then returned to *Tirak*.

I read through my mail and there was a letter from my agent. She seemed to understand the need to keep the information light but gave me a general outline of what we were up against. She wrote that if a child had parents in good standing it would be impossible to become a guardian without some form of written permission from them. She had made a few quick inquiries about the man who had purchased Mei but it was sketchy at best.

The next day I went into town alone and wandered around, seeing the sights. I found a small internet shop that also had a private room for telephoning. I made a hard line call to my agent and heard her sleepy voice for the first time in over a year. I wasn't sure if anyone in the shop could listen to my conversation so I kept my end simple. I told her I had a friend in Hong Kong who wanted to adopt a child but was having trouble finding the parents and gaining all the information needed. She went into more detail and I soon saw it would not be easy but might be doable. My lawyer had been brought in and he was exploring the avenues available to me.

She then asked if I were writing again and I said no. She said my fans missed me, and I had to laugh. She said she was serious. She had been getting several letters asking about me and when my next book would be out.

She also mentioned a woman who was trying to get in touch with me. She said the woman mentioned that she had met me once in the Marianas on Rota Island. This instantly had my attention and I asked her to forward the letter to me.

She told me of two phone calls within the last two months from a man who said he was trying to get in touch with me for some work. He had mentioned Team 5 several times but she had offered him no help. He left a phone number and email address and asked that I get in touch with him. The term Team 5 struck a chord in me but I couldn't bring the information forward. I told her to include all the information she could remember and send it along with the letter from the woman.

We made small talk for a few minutes and I asked her if I was paying her enough for all this help. She was a little offended at that but then, knowing me as she did, she forgave me. She told me I had just bought her a new car from my royalties and that I needed to spend more money before the banks send out a search party. I said goodbye and then went to a computer to do a little research on my own.

I looked up information on the Chinese Tong and got only general data. I put Blue Dragon Tong into *Google* and it came back with nothing on organized crime, just a few bars spread throughout Asia and the Pacific. One of the bars, called the Blue Dragon, was located right here on the island. I would take a look later tonight.

When I returned, Mei was bored and sat looking at several packages I had received but forgot to open. I smiled and asked her to open them and see if it was anything important. She brightened immediately and sprang at the plunder. It was for the most part spare electronic boards for the navigation equipment but also several books, including a southern history book and a technical book on navigation. To my surprise she went for the navigation book. It had taken me several courses and how-to books to get a firm grasp on navigating the sea.

It was still a daunting task without the aid of my electronic gear. I had learned to use a sexton from my friend years before and used it for quite a while until I felt proficient. I still make sun shots from time to time. It was a useful instrument and in emergencies I was sure I could get close to my destination.

I went on deck and lay down on the bench and my thoughts leaped at me with a crush I hadn't felt for more than a month. Who was I to think of taking on a child? If she turned out as screwed up as I was, it would be a great disservice to mankind. Maybe I should start thinking about finding some authorities to protect her from this man. I would go into town tomorrow and have a talk with the official who came to see me at the dock.

At the thought of losing her my depression dragged me back towards the hole that I deserved to flounder in. I didn't merit or even want the warmth and contentment I had felt since she came to me. I needed to get back to my solitude so I could drift and wait on the next stage of life. I wasn't worth...

A pain shot through my side that launched me back to reality. I sprang to a sitting position holding my side and looked into the blazing black pools of Mei's eyes. She was hunched down out of sight of land but her demeanor was that of a mother catching her child with a cigarette between his lips. I recoiled a little but she put her finger to her lips and motioned for me to follow her below.

I slunk to the cabin and she punched me in the gut with enough force to hurt. She then took my hands and sat me down in the salon. She jumped in my lap and kissed my cheek and softly ran her right hand down the other cheek. The term schizophrenia jumped to the forefront of my thoughts as I looked into the liquid orbs looking up at me.

She smiled and said, "You cannot step back. You must step forward— for me! I watch you all time, except when you go to angry toilet, so stop feeling sorry!"

It took me a moment to digest what she said but I burst out laughing at the *angry toilet*. What a perfect description of the vacuum head in *Tirak*. It sounded like the howl of a mad beast when activated.

She looked at me and said, "Wha?"

I laughed even harder and she became exasperated with me, jumped down and stormed to her room.

I looked in on her and all she would say was, "People watch us from window near dock."

I went on deck and casually looked around but since we were several hundred yards from the dock I could see nothing amiss. I went to my cabin, closed the door to block the backlight and observed the area with binoculars. I saw the official who had visited earlier watching *Tirak* with a pair of high-powered binoculars. He was not in his uniform and it dawned on me that I had not asked to see his ID. I decided we would leave in the early morning but first I wanted to visit the Blue Dragon bar.

I entered the bar from a dimly lit side street several hundred yards away from the marketplace. There was Chinese script above the doorway and multicolored rice paper lanterns softly glowed over the bar. The room was about twenty-by-twenty and had tables lining the walls. A single candle broadcast from the small table tops but only outlined the few patrons. I chose a table near the entrance and was pounced on by two chubby native girls looking to offer me their services for a nominal fee. I told them I wasn't interested but bought them each a drink to succor their disappointment. As the drinks arrived something caught my eye near a door by the bar.

I looked and only caught a glimpse of a man's outline as he passed through the doorway. It was the official, I'm sure, that had questioned me on the dock. I ordered a bottle of *John Courage* and as soft, slack-key guitar music filtered about the room I tried to listen to the other conversations going on around me. There were only two other tables occupied and the language was Chinese being spoken. I finished my beer and went to the bar and spoke to a giant Chinese man behind the bar.

I could tell if trouble ever started he was not the one to antagonize. I put on my bland, no accent American English and asked if there was anyone around who could be my guide on a tour of the island. He nodded at the two eager-to-please native girls and I smiled and said I wanted a tour of the island, not the natives. He shrugged and said try the market. I ordered another beer and took a seat at the bar waiting for the door beside the bar to open. The barman told one of the girls to get some more beer from the back and as she opened the door I heard the dialect Mei had been teaching me.

It was the secret language of the Blue Dragon Tong. The talking ceased when the door was open but I knew what I had heard. I finished my beer and casually walked out. I tried not to hurry and made several turns and stops, looking at the reflection in the storefront windows. I saw movement twice and knew someone was following me. I walked through the market and only a few stalls were still open and they were preparing to close up for the night. I bought some fried something and continued on toward the dock. As I reached my tender I prepared for an assault but no one came near me. I motored slowly back to *Tirak* and watched the dock behind me. No one had followed. I went onboard and Mei was waiting for me in the cabin.

She said, "Someone followed you to the dock! They went to the room where they were watching before."

I handed her the packet of fried whatever and she attacked it. I tried a piece and found it was fried squid and very tasty. She looked up at me and asked what I found out. I didn't want to frighten her but I didn't want to withhold from her so I told her everything and she smiled at me.

"Why you don't bring pretty girls back to boat? I no watch you."

The look on my face caused her to giggle until she had to sit down.

When I asked her what she thought of what I had heard, she said, "It's time to leave."

I agreed but set our departure time for a half hour before dawn.

As the dark of night took on lighter shades of gray-blue in the east, I motored out of the harbor. I set the main and jib and once outside I turned *Tirak* to fill the sails, shut down the engine and unfurled the staysail. The wind was light, the sea calm, and I put *Tirak* at her best point of sail and we raced for the horizon. Once we were well off shore Mei came on deck and took a deep breath. She looked at me with a smile of freedom. I turned *Tirak* on a starboard tack and with the wind on the beam we sailed toward a small atoll only a day's sail away.

To celebrate her release from incarceration, Mei grabbed the bucket and rope, stripped down in front of me and raced to the foredeck to bathe. She was laughing and twirling as the cool water raced down her willowy body. She looked up and motioned for me to join her but I declined. She went to the bowsprit and leaned on the rail, letting the wind dry her. I smiled at her uninhibited display and watched her try to call up the dolphins. Her happiness filtered back to me and I leaned back to enjoy the placid sea.

We entered the pass in the reef at sundown, the next day, the water turned from blue to turquoise to clear white from the coral sand. Mei was a little taken aback at how close the coral heads looked below *Tirak* but I assured her there was twenty feet of water below us. She kept pointing out the multicolored schools of fish as we moved into the lagoon.

My elation at being away from the harbor was dashed as I saw two native huts within a coconut grove. The lagoon was about a half mile wide but the only anchorage was near the huts. I dropped the anchor and made sure it bit into the sand and then we furled the sails and prepared for the evening.

I could see people coming down to the beach to look at us. It appeared to be two families with four young children who were dancing around their parents in excitement. The sun had set and darkness covered us from their view. Mei insisted we stay for a few days and I said we would take it one day at a time. She smiled her knowing smile and dove in the water for a quick swim. As she moved through the water she left a phosphorescent trail like a comet passing through the constellations.

Early the next morning I heard voices and went up on deck to find one of the families in a small boat lying off from us about ten feet away. I greeted them and the man paddled closer to the stern. The small male child offered me two coconuts and a bunch of bananas. They spoke only a little English but I gathered they were inviting us ashore to visit them. Mei came on deck and excitedly jumped in the boat with them. The man looked to me to see if it was all right and I smiled and nodded.

Off they went toward shore with Mei laughing and talking animatedly to the boy. I launched the tender and soon joined the group at their huts. We had breakfast of fish and something like taro paste. I introduced ourselves as father and daughter and could see no suspicion in our host's eyes. Mei's eyes gleamed at the introduction but said nothing.

One of the men and a young girl and boy were preparing to go fishing and invited us to go along. I declined but Mei accepted readily. As they walked down to the small boat, Mei ripped off her shirt to be dressed like the other girl. The women looked at me and smiled. One said I looked like a good father and I felt a lump in my throat.

I wandered the island for most of the day and the families allowed me my solitude. In the late afternoon the fishing party returned and Mei ran with a sack toward me to show off her catch. She had two large Langoustines and several nice Parrot fish. She handed the bag to me, raced to the tender and sped off toward *Tirak*. She returned with a small cooler filled with spices, vegetables and my favorite, butter.

Mei and I each prepared a sampler to add to the banquet. I charcoaled one of the fish sprinkled with *Old Bay* and Mei stir-fried a portion of lobster and fish with vegetables, soy and hot peppers. I went back to *Tirak* and brought back some beer and a good bottle of wine. It was a glorious meal and just to watch Mei laughing and playing like a child with the others was another happiness to add to my growing list of good times.

The high point of the meal was when the families tried Mei's concoction, which was delicious. When they bit into the hot peppers it was something none of them had ever experienced. An impromptu dance and running about ensued but once everyone calmed down they went back in for more. I broke out the beer and wine and even the children were allowed to taste each. I gave them watered wine and they sipped it until it was gone. The men and women began to feel the effects of the alcohol and put on a concert for Mei and me.

Their singing was high-pitched but harmonious and their dancing was peculiar from western standards. I had seen it before but for Mei, it caught her by surprise. She had expected the Polynesian rhythmic drums, swaying hips and flowing hands and arms. What she saw stopped her for a while and I explained what I knew about it. They danced, barely moving their upper bodies, moving only their feet and taking small steps to emphasize the feet. Once she understood the purpose, Mei watched as the men and women moved around each other and their ardor increased. It became very seductive but was more felt than shown.

Mei then sang *a cappella* and we were all entranced with her gentle pentagonal sound as it flowed up and down the eastern scale. I had only my harmonica to add but found that the high reedy sound fit right in with the performance.

We spent a week with these people and the experience brought me closer to Mei Yue. I found my happiness was based on hers and we learned many things about island living. The men made us *love sticks* and it surprised Mei that love could be so casual among people.

The *love sticks* were originally made by young men in a village. They displayed the long, thin, intricately carved stick during the day as they walked around the village for all the maidens to see. Late at night they would go to their intended lover's hut and push the stick through the wall of the girl's sleeping area. In the dark she could feel the carvings and know who waited outside. If she wanted him, she would pull the stick through the wall and he would slip in for a tryst. If she didn't want him, then she would push the ornament back outside and he would move on until he found a girl that desired him. The young men and women were allowed this time of awareness until they decided on a mate and then they became monogamous. Often children were produced through this joining but there was no stigma associated and the children were a part of the family, to be loved and cherished. When the woman married, the man took the child as his son or daughter.

We took them sailing and it was a delight to see these people of the sea smile and laugh as I put *Tirak* through her paces.

We left them in the afternoon of the seventh day and there were tears flowing from Mei and the women and children. We exchanged a few gifts and I secreted some money away in each of the men's gear, to be found later.

We visited several more atolls and were a little disappointed to find them deserted. I would occasionally be swept by depression in moments of solitude but it was a mild state until Mei continued her inquisition into my past.

On a night where the Milky Way looked like a silver belt across the sky that was filled with sparkling diamonds as numerous as the sand on a white coral beach she came to me.

"It is time. I know you trust me and I will never betray you. I could live like this forever but I know there are bad times coming. I will need your help. I want to hear about your life after you finished school."

I began with the resolve of telling her everything but as I went along I found great holes in my memories. She listened closely and when I came to a large gap she took me back and pried the door partway open and some of my dread slipped out.

I had met a man who saw my physical abilities and he began to restructure my confidence. It went much quicker than he had expected as I was eager to shed my insecurities and embarrassments. In the end he introduced me to a group of hardened, confident and happy men. They were Navy SEALs. I was recruited into the Marines and selected for SEAL training just after boot camp. This was unusual but my friend had cleared the way. It became a happy time and as I trained the instructors took me to and beyond my limits of endurance. I found a confidence I never knew could exist. After SEAL training a few men were selected for an even more elite team that combined with Army Delta select members.

We were inserted into hostile areas and sometimes stayed for weeks, if necessary, to accomplish the mission. We would go in alone or two or three at the most. I was picked for the individual insertions most of the time. I could remember being in Central America, South America, Africa, Middle East, and numerous times in Afghanistan. Our mission was in part to observe but when a known target appeared they were taken out.

At times I was sent out to track and find certain individuals and remove them quietly from the field of play. They were all terrorists or people of influence with the bad guys. I was very good at what I did and never came close to being detected.

One mission I remembered as I spoke was a two-man insertion in Afghanistan on which we were to take out a cell of five men. We found them in a house in the foothills of a northern pass through the mountains. They were waiting for us, alerted by some electronic gear we hadn't expected them to have. A firefight ensued and my partner was critically wounded. We had managed to kill all but one of the men and I was moving around for a better position, and just as I pulled the trigger and took the man down someone jumped me from a rock ledge. I spun, had my knife in my hand and plunged it into...

My memory came to a violent, sudden stop that left me with a tremendous headache and shaking badly. Mei flew into me and hugged me close as her voice soothed me. She even brought a momentary laugh out of me when she spoke as she helped me to my bed.

She said, "You must sleep now. You're shakin' like a hound dawg shittin' peach pits."

She put me to bed, removed my clothes and wiped me down with a cool cloth. She then sang me to a dreamless sleep.

I awoke the next morning refreshed and found her lying next to me with her arm laid across me and her fingers laced through the hairs of my chest. I looked down at my nudity and pulled the sheet up to cover myself. I looked into her eastern angelic face cuddled into the side of my chest and I relaxed in the warmth of this woman-child. Her innocence lay on top of her face as she slept but inside she was a hard taskmaster when she tried to open the doors in my mind.

The knowledge that I had been in the military and an assassin was something I had never envisioned coming from the holes in my memories. I knew the holes were there but also knew instinctively not to open the door that would shatter my melancholy life. As I thought, faces and names began to pop before my eyes. I got up and went to the cockpit and dove over the side to clear my head. I swam to the bottom of the lagoon where a cooler layer of water hovered and let the coolness soak into me.

I heard a muffled splash and looked up to see Mei driving toward me. She was nude and smiling with tiny bubbles flowing from her nose. I gave her a critical look, pointed at her body and wagged my finger at her. She pointed down at my body and I realized I was also nude. The look on my face caused a rush of air to explode from her mouth and she was forced to surface. I swam directly to the boarding ladder and went below for my trunks. I returned with her bikini bottom and tossed it to her. She stuck her tongue out at me and climbed into the skimpy cloth. We spent the whole day relaxing, swimming and exploring our little piece of paradise.

That night she relented from my therapy session and we discussed our next big move. I decided we would go to Fiji and blend in with the tourists for a while. I told Mei we would have to return to our entry point for the Cooks to clear immigration and customs. She looked concerned but only asked how long we would be there. I told her only as long as it took to top off our tanks and clear immigration. I said we would leave day or night, high or low tide, just as soon as I finished the necessary tasks.

We sailed out of the little lagoon at daybreak with streaks of golden light streaming out of the east like beacons to burn through the night. I was rummaging in the cabin and I noticed the packet of letters my agent had sent me in between two books on the shelf. I had forgotten all about them so I took them to the cockpit. My agent had told me a few people wanted to meet me so I fully expected to jettison them to the deep soon after reading.

The first printed email was from a man named Moe Justice. I felt a memory tickle the back of my brain at the name. The letter was somewhat generic but it mentioned Team 5 and spoke of a need to contact me. He gave a different email address from the one at the header and asked that I respond in *'kript'*, a word I knew meant send in cipher or code.

I decided to keep the message until I had time to think about what had been said so I put it back in the packet. The next letter was also a copied email from a woman named Sharia. The name did not ring any bells so I continued on. She spoke in platitudes about my books and how much she enjoyed them.

A line that stood out like a beacon in the night said, "My memories of Rota Island are so vivid and pleasant because of your skills."

She seemed to speak of my writing acumens but the island was one that visited my dreams because that was where my six days of paradise was spent with Jamila. I finished reading it and went back, looking more closely at the words. There was a message within it and she was telling me to meet her again but no location was given. At the bottom of the copy a few lines below her name was a series of numbers with two arrows, one at the beginning and one in the middle of the series.

There was something familiar about the sequence and as I studied them Mei sat beside me, took one look and asked, "Where is that?"

She was pointing at the numbers and it suddenly struck me that I was looking at latitude and longitude coordinates. We went down to my charts and found that the numbers pinpointed one of the main islands of Fiji.

Mei was reading the letter and she said, "Who this woman? Why she say she be there until you come for her?"

I knew that she was agitated because of her English. She now made only a few mistakes when she was not excited or upset.

I told her I didn't know anyone by that name but she looked at me and said, "You meet her on Rota?"

She then let it drop as if it hadn't happened and went to her books and remained silent. Mei was a complex girl that I could never hope to understand completely.

That night as we sailed over the black soup and under the glittering performance put on by the heavens she came to me in the cockpit with a glass of brandy, which she handed to me and sat down to wait. I knew another session would ensue after my brandy so I took my time. I put the glass in a holder and felt her hand clasp mine.

"Will you tell me about Rota Island and the woman you met there?"

It was a subject that I thought would be safe for me so I told her everything about my interlude with Jamila, leaving only some graphic details out.

She asked me, "Do you love her?"

I responded with the truth as I knew it and said that I didn't have time to find out but it might have been the case if she hadn't left for her duties.

Mei thought about this for a while and said, "I think you do love her but you don't understand obligation like Asians do. I think we will meet this woman and I will judge her." After a moment she asked, "If you do find someone else to love... will you still want me?"

I pulled her into my lap and said, "Little Bit, nothing in this world could change what we have. You are my family. I... You have chosen and I won't let you change your mind."

She smiled with glistening eyes and said, "I would like to meet this woman."

Since we were going to head for Fiji anyway, I didn't object. I could see by the set of her body that I would be seeing this person who wrote the email even if it was over objections.

We then relaxed, watching the small rollers pass us by, when she began to talk. She spoke of her fear of being separated from me and then drifted back to the time she had spent with her family just before she was given to the man.

It was a hard time for her. She studied every moment she was not working as a servant to her aunt. Her aunt disagreed with her being allowed to attend school. She said it was not a woman's place to be educated outside the home; her training should be in caring for the household and pleasing her husband. So she found many mundane tasks to fill Mei's time.

It was almost a relief when her father called her home, but when she heard the news of her imminent departure she was devastated. Her mother spoke of duty to the family and of the wealth she would bring to them. When Mei protested, her father beat her and spoke of her duty. In the end she was taken away without any praise or words from her father. When she spoke the word *duty* she spat the word from her lips in disdain. She was trembling as she spoke and I pulled her back into my lap and soothed her with words of praise and comfort.

She held me tight and cried for a long time at her loss of family but then she looked up at me and said, "You are my family now. Will you always come after me?"

I told her I would never let her go and would always be there for her. I wanted to tell her I loved her but the words stuck in my throat. I was afraid if I uttered those fateful words they would drive her away, like they had done with Jamila. She seemed to understand and smiled up through the darkness and I could see the glistening love in her eyes.

Chapter 12

She spent the entire next day in her books and one time I noticed the sat-phone hooked up to the computer. I said nothing and she offered no response. That night she spent the night in the cockpit with me, touching and staying close. She had become the contentment I had sought for years.

We spoke of our future after the legal trials we would have to overcome. I could see my life more than port to port. She would receive a proper education and I spoke to her about home-schooling and then university. She told me it would have to be a school near the ocean and I would have to remain close. I would not be allowed to wander the high seas alone. I asked her what she wanted to be and her reply took me unawares.

She said, "I want to be your daughter."

I hid my tears in the dark but she knew. She kissed my cheek and before she could turn I returned the kiss. I could feel the joy in her and we slept cuddling in the cockpit until the dawn overtook us.

The island was a dark smudge on the horizon and I knew it would be late afternoon before we reached the harbor. She went below and continued her studies in the navigation book. Just before entering the harbor she took her place in her hidden compartment.

I went directly to the public dock and sought out the government officials to clear port. The man from Immigration said I would have to go with him to his office to answer some questions. I protested but it was plain that he would not relent. I said I needed to put my boat at a mooring because I didn't want to leave it unattended at the dock. He agreed so I motored out to a mooring and whispered to Mei what was happening. I told her to stay in the cabin until I returned and then we would leave. I took the tender back to the dock and chain-locked it to a large cleat.

It was nearly dark when we reached the official's office and there were several men waiting for me. One was a policeman and he questioned me about my last visit to the town. He wanted the name of the child I had spoken to and hired to aid me with my packages. I explained that I had already answered these questions to the police two weeks before. He looked surprised and made a quick call to the station. He then told me there was no report of my being questioned before. I told him the name of the man in uniform that I had spoken to and he said that no one by that name worked for the police or any other government group on the island.

He began again asking about the young girl and her parents and I answered in the same manner as before. He went out of the office and the customs man began to ask about the items I had bought and packages I had received. I answered all his questions but when the Immigration man stepped forward I became angry and asked why I was being questioned. He told me it was routine when a child was involved. I explained I had been gone for two weeks but he continued to ask where I had been. I named a few islands but left out the atoll where we had met the families.

It took over two hours of questions and answers and anger on my part before the policeman returned. He said it had all been a mistake. Someone had reported a young girl missing that fit the description of the girl seen with me but the child was found a few hours ago. He said I was free to go and if I required any further assistance to please ask. I withheld the expletives that burnt my tongue and only nodded and then walked out.

I hurried to the dock and raced to *Tirak*. As I stepped into the cockpit I knew something was wrong. A cabinet door below slammed as the wake of a passing boat rocked *Tirak*. She seemed angry but I knew that it was only my emotions projecting to her.

I went below cautiously, picking up a deck knife from its holder on the bulkhead. The only sounds were the lapping of water on *Tirak*'s hull. I checked my compartment and found it in disarray. Someone had searched my room. I moved to Mei Yue's room and found it tossed. I went to the other compartment, where Mei concealed herself, and found it barely touched. I said a prayer and lifted the mattress. She was not there but I saw that her small bag of possessions was still tucked into a cubby against the hull. I quickly went through the boat and the panic of my past began to freeze my blood.

I forced down my feelings of despair and panic and went through the cabin again. I went on deck, turned on the spreader lights and searched for clues. Nothing was out of place so I turned the bright lights off and sat down.

A single thought came to me. They had found us and had taken her away. I fought the emotions of my past and let anger come to the forefront to burn away the others. I had to move quickly while she was still on the island. I leaped into the tender and sped to the dock. I ran all the way to the market looking for anything unusual. The Chinese vendors watched me but when I looked they turned away. I went to a man about my age selling handmade trinkets and questioned him. He knew nothing but told me if it was a Chinese matter… I should not interfere. As he spoke he looked off toward the side street where the Blue Dragon bar was located.

I ran halfway there but then slowed, trying to make a plan for entering the bar. I was calm until I stepped through the doorway. Then a fiery demon rose in my soul. I raced toward the door beside the bar and burst into the waiting arms of a gang of men. I'm a strong man and I struggled to free myself but iron grips held me.

I continued to struggle and a voice spoke in the Tong dialect, "Do not hurt him! If necessary, we will kill him later but for now try to be gentle."

I struggled for a while longer, not wanting them to know I knew their dialect, and then I relaxed a bit and looked around. The official who had spoken to me several weeks before stood off to the side. This was the same man I had seen observing *Tirak* with binoculars. He was dressed casually and he had a pleasant look on his face.

He said in flawless English, "Please try to calm down, Mr. Durian. We have no wish to harm you."

"What have you done with her?"

"She is being returned to her guardian and he sends his warmest appreciation for your assistance in saving the child's life. If there is anything we can do to repay you, it will be done."

I said, "I want to speak to her!"

He looked at me with a smile and replied, "Of course. If you will kindly calm down, I will put you in touch with her."

I relaxed and felt the hands ease their grip on my arms. I looked at the men holding me and recognized the large bartender but the others were new. The room was drab but had a sturdy table under a stained glass hanging lamp. There was Mahjong tiles stacked neatly on the table, waiting for the contestants. The rest of the room appeared to be used for storage. The man stood nearby and spoke into the phone using the dialect.

He said, "Has she been warned what to say? Listen closely and take the phone if she strays. I will listen to the white monkey. If he is not satisfied, then we will take him and drop him in the sea. Is she on the plane yet...? Very well put her on."

He turned to me and smiled brightly.

"Mr. Durian, she is excited to thank you for saving her."

He handed me the phone and the hands released me.

I put the phone to my ear and said, "Hello?"

Mei's voice came over the line, soft and sweet. "Hello, this is Jing Wei. You not forgot me yet, yes?"

I told her I had not forgotten and asked if she was all right.

She replied, "Oh, very much yes! I go back to my duty. You know about duty?"

"Yes, I know of duty but can I see you again?"

"No, not possible. You must forget Jing Wei. She go to duty, very happy."

Her voice had the animation of joy but her English told another story.

She continued, "I must go now. You don't forget to sign the book. Don't let that damn hound dawg eat no peaches. Y'all git back to yor rug rat now, ya heea!"

I heard talking in the background and she answered in the dialect, saying it was just a way of saying goodbye. They told her to end the conversation.

She spoke into the phone and said, "Wha?"

I said, "Surenuf, Little Bit." I could feel her waiting for more and I softly said, "*Paw rak luk sau mach. Paw ja gap maa lap luk reo.*"

She said, "*Ka...* I no understand wha you say. I must go now to my duty. Have a much good life." As she finished she whispered, "*Luk sau rak Paw duay.*"

And then she hung up.

I handed the phone back and the hands did not return to hold me. I wanted to pound these people and make them tell me where she was but I knew I could not overcome four men so I stood calmly.

The man said, "Do you see that Jing Wei is fine and happy to be returned to her guardian?" I responded that I understood and was pleased to help.

They all gave me a half bow and he said, "My mas... employer is in your debt."

I asked how I could get in touch with him if I ever needed a favor and was told to come to this bar and all would be taken care of.

I was allowed to leave and I walked slowly back towards the dock, trying to remember every word Mei had spoken and all I had heard from the others. I went to *Tirak* and sat at the chart table and wrote everything down I could remember. I opened the cooler for a drink and found a sandwich on a plate waiting for me. Mei had made me supper and put it away until I returned.

Tears flooded my eyes and despair raced through my soul. I collapsed on the bench and sobbed like a child at my loss. I lay in my sorrow for a long while and suddenly in my ear her voice told me to get up and help her! I jumped up but no one was there. I washed my face and went back to the dock in the tender.

I walked the streets the rest of the night and even started off across the island to the small airport. A few miles out of town an old man in an ancient truck offered me a ride. He was a kind man and saw my distress.

He laughed and said, "I can see you have woman trouble. Let her go and find a new one, unless you love her. If you love her, you must remember and go to the ends of the earth to find her."

He laughed again and then became silent. He stopped near the airfield and we shook hands and then he drove off. The airfield was deserted except for one old plane partially disassembled. I walked over to the hangar and sat down and watched the sunrise.

It was dull and lacked any color but as I looked around I felt Mei had been there.

I waited two hours until a dark-skinned man opened the hangar doors to begin his work day. He was surprised to see me but offered me a cup of java, coffee, and even a few bananas. As I ate I asked about any planes that were there yesterday and he remembered one small jet coming in around sunset but it must have left during the night. I asked if he knew the tail number and he went to a ledger and wrote down the information on a scrap piece of paper. He laughed and said he was the mechanic, fueler, groundskeeper and secretary. I thanked him and started off back to town.

I had only gone a few hundred yards when a young man rode up and offered me a ride on the back of his small motorcycle. He said he was the son of the man at the airport and his father asked him to give me a ride. The people here were easy to like, even in my haze of need. I made it back to *Tirak* and collapsed in the salon, asleep before my head hit the cushion.

I awoke and could see by the dim light that the sun had set and night was rushing in. I went to the chart table and looked over what I had written down. Mei used the name Jing Wei, which meant *little bird*, and the name struck my memory lightly. I thought back to all the conversations we had had and remembered one night when she used that name.

It was the first time she had used my name and commanded me to protect her. She had calmly told me I had to remember my past so I could protect her in her times of need. She had told me that I had been a dangerous man but now I was only a danger to myself. Just before she finished she had said that Jing Wei- Mei Yue loved me and called me by my full name. Jing Wei was the name known to these people who held her, but Mei Yue was a name only I knew her by

I read over what I had written of our phone conversation. She spoke of duty, and I remembered the last time she spoke of duty was after I told her about Jamila. She almost spit the word out as something so distasteful she wouldn't let it sit on her tongue. Her English was more broken than when I had first found her so she was putting on a show for her captors. Then near the end she spoke with a perfect southern accent, which must have thrown her listeners off. She told me not to let the dog eat peaches. I had used that expression once when my hands were shaking while I tried to put a winch back together. She made me explain it and then our *Southern English* lessons started in earnest. She was telling me not to start shaking and to be strong. She told me to come and get my rug rat. She was my *rug rat* and she was telling me I had to come and rescue her. I started to make an outline of important phrases she had used.

She said not to forget to sign the book. That made no sense to me so I wrote it down and drew a star by it. In the last part of our conversation I spoke a quick phrase in Thai, which we were both competent in. I told her, "*Paw rak luk sau mach. Paw ja gap maa lap luk reo.*" This translated to, "*Papa loves his daughter very much and Papa will come and get his child quickly.*" She had used the word "*Ka*" before she said she didn't know what I had said. *Ka* was used by Thai women in polite conversations. It also meant agreement or yes in normal conversations. She had whispered, "*Luk sau rak Paw mak duay,*" which meant "*Papa's daughter loves him very much also.*"

It had been the first time I had said I loved her, even if it was in another language. I would change that when I saw her again. I did love her and would go to the ends of the earth to find her.

I went back to the Blue Dragon bar and found no one I recognized there, including the bartender. I spoke to the new bartender and he told me he had worked there for years. I asked about the big guy who was there last night and a few days before. The man said he had been sent away by the owner a few weeks ago to work in a bar on another island. He didn't know who took his place while he was gone. He called one of the bar girls over and after I bought her several drinks she opened up. She said that the big guy and several others just showed up one night and told the girls that it was none of their business.

She said, "I think it was the day before I saw you the first time."

She smiled and looked at her empty glass and I motioned for a refill. I asked if I could go in the back room and the bartender shrugged his shoulders. I walked in the room and flipped on the light. The table was gone and the only things there were cases of beer and liquor. The people were gone and so was Mei! I made my way back to *Tirak* and sat in the cockpit without a clue of what to do.

The next day I went to the government house and tried to get information on the aircraft that had landed two days before. It was abundantly clear after about twenty minutes that I would not receive any help. Government workers everywhere seemed to think their stations in life were well above the civilian population. They guard their positions as if state secrets might slip out to the wrong ears.

I went to the internet shop that had long distance telephone service and called my agent. It was early in the morning her time but she sounded happy to hear from me. I explained a little of what had happened and then gave her the aircraft tail number of the plane that had been here for only a few hours. She asked if I had received the package she had sent several weeks before and I told her I had. I told her I would try to check my email daily and she hung up with a promise to find the information I needed. I went back to *Tirak* with the weight of the world on my shoulders.

Something my agent said made me take the letters she had sent out again and reread them. I wouldn't be going to Fiji for a while so I put the letter from the woman aside. I would not believe that it was Jamila. When I read the other letter the name Moe Justice again touched my memory but I couldn't draw it forth. I put both letters aside and hunger drove me to make a simple fare. I went to the cockpit with a cigar and brandy but neither brought me any satisfaction. I lay back on the bench and let my mind drift.

I went back to Mei's demand for me to remember my past so I could protect her. Misery of my failure crashed down on me and the failures throughout my life choked me until I cried out in despair. *Tirak* remained still on her lead and she offered no comfort. She seemed to be waiting. Through tear-clouded eyes, I looked out and saw Mei's eyes looking back at me with anger at my weakness. I drifted off to sleep with her stern look piercing my soul.

Chapter 13

#

A young black man about my age was walking toward me smiling. He was not tall but I could tell by his build he was a powerful man. He walked on cats' feet and even with his smile he was conscious of everything around him. He could be a dangerous man when necessary.

He sat on the park bench next to me and put out his hand. I could see a tattoo on the inside of his forearm. It was crossed scimitars above a skull. I don't know how I knew but it was a military insignia. He began to talk like we were old friends and he spoke of confidence and ability. Why was he speaking about things I had no knowledge of? I tried to rise but he shoved me back in my seat and locked his eyes with mine. Slowly his face became familiar and his white toothy smile grew wider.

He said, "Dougy, it's time to suit up. The past has forgiven you but the future of the next child is completely in your hands so buck up, buddy." He stood up in front of me and said, "Because you saved my life and I love you, Dougy, I'm going to open you up and let the bad spill out. You are about to receive more justice."

He swung his right arm in a short cross to the left side of my head and stars and pain filled my being.

#

My eyes flew open and a stabbing pain that nearly blinded me forced me to the side and I threw up into the water. I stripped down and dove in the clear water of the harbor and went as deep as the pain would allow. When I looked up I could see *Tirak*'s underside as she lazed at her mooring. She was beautiful from every angle.

In the cool clear water near the white coral sand floor of the harbor my pain eased until it was only a painful memory. My need for air forced me to the surface and I climbed back aboard *Tirak*, dried off and dressed. I looked around to see if anyone viewed my nudity but it was early morning and I had no onlookers.

I sat down to think about my dream. The man said he was giving me more justice... Why was that important? Like a flash, the name Moe Justice rushed in from my past. Moe Justice... More Justice. This was the man that took me on as a project and made me into a confident and dangerous man. We stayed together all through Team 5's training and incursions. We were a team when the mission required multiple assets.

I ran down to reread the letter from Moe Justice. It didn't say anything specific but there was enough there to see he was trying to get in touch with me and knew who I was. I opened my laptop and composed a generic response with my email address. I used a 128-bit encryption code to send it off. I also told him my agent's name and number and made sure he knew she was only a go-between and had no knowledge of the past.

I then wrote to my agent and explained to her how to handle any contact from the man. I told her to use her own judgment as to how much information she passed on.

Just before I sent the coded emails I decided to write to this Sharia in Fiji with a generic letter of introduction but I also encrypted it. I hooked up my sat phone and transmitted the letters and quickly checked my inbox but found nothing worth looking at.

I was at a loss of what to do next. Should I go on to Fiji or track back to where I found Mei and try to determine where she had come from by looking at the currents? Surely they wouldn't take her to the same place.

In the end I walked the streets of the town and wandered back toward the airfield. The same old man stopped to give me a lift, but when I said I didn't know where I was going he said get in and took me to his house located in a small bay about ten miles from the town. He introduced me to his wife and grown children and then two young grandchildren came to stand before me. He told them to entertain me while he went off on some business and they both took a hand and led me to the water. I spent the day in their company and their laughter and joy made it all the harder to be without Mei but it also gave me consolation as I ran and swam with them.

I ate lunch with the large family and the old man spoke again of love worth tearing the world apart to find. They wanted me to spend several days with them but my conscience wouldn't let me. I promised to return again and the old man's son took me back to the town. Once back onboard *Tirak* I decided I would invite them to go for a day of sailing in *Tirak*.

My spirit had been lifted in the company of the children and their families. It was something I wanted with Mei Yue. I went over my short life with Mei and kept coming back to her forcing me to remember my past so I could protect her. She somehow knew that these people would find her again and she had put her full trust in me. I had failed her. I could see her in my mind's eye scowling at me and telling me to stop blaming myself.

"Don't be a child! You are my only hope. I love you, Papa."

I jerked at the words and looked around but only *Tirak* sat with me. I steeled myself to break down the doors blocking my memory but each time I attempted it my mind jumped to my childhood and refused to come back to the issue at hand. In the end I went to my cabin and fell into a fitful sleep.

I received two emails the next day, one from my agent, giving me the corporate name the aircraft was registered to and the address in Hong Kong. The name was BD Products. The other was from Moe. He confirmed who he was with a few details of some of our missions. He offered to do anything he could to help me if I ever needed it. He finished by saying he owed me big time and it was time to pay me back.

I wrote him back and gave him some minor details of what had been happening. I asked if he could get any information on a group called the Blue Dragon Tong. I said it had to do with a kidnapping but did not offer details. I finished the email by giving him my location at the present and the name of my boat. I sent it off.

That night I fell back into my hole of depression, feeling as if I had failed everyone in my life. I began to drink from a bottle of Red Label and when it was empty I let it drop to the deck in the cockpit. I heard *Tirak*'s irritated clinking but was in no shape to care.

I passed out with my hand on the wheel and soon I was sailing in a storm with giant seas and contrary winds. Every time I trimmed *Tirak* the wind would back 180 degrees and the seas would reach high above her mast. I was thrown about but didn't really care. This was what I deserved. As I trimmed the main sheet I looked at my hands and I carried an M-4 assault rifle in my right.

#

I could hear the soft crunch of rocky sand beneath my black combat boots and feel the weight of the pack on my back. I looked over and in the moonlight could see Moe five feet away, moving with me. I looked ahead and saw a cluster of dwellings about one hundred yards ahead. Moe signaled a stop and moved to my right ear.

He said, "Be alert. There were five targets but they may have others with them. We take the five out and then bug out."

I gave him thumbs up and we moved out. I lowered my night vision monocular eyepiece and double-checked my weapon. I was set on single-fire and Moe would be set on a three-round burst. If we got into it, this would stagger our reloading. I felt the small round grenades clipped to my vest and the Kay bar strapped to my upper left thigh.

Some of the guys laughed at me for carrying the big knife but my pat answer was, "It don't run out of bullets."

As we got to within thirty yards we clicked on our comm gear but remained silent. Suddenly arrows of light streaked out of the night towards us. There were at least four gunmen using tracers. I was behind a small boulder and followed the trail of fire back to its source. Twenty yards behind where the streaks began I could see muzzle flashes. I aimed, heard the spurt of my silenced weapon and saw the opponent drop. I moved to the next and could hear Moe's weapon spurting out three at a time. The ambush was poorly designed. They must have had some kind of a motion detector but only moments to move into a position. No planning in this or Moe and I would be dead or wounded at once.

Four were down when I heard the distinct thud of bullets striking flesh and then heard Moe say in my earpiece, "I'm hit but still moving."

As he continued to fire, I moved closer to the house and around to the left to stay out of Moe's line. There was an outcrop near the stone wall surrounding the houses and I moved between it and the wall. I bounced up for a quick look and saw the last man stooping under the window.

I pulled the pins on two grenades and lobbed them towards the enemy. I raised my weapon, flicked the lever to fully automatic and depressed the trigger. There was a low, long blurb and a tongue of fire and the enemy spouted blood like a fountain in an Italian piazza. Then the grenades blew the wall out of the house. I reloaded and listened. Dead silence.

I moved along the wall and just as I passed the outcrop a body fell on me from behind, taking me to the ground and knocking my weapon from my grip. It was still attached to me by a lanyard but my hand went to my knife and I pulled, twisted, blocked a knife coming in at me and plunged my blade into the enemy. I twisted the blade out and rolled over, listening for anyone else.

Over my earpiece Moe said in a strained voice, "I don't see anyone moving but we need to be on our horse."

I could hear small breathing coming from my opponent and felt for movement. The man was very small and his breathing was high pitched with fear. I pulled out my flashlight and shielded the beam. The face of a child lit up before my eyes. It was a girl maybe ten years old. Her startling green eyes stared at me in terror. I checked her wound and saw there was no hope so I tried to calm her with words she would understand.

Her green eyes stared, then turned to hate, and she whispered in her dialect, "You killed my father."

She died right before my eyes and her eyes remained wide as they stared back at me.

I started to lose it but over my earpiece Moe said, "Dougy, I'm hit pretty bad and I hear a vehicle coming. We've got to get out of here now! Help me, please."

I broke my gaze with the child but knew those eyes were burned into my brain. I moved over to Moe, quickly tied off his upper right thigh and left shoulder wounds. He was bleeding but I had staunched the flow and I could now hear the truck approaching. I lifted him up on my shoulder and moved out. We had six hours of normal moving to our extract point but with Moe injured it would take much longer.

As dawn broke across the rock-strewn mountain pass, we were moving along the rise of the mountainside and I was at the end of my strength. I found a small cave and we moved into it for a break. We rested through the day and all I could see were those green eyes accusing me. At nightfall Moe had to slap me a few times to get my attention.

He said, "Keep it together, Dougy. There have been a lot of patrols out today looking for us. I damn sure can't carry your ass so snap to SEAL and get me out of here."

We buried all of our gear except weapons and water to lighten the load and I shouldered his weight and set off. The exertion and knowledge that I was responsible for getting Moe to safety kept my mind focused and I was determined not to let my friend down. Moe was in a great deal of pain but we moved at a better pace than the night before.

Moe sent out a call and then painted a large rock with infrared near us. The helicopter confirmed his beam and swooped in. We loaded up and were airborne in seconds. I made sure Moe had medical care and...that's the last thing I could remember. The girl with green eyes looked at me with hate and I woke with a scream on my lips.

#

Chapter 14

I looked around, confused as to where I was, and saw the harbor and boats moored around me. It all came back to me along with a splitting headache. I staggered into the cabin and found I was out of liquor. I normally only had a glass of wine or brandy at night, no more, but I felt a craving for oblivion. I drank a small can of pre-made coffee. It was sickly sweet but had enough caffeine and sugar to jolt an elephant. I showered quickly, dressed in a tee and shorts, jumped in the tender and headed for shore. My headache got a caffeine bump and I threw up over the side, making me feel a little better.

I went to the chandler, the only shop on the island that opened that early in the morning, purchased a case of scotch and then made it two for luck. One of the workers carried the boxes to my tender. I could tell *Tirak* was not happy and wanted to be out on the blue but her disposition did not concern me at the moment.

I slouched in the dark and closed my eyes and saw two pair of eyes looking at me. The green pair had a look of hate and the beautiful dark brown pair, terror. Everything I touched withered and died all through my life. I knew I had to help Mei but it was too late. She was gone without a trace and I could sail the oceans for years and never find her so what was the point? She was better off without me. Yes, the man was going to... take her power but at least he could protect her from everything but him. Take her power... what a joke. Stupid little girl thinking she had some power to give or to be taken. I didn't need any of this. I wanted my old life back, the life where I didn't remember those green eyes and the life where I lived in the sameness of mild depression.

Depression has been given a bad name. It's true that depressed people move through life only looking for the end of the tunnel, but they keep out of others' way and make few ripples in life. More people should live like that. The bumping and pushing through life thinking you are better than the other guy and always trying to prove it was a waste of time. My biggest ripples were made when I raised my head above the hole I tried to live in and look where it got me. I killed a child trying to protect her father and I lost a child trying to escape a life of duty she didn't want.

I opened my eyes and they were there, those damn eyes. I cracked the seal on my second bottle of Red Label and moved to the cockpit. One of my last coherent thoughts was maybe I could drink my way to the end of the trail. Would that count as killing yourself?

I continued drinking and everything became a fog with short bursts of a dismal life playing itself out in my brain. Every mistake I've made came to me in short episodes and my eyes turned to the children and they were my only audience, sometimes laughing, sometimes throwing rotten things at me, but most of the time just staring into my eyes, blaming me.

I had no idea how long I remained in my state of self-pity nor did I care but I could tell I was dying slowly and I only wished it would hurry. I remembered eating some kind of food from time to time but had no idea of the passage of time.

I guess I was in the throes of alcohol poisoning but suddenly the green-eyed girl was standing in front of me in a pure white robe. She smiled and reached out and touched my face. She told me I had paid enough and it was time to return. I argued that I didn't want to return, that I could stay with her. She said that I could not because I had to save the one that needed me. She said she was sending help and that I had paid the price of suffering long enough. She said stop being such a baby. She knew I didn't kill her because I wanted to and now she told me it was all right. She commanded me to return and then disappeared. Next Mei Yue stood before me and she too was smiling.

She said, "You such a big baby!"
She told me to get up, sign the book and come and get her. She said she missed me and needed me. She began to cry and told me the old man had her power and she would not live if I didn't come to her and tell her it was all right. Mei said she was so ashamed and wanted me to forgive her.

She said, "Get up and move," and then she slapped my face.

Next two people I loved were standing in front of me, not as judges but as people who loved me. Moe and Jamila stood before me and talked at the same time. I couldn't understand them. Finally Moe stopped talking and let Jamila proceed. She told me that she had come to help and that I had to get up.

She leaned forward and whispered, "I love you, Douglas. You have a job to do and no one else can do it."

Moe stuck his face in front of mine and said, "Dougy, you look like twenty miles of bad road. Now git your ass up and tell me what is going on. By the way, buddy, I love you, too."

What a crazy dream. I needed another drink. These people didn't care about me and I didn't blame them. Why were they in my head? They had no idea of the stupid, self-satisfying, embarrassing, careless and thoughtless things I had done until I learned to dig my hole and crawl into it. That's where I belong, until the next step.

Suddenly I felt like I was flying. I thought in my fog— 'Now what?' I was flying just like a bird and it was nice until I hit the icy water and went under. I thought, 'This is almost like it is real,' as my lungs took in saltwater and I started coughing and flailing my arms. I felt a hand grab me by my hair and raise my head above the water.

I opened my eyes and realized that this was real. I was coughing, trying to clear my lungs and felt my face hit the boarding ladder. I clung to it as the hand released my hair. I looked up but saw no one so I started to climb. As my eyes passed over the gunwale I looked into the eyes of Moe Justice. He was grinning at me and shaking his head in disbelief.

He said, "You look like shit, Dougy. I didn't know if you were dead or alive until I saw your picture on the back cover of a book. I couldn't believe you knew how to write, and after I read the trash you wrote I knew I was right. I went back to the store and asked the lady how many people bought this kind of junk and she said only about fifteen million. Dougy, you owe me twenty bucks and I want it back."

I was still unsure if he was real or something from my alcohol haze until he lifted me up and threw me back in the water.

He said, "Clean yourself up! This thing smells like a garbage scowl and looks like one, too."

I crawled back up the ladder, pulled my tee-shirt off and a bar of soap hit me in the chest. I opened the hatch in the bench and retrieved the bucket and line. It was broad daylight but I didn't care as I stripped off my trunks and filled the bucket with seawater. I dropped the safety rail beside the cockpit, stood on the gunwale and poured water over my head. I soaped up and cleaned everywhere. I pulled up another bucket and washed down my front and then turned to wash my backside.

As the water cleared from my eyes I opened them and looked into two black, liquid pools so large I could have swum in them. I looked into the face of Jamila. In my shock I took a step back and plunged back into the water. Moe was laughing so hard he had to sit down next to her but as I crawled back up the ladder I could see she was smiling, too.

She said, "Hello, Douglas. Did you miss me?"

As I came up she threw me a pair of shorts to put on but didn't say anything else.

I asked, looking at both of them, "What are you doing here?"

She stood, moved close to me and asked, "Did you miss me?"

I looked at her and knew I had been searching for her ever since she left.

I said, "Yes, I have missed you very much."

I leaned in to kiss her but she put her hand on my chest and said with a smile, "There won't be any kissing until you wash that dead animal out of your mouth."

I gave her a questioning look and heard Moe laughing loudly.

He said, "I told her when we first came on board that your breath smelled like something crawled up in there and died."

Nausea and dizziness swept over me and I lunged for the side, practicing my hurling technique.

Moe laughed again and said, "When is the Summer Olympics, anyway? Hey, Dougy, you've built up quite a shoal of fish under the boat. We won't have to go into town for supper."

I smiled sickly at him and turned for another attempt at perfecting my form.

Jamila took pity on me and laid me down on freshly cleaned cushions and wiped me down with a cool towel. I drifted off into a fitful but needed sleep.

I woke at sunset and could smell one of my best cigars. I sat up and looked at Moe as he puffed on my cigar and he had a large glass of brandy in his hand.

He smiled and said, "You know, for a bum you got some good stuff."

When I spoke my throat felt like I had drunk gasoline and set it on fire as it came back up.

"What are you doing here, Moe?"

"I came to help my best friend and the man who saved my life. Say, Dougy that is one fine woman you've found. She's been cleaning this boat all day trying to get the dead animal smell out if it. You have managed to puke in places I wouldn't have believed. You better tie a rope around her because she's a keeper. Just looking in those eyes makes me want to... Oh, never mind. She is beautiful."

He told me how they had met as they deplaned from the small commuter jet that brought them here.

He said, "An old man with a truck as old as he was gave us a ride. I described you and he told us you were in trouble. Jamila and I exchanged information while we waited on a boat to take us out to your boat. She told me right off that she loved you and was here to help you find your little girl. For someone who stays hidden, you've been busy." Moe looked at me and asked, "Do you really have a daughter, Dougy?"

Jamila came up to the cockpit and gave us each a cool glass of Coke and sat down and took my hand. I started to talk but she stopped and told me to go brush my teeth, twice. Moe laughed and I even smiled.

I returned and when I sat down she turned my head and kissed me softly. I drew in a breath filled with the scent of jasmine and fresh ocean air. I began my story at a point just after Jamila left. I could see her eyes glisten but she said nothing. I didn't have much of a story to tell. It was filled with gloom and colorless woes until I found Mei Yue floating in the middle of the ocean. I told them about the happy times and ended with her abduction.

Neither one spoke until Jamila said, "Let's go get something to eat."

They helped me into the tender. Jamila took command and led us to a restaurant where the two of them ordered a massive meal.

Moe said, "I was afraid to eat anything off that boat of yours."

I told him her name was *Tirak* and she had been taking care of me for several years.

His eyes laughed but he said, "I guess that's a new one for me. I had a dog I loved like a brother once, but I never had a car or boat I was intimate with. I have a few things to say to you but it can wait."

They both ate like they hadn't had a meal in weeks but I could only handle a light salad.

They supported me back to the dock and I asked, "How long have I been like this?"

Moe said, "Judging from what the guy at the boat store said and the number of dead soldiers lying around, I guess about two weeks."

Jamila asked what were dead soldiers and he explained the term as empty liquor bottles.

We sat down in the cockpit and Moe said, "I'm going to bed but let me say this one thing until tomorrow. You are the best man I know, Doug, and I will lay down my life for you, but you need to look around you and see this beautiful boat and the world you live in. Stop feeling sorry or I'm going to kick my best friend's ass, proper."

He stood, kissed me on the forehead and went below.

Jamila snuggled closer and kissed me hard on the lips.

She said, "You are going to tell me what happened to you before we met but not tonight. Now I am going to tell you what happened to me after I left."

In the darkness of the night I could feel her shiver and take a deep breath. She began by explaining again why she had to leave and then she told me about being married to the older man her father had made the agreement with. She spoke without emotion about going to his house near the Red Sea. She was his fourth wife and in the hierarchy of the household she was just above the concubines and servants.

She went to him on the night of their wedding and he took her roughly and sent her back to her part of the house. He called for her every night for two weeks but she didn't participate in the acts he demanded. She said she was like a dead fish under him.

When her moon time began he sent her away and didn't call her back for months. He was not unkind but did not love her and had little time for women except for his pleasure. She had promised her father to do her duty but refused to take any pleasure in it.

Her father and mother died over a year ago and the man, her husband, never called her to his room again. Under the laws of Islam she divorced him for this and he made no protest. She moved away quickly.

Jamila continued, "I had saved enough money before I had to marry and I used it to move around until I got a visa to the U.S. I had gone to university in the U.S. so I found work quickly and soon had my *Green Card*. I started right away trying to track you down but the only information I had was the name of your boat and the literary agent you used to publish your books. There was no way to track *Tirak* without help so I wrote your agent several times.

"A month ago I received an email from a woman who was with you and she told me you missed me and that I needed to find you. She said you needed my help. She told me what part of the Pacific you were in but not which island. I packed my bags and flew to Fiji in hopes of finding you. I received your email a few weeks ago and a friend helped me track your computer user ID to the Cook Islands."

"Who was this woman who wrote to you?"

"It could only have been Mei Yue but she never gave me her name."

"How did she get your email address?"

She smiled at me and said, "I wrote it in your book, hoping you would see it."

I told her I never looked at my books.

She took me in her arms and with tears flowing down her face she asked, "Do you love me, Douglas, even after all I have told you?"

I kissed her lips softly and looked into her beautiful eyes, thinking I could stare at her face forever.

"I could not stop thinking of you after you left. You came to me in my dreams and once you told me you loved me. I wanted to go look for you but I knew it would put us both in danger. I think I have loved you from the first time I saw you, Jamila. That is your name, isn't it?"

She looked at me through her tears and said, "It was a pet name my father gave me as a child. You are the only one who knows it now that he is gone. Yes, it is my name and no one will be able to trace it back to me. Do you love me, Douglas? I need to hear you say it."

"My love, I don't know why you would want someone like me but, yes, I love you. I tried to convince myself that you were better off without me but my love has always been for you." I lost myself in her eyes and asked, "Will you stay with me?"

"Yes, but it will have to be with Mei's approval as well. Until then I am yours and we will get her back!"

She took me to my cabin and undressed me. I was so wrung out I simply followed her lead. She put me in bed and stripped off her clothes and moved in beside me. She laid her head on my chest and crooned to me until she heard my even breathing and joined me in my dreams.

As the dawn of the new day crept through the porthole my dreams were so vivid; they felt real. Jamila was kneeling over me, letting her dark firm nipples brush my lips and she guided me into her and began a soft dance. Oh, what a dream!

I opened my eyes and looked up into her large, dark, depthless eyes that were filled with passion and I could feel now this was no dream. Her dance changed to a Beguine. The Latin rhythm charged through me and as her release came she grabbed a pillow to muffle her cry. I pulled her tightly to me and filled my senses with her as I followed.

We went on deck to find Moe smiling but he didn't say a word. Jamila blushed furiously and went down to make some breakfast. I told Moe to wipe that grin off his face and tell me how he got here.

He started back a few years and he told me that after six years with the SEALs he was recruited into a government agency that did work similar to Team 5 except they didn't wear all the gear and had few rules of engagement. He spent three years in the field and now he worked in Washington in a management capacity. He tried marriage once but his job was not conducive to stability. He didn't give up a great deal of information but he said he could provide almost any kind of help I needed.

He said, "Dougy, I have wondered and worried about you ever since you flipped out, but once I knew you were better I left you alone, hoping you would get in touch with me one day. I owe you a lot, not just for saving my life but for everything else you did when we were together. You really are my best friend, maybe my only real friend, and it has been hard for me not to get involved until now. I have to go back in a few days but everything I can do is at your disposal. When you find this child let me know because I can give her everything she needs to have a new life."

I told him I was sorry I left him out of my life but my mind closed down doors on the past and he was behind one of them until a few days ago.

I said, "I want you to meet Mei and get to know her as well as Jamila. I think you would make a good godfather for Mei."

He looked at me with a startled stare that turned to a big smile and glistening eyes and said, "Dougy, of all the things I might have wanted or needed from you, this is the one thing I never thought of. I would be honored to be the godfather of your child! Heck, I'll even take care of that pretty thing downstairs if you want."

He laughed so hard that the noise brought Jamila up on deck. She looked at me and then at Moe and knew she had been a part of the conversation.

She asked, "What were you two talking about?"

Moe's dark face darkened even more and he said, "I've just been made a godfather and... I guess a godbrother! I accepted with the provision that I get to kiss my new sister."

She looked confused for a moment and Moe grabbed her arm and pulled her into his lap and gave her a big kiss. She looked to his face for any guile and found only happiness and a stalwart commitment. She gave him a bright smile as tears sprang to her eyes and then she leaped into my lap and kissed me hard on the lips.

I looked at Moe and back to Jamila and said, "I love you both, Moe as my brother and you, Jamila, as my... soon to be wife, if you'll have me."

She told me she had waited for four years to hear those words and there was no way I would get away from her again.

She then said, "Yes! I'll be your wife if Mei will accept me as her mother. I know she will because she loves you so much."

My words were caught in my throat for a long moment and finally I said, "Let's go sailing."

Moe laughed and said he was wondering if this was really a boat or just a holding pen for drunks. A bow wave from a passing yacht rocked *Tirak* and she clattered angrily. I told Moe he was about to get a quick course in sailing etiquette so he better pay attention.

Jamila said, "Don't worry, brother; I'll teach you all you need to know about your other sister, *Tirak*."

I gave Jamila money and she took the tender in to buy food for a few days and I checked over *Tirak* for problems she might have developed during *my absence*. We dropped our mooring at sundown and under full sail left the harbor. The wind was at twenty-five knots and the seas had built to five feet and I knew the only direction *Tirak* wanted to go was close-hauled. She had a few lessons for this black man who needed to show more appreciation to her.

Tirak leaped and drove into the oncoming swell and I could feel her joy at being set free. Moe, however, for the first two hours applied to be a member of my hurling team and showed us his form off the transom. Jamila gave him some watered-down coke and his body settled down. By midnight he was enjoying a beer and was fascinated at the power of the sea and the dexterity of *Tirak*. He had seen stars like this in the desert, but with the combination of large rollers and the soothing hum of *Tirak*, he was soon in love with the elements. I put him in the port cabin, Mei's room, and with the bow wave passing just a few inches from his head he slept in a cocoon of movement and orchestrated sound.

After I set a course in the navigation system, Jamila and I talked, kissed and cuddled until late in the night. I told her more about Mei and left nothing out. Jamila laughed at my many dilemmas and when I told her about hiding in the head she rolled on the cushioned bench in laughter. I then told her about the test Mei Yue had given me to finally make our lives begin to grow together. Jamila stopped laughing and looked at me in wonder.

She said, "That's the very same test I gave you, my love. I was so embarrassed to expose myself to you like that but I knew it would show me the true you."

"Did I pass?"

She smiled shyly and said, "Yes, with flying colors. You're a very good man in many different ways, Douglas."

We went to our cabin and made love and fell asleep in each other's arms.

The sea had calmed and the wind dropped a few knots but *Tirak* still put her best foot forward, leaping and humming as we slipped across the wet prairie. Moe sat on the safety rail at *Tirak*'s bowsprit and seemed to be talking to her for two hours and then he came back to the cockpit. He told me he could get used to this but had a lot to learn.

He then gave me a serious look and called Jamila up from the cabin.

He said, "I want to talk about the guy who has Mei. You say he is the leader of a group called the Blue Dragon Tong? Well, brother, there ain't no such group, at least in eastern organized crime. I ran a check of the bar and it is owned, along with a string of other bars, by a company called Dragon Distributers. It is a corporation that imports mostly paper products into Hong Kong. They have several large cargo vessels and import and export whatever is on the menu. There may be some illegal activity but it is small time. The real Tong would step in if there was too much under the table stuff going on. The guy who heads the corporation is a seventy-five-year-old man who profiles as a wannabe big-shot. He is rich, very rich, but he does not come up on the radar as tough guy. He has built his little kingdom hauling toilet paper, napkins and anything made with paper into Hong Kong. I guess we can call him a paper dragon."

This was information I needed to make a plan for getting Mei back. Now all I had to do was find out where she was. Moe said he had checked on property owned by the corporation and their owner but it was almost impossible to trace everything. He said the Chinese had lived with secrets for thousands of years and had become extremely adept at hiding things from the west.

He said, "When I get back I will get started on breaking these walls down and get you some information. In the meantime you need to go back over everything that has happened since you found Mei and see if you've left something out."

Just as the sun touched the edge of the world we were only a few miles west of our island destination. I furled the staysail and sat back with the others to enjoy the submission to night.

As the golden orb dripped below the horizon, the *green pop* flashed and Moe exclaimed, "I always thought that was a bunch of crap but I saw it with my own two eyes."

We sailed into the small lagoon and my friends, the two native families, were still in residence. They rowed out to greet us and the children were disappointed that Mei was not with us.

The next day the kids took Moe under their wings and were gone most of the day fishing and playing. The women took Jamila with them to do... women things. I helped the men repair a few nets and fish traps. The men knew something was wrong but didn't press. The people of the island were such happy people — they kept my mood light. Moe returned with lobsters and three large fish. He was smiling like a proud father as he told how the children had taught him everything about *tickling* lobsters out of their holes.

At the evening meal Jamila came out of one of the huts wearing a sarong-like wrap, complete with braided cowry shells in her tresses. She was breathtaking. Her skin glistened from coconut oil and glowed in the light of the fire. Her hair was shimmering as it fell down her back and swayed with her rhythmic walk. And those eyes... those eyes shone with love for me and a happiness she hadn't felt in many years. I looked at Moe and he had his eyes fixed on her in awe and love.

He broke his gaze and looked at me and said, "I wonder if she has a sister. I never knew women from the Middle East were so beautiful."

She smiled and said, "Thank you, Moe. We keep ourselves covered but never again for me, unless it's to help my new family."

Moe stayed on shore with the families that night and I escorted my sultry beauty back to our home.

The next day everyone went to the other side of the lagoon and we snorkeled in a forest of living coral, with florescent fish and a myriad of other strange and beautiful creatures. We were swimming through the crystal clear water with a pure white coral sand bottom.

The children led Jamila on a chase among the Brain and Staghorn coral that looked like a forest of antlers. At the small coral heads they showed her the Neon Tetras, small black fish with florescent strips, and a myriad of schools of brightly colored fish. They watched the Parrot fish take small bites from the coral and discharge the waste behind them in small clouds of gray.

I watched Jamila playing and could see how she enjoyed being with the children. It struck me that she would be a good mother to Mei. My heart wrenched at the thought of her but I pushed the hurt away. I would save all these lost moments and add them to the response I was planning for the man who took her. I forced myself to think of these families playing as something we would not miss with Mei.

Moe was moving close to a Lion fish as it displayed its long, beautiful orange and tan feathers. I swam over to him to warn him of the danger. Although beautiful, the feathery fins carried a deadly poison at their tips. Moe backed away and went to help the men gather shellfish lying just under the sand. Suddenly I was surrounded by children and women splashing and tempting me into the fun. I couldn't resist and was soon engaged in seeing who could squeal the loudest as I chased and grabbed at them. Jamila stayed close to me after she saw the mood that had tried to take me, but I had her squealing with the rest. It was a good day.

That night we feasted on roasted fish and a large pot of shellfish, local vegetables and large land crabs. More of the fierce local brew of coconut wine was brought out and I had *Tirak* in close to shore. I cranked up music and we tried to learn the native foot dance. Moe taught them some of his smooth moves and it was a night we would all remember.

The next day we sailed back toward Hondo Island and it was with a few tears that we left our friends. The women and children had made a special Puka and tiny Marlinspike shell necklace for us to give to Mei Yue and they presented it to Jamila with hugs and kisses. The men had made beautiful Tiger cowry shell necklaces for Moe and me and it made our parting even harder, but promises were made and I meant to see them fulfilled. I wanted to offer them something for all they had done but could tell from their faces that nothing would be accepted. In the end I gave them all but a few cans of our coke and beer.

One of the men spoke for all of them when he made a speech in his own language and then translated it by saying we were their friends and we would be together again for a real celebration. As I sailed out of the lagoon Jamila stayed close to me holding Mei's necklace.

She said, "They told me this necklace was one that a mother gives her daughter as a show of love and they told me when we return they will have a mother's necklace waiting for me."

She cried for an hour as I set *Tirak*'s sails and trimmed them. When I finished and sat next to her, I took her in my arms and held her.

I looked down into her beautiful brimming eyes and I saw an animal looking back at me as she said, "If they touch a hair on her head they will pay for it and will never forget however long they live."

From her look I didn't give them a long life.

I said, "Yes, they will pay and we will get her back."
Moe was watching and I saw tears in his eyes for the first time and he could only nod his agreement.

As Jamila made dinner, Moe and I discussed some of the things I might need when the time came to retrieve Mei and what it would take to make sure she was safe afterwards. Moe told me he would do more checking into the company, Dragon Distributors.

He looked me in the eye and said, "Dougy, one thing I don't want you to worry about is what will happen after you get her back.

I will take care of everything for her and Jamila. I won't tell you everything but I have friends in high places and they owe me some favors that I intend to collect."

We moored in the harbor early the next morning and took Moe to the airport to catch a flight back to the States.

Moe kissed Jamila like more than a friend and smiled at me as he said, "Jamila, he is one lucky man and if he ever doesn't treat you right, you come and see old Moe."

We all laughed and I grabbed Jamila away from him.

It took two days to provision *Tirak* for a long voyage and then we cleared immigration and sailed out on the evening tide heading for the blue. We had decided to make a passage to Fiji and plan our next move as we sailed. Moe had promised help and equipment when we arrived.

Chapter 15

As we sailed out into the blue, shimmering sea I set up our course, trimmed the sails for a broad reach that would last for several weeks and settled down to hand steer *Tirak* for an hour or so. Jamila was below preparing something for us to eat.

I was extremely happy but thoughts of failures in my past began to creep in on me. The time I had spent with Jamila and the day and night dreams I lived with after she had left were some of the few good thoughts I carried around with me. Mei was different. We spent a long time getting to know one another and she was so intuitive that she refused to allow me to crawl back in my hole.

Jamila had professed her love and I mine but now that we were alone on a long passage would Jamila see the pitiful man I truly was? I did love her and wanted to make her happy and that was the problem that slunk in from my past. Could she bring out the truth in me and not be driven away? We had only been together for a short time. I would take it a day at a time and let her view the real me and not the man of my daydreams. If things got to be too much for her, I could always change course and drop her off in one of the many island groups we were bypassing. I knew I was setting myself up for failure and I didn't want to fail. I had missed her, wanted her, loved her, and in my mind I knew I needed her as much as I needed Mei.

I thought of the time I had spent with Mei and let that feeling spread through me. I wanted this woman and would fight anyone, even myself, to keep her and make her happy. She must make up her own mind but I would give her no reason to reject me. I was in love with her and I would tell her often.

Jamila brought our dinner up to the cockpit and I set up the small table. She had made a simple but delicious meal, one that could be enjoyed while *Tirak* raced on a starboard tack and heeled over nicely.

She said, "It will take a little getting used to living in a home that leans but *Tirak* is so beautiful I will enjoy any of her attitudes."

I laughed and told her she didn't always heel but sometimes wallows and swishes as well. She took the plates and cups down below and returned in a moment with two glasses of brandy and one cigar. She told me that she had tried wine only a few times and would be willing to try whatever I liked, except my cigar.

I told her I would give them up if she preferred and she said, "You will never have to give anything up if you will keep me, Douglas, except one thing."

I asked her what the one thing was and she told me that I must give up the thoughts of failure and pity I carried around with me. I bridled at the word pity but in reality I knew she had spoken the truth. She went on to tell me that she already knew what kind of man I was and what kind of man I would be again. She told me that she saw the real me when we were together before and she saw that same man when we were on the small island with the families.

She said, "Mei did that for you and I will continue to do it. When Mei is with us and if she wants me to stay, we will make your life happy and blessed. We will give you no choice in this matter."

Her laughter peeled across the water and resonated with the hum of *Tirak*'s rigging. It touched my soul but I could find no words so leaned over and kissed her softly. We sat holding each other through the first watch and my mind was at rest. I sent her to sleep while I stood the next watch alone.

As she descended into the cabin she turned and said, "Don't think too much. You have nothing to worry about."

We spent the next several days getting into the routine of a long passage. She was learning to care for *Tirak* and I could see the love she put into her with everything she did. *Tirak* seemed to be at peace with her onboard. She cut through the water, her bow slicing and stern bubbling.

Jamila found enjoyment at gathering the harvest of flying fish each morning and sharing the prize with the herders. She also took great care with releasing the ones selected for freedom, not wanting to be tricked by the dolphins into more than their share.

She made dishes of eastern delights with them and I enjoyed everything she created. Usually when sailing I found eating fish too much after a few days and gave them a rest for a week or so. She would even prepare macaroni and cheese in ways I would never have thought of but would allow me my plain fare with hot sauce from time to time.

The sea remained subdued with rollers marching in forward the beam in a regular smooth motion. We made a point to sit and enjoy the sunset each day and I was seeing it with new eyes as she snuggled at my side. There were days of golden pinks and days of vivid oranges and some days of muted pastels as the evening prepared the stage for the sparkling silver stars and planets to put on their performances. The moon was waxing to full and each evening it appeared a little earlier with the anticipation of dominating the entire sky for its gala.

I found the solitude of the late night calming and did as I had been told and left my pity stored in its box. These were days of joy for me except when I thought of Mei's plight. She was the one thing that would complete my transition and I would find her if I...we had to circle the globe to do it. As I thought of the strong child that had captured and commanded me— something kept tickling the back of my mind. I was missing something and it would not present itself.

Jamila came from a society that insisted that the women cover themselves, and even with her new-found freedom and being alone with me far from land, she was not completely ready to shed her garments. Every day she would sit in the sun and she removed her top but only after carefully scanning the horizon and then only for a few minutes. I laughed at her and she glared and told me that it was not easy to break a lifetime of behavior. I told her that I did not expect her to do anything she felt uncomfortable with and she could wear whatever she liked. Each evening with the sunset she would remove her top and sit with me in the cockpit. She said she wanted to feel the freedom but I must give her time.

Late one afternoon as we sat with the sun in our faces I asked, "Tell me again how you found me."

Jamila said, "I received an email from Mei and she told me you missed and needed me. Then I got your email and traced you

~ 148 ~

to the Cook Islands. I didn't know at the time that she was a child. Her email made her sound so much more of a grown woman. I had made up my mind before, that if I was given the chance I would come to you and ask you to take me back. I missed you so much, Douglas. After her email I decided I... I loved you so much that I would be your second woman if that was all that was offered so I came to you not knowing what to expect."

I kissed her and touched her and told her that there would never be another woman in my life as long as she was with me. We made love in the cockpit as lightning flashed far off to the northwest and outlined the layers of clouds in the giant thunderheads.

We had had perfect weather but there might be a change coming in a few days. The sky was filled with the sheep herds of the Alto cumulus, forewarning of an approaching front. The front appeared to be moving to our north but ocean storms could well up, fed by the warm moisture of the sea. I checked all the reports and set the radar to sweep every fifteen minutes. We were far from any shore and not in a heavy sea-lane so I decided we would sleep together that night. It was a break in routine but I wanted Jamila beside me.

The wind shifted during the night and the change in the movement of *Tirak* woke me immediately. I went on deck, trimmed her sails and watched for a few hours. Just as I was returning to bed the wind shifted back and I had to do it all over again— so much for lying in Jamila's arms. At dawn she relieved me and I went to sleep as she stood watch. The barometer had fallen but only slightly.

I awoke early in the afternoon and the pressure had fallen a little more. I anchored a safety line fore and aft on the port and starboard sides. I got out the foul weather gear and fitted Jamila's new outfit and let her clip in and walk the deck to get the feel of being snapped in. I laughed and told her she would feel more comfortable with all that gear on, in case a bird was checking her out. At least I thought it was funny. If a storm approached I wanted her to understand the things I demanded during bad weather. She laughed and saluted me but then kissed me and thanked me for my concern.

We stripped down and took turns pouring saltwater over each other to cool down from wearing all the gear. It didn't work. I pulled her downstairs and laid her on the bench in the salon and kissed her everywhere. The salt mixed with her own taste and we were soon tangled together frantic for release. We lay together kissing after and then the proximity alarm went off on the radar set.

Chapter 16

I went on deck and looked forward at a great wall of gray and black clouds that flashed with bright streaks of lightning. The storm was five miles away and approaching fast. I furled the staysail and turned *Tirak* up into the wind to reef the mainsail.

As I operated the winch I looked toward the southeast and saw a giant container ship bearing down on us from about a three-mile distance. I yelled to Jamila to hail the ship and alert them that we were dead ahead of them. I heard her calling but there was no response. Even from this distance I could see a lookout in the bow of the enormous ship.

I finished reefing the main and turned *Tirak* back to our course. I then steered more to the north to meet the oncoming storm close-hauled on a starboard tack. When I looked back I could see the ship changing course with us. I trimmed the sails and told Jamila to get into her gear. She stopped trying to hail the ship and stuck her head above the hatchway and saw the ship bearing down on us and then turned to see the wall of the storm only a mile ahead of us.

Already the wind had picked up and veered. The wind was on our stern but I knew as we entered the storm it would swing to our stem. The waves were building and confused into a frothing at the counter wind. The ship was now only a mile away and moving fast. I knew we could not outrun her in normal conditions but in a tropical storm she would have to slow as the waves built up.

Large ships had to proceed carefully in steep, large waves. They were not designed to have their bottoms unsupported and in large waves they could break their backs at the top of the giant rollers.

With *Tirak*, she was small enough to deal with that but the wind and waves would throw her about if not handled properly. If the waves and wind were strong enough, she could be flipped over, ripping her mast and rigging away, but she could survive. I did not relish meeting the storm head-on but with the container ship bearing down on us I had no choice.

Jamila was on deck and I had her man the jib winch and as the wind suddenly veered we sheeted in the main and jib. I eased both out to spill some of the power but *Tirak* leaped into the fray. The waves had built to twenty-five feet and she danced to their rhythm with glee. The container ship was only two hundred yards away from us and I could see the lookout using binoculars and talking into a radio. He was guiding the ship toward us.

I was still nude but had the wheel to support me. Jamila was clipped in with her gear properly fitted. She helped me into my jacket, zipped me up and attached my safety line. She smiled at my bare legs and I took time to give her a big grin.

I had to do something to get away from the ship. The wind was up to near fifty knots and the sea building. We were carrying too much sail but first thing was to give us some room from the behemoth bearing down on us.

As we ran down the back of a massive roller I turned *Tirak* to port to show I was tacking. I watched the ship begin to turn with us and as we crested the oncoming wave and disappeared for a moment, I turned the wheel hard over to starboard and ran down the trough on a starboard beams reach.

We came up the back of the wave and the ship was still turning to port but trying to change direction. Even though the ship could crush us and outrun us in normal weather, she was no match for *Tirak*'s agility. As we started down the next roller I brought her back close-hauled and *Tirak* leaped in delight. The wind and waves were continuing to build and I had to get her sail area reduced.

The sun had set below the horizon and darkness quickly overtook us. Down the next wave I turned once again to run the trough, put the autopilot on for a moment, released the sheet on the jib and winched the furling line in to leave only a small patch of jib exposed. I trimmed the reduced jib and came back close-hauled. I still had too much main but she was handling better. I positioned Jamila at the helm and told her to maintain this course but when I signaled she was to turn her up into the wind and keep her there until I reefed the main again.

I moved carefully to the mast and took the two special halyards that held the radar reflector in its carriage. I untied the locking knots in the bitter ends and released the halyards from the mast cleats at the base of the mast. I gave the halyards a little slack until I could see the ball bouncing at the spreaders and then let go. The ball lifted like a helium-filled balloon as the wind clutched it and flung it away with the lines trailing like a jellyfish caught in a riptide. That would help hide us from the monster trying to crush us.

I turned back to the mast, prepared the main halyard and the third reefing line. I would use the hydraulic winch on the reefing line and ease the main halyard on a manual winch. I was ready and looked to Jamila at the helm. The small glow from the cockpit instrument and binnacle lights showed the controlled terror on her face. She smiled as she looked at me and nodded. I looked ahead as we raced down the back of a forty-foot wave and I waved to her as we entered the trough. The main began to clap like the thunder of big guns and I stepped on the winch switch and eased the halyard. I also had to pull the second reef line to take up its slack.

Tirak was built for single-handed sailing and all of the gear and lines were accessed easily. She crested the wave and I felt her try and turn her head but Jamila kept her dead on into the wind. As the reef line came taut I released the switch and secured the halyard. I would tighten it up after I secured the sail. I had the reefing webbing slipped under my safety belt and moved quickly to tie in the loose sail to the boom.

After all was done I waved and pointed off the wind and Jamila let *Tirak* fall off. The main thundered one more time and went as stiff as steel. *Tirak* leaped away with a scream of delight in her rigging.

I moved back to the cockpit and when I tried to take the wheel Jamila pushed me with her butt and refused to let go. She had the smile of a great accomplishment on her face and I kissed her and screamed my delight to the storm. I looked around and saw the lights from the container ship coming back at us. I told Jamila to go below and make us something to drink.

I watched the ship moving closer to us as the waves continued to build. She couldn't keep that speed for much longer or she would take a chance on severe damage. She had her deck lights on and I watched as her bow reached far out above the giant wave she had just climbed. I saw a shift in her forward portside containers and she dropped ponderously toward the trough. Water completely engulfed her foredeck as she tried to climb up the next set.

As her bow came clear I watched several containers break loose and wash over the side. She crested the wave and the wind took the whole group of forward portside containers over the side. She would now be unbalanced and in real trouble if her captain didn't take action.

He did and immediately the bow began to fall off as she turned broadside to the wind but she was in the trough and had her head turned enough not to be broached by the wind and waves. We separated at a fast pace and then I lost sight of her. Those containers would become a dangerous hazard to navigation but we were ahead of them and I had no plans for the moment to alter course.

The storm had reached its peak and *Tirak*, still carrying too much sail, flew into it. Jamila brought me soup in a child cup, the ones with a spout, and I relaxed for a moment while she took a turn at the wheel. After a brief respite from the storm, I took over and let *Tirak* fall away from the wind to take the wave at an oblique angle. We had no worries of land or reefs so we would ride with the storm and wait for it to blow itself out. I would not turn to run for that was the direction that the huge ship had taken.

I had little time to think about what had occurred but instead concentrated on sailing *Tirak*. The sea was an organized maelstrom which *Tirak* took in stride. If we blew out a sail, then we might have to turn and run bare pole until I could change the sail out. The gale was at 70 miles per hour and the waves were somewhere around forty to fifty feet. I watched the main and jib carefully. They were tight as boards but so far showing well. I sent Jamila below and told her we would do one hour on, one off through the night.

When her watch came I stayed in the cockpit but she was keeping a steady course and I watched her let *Tirak* fall off a bit if the wind gusted. She was learning the hard way but carrying on well and without complaint. At the end of my second watch I went below after kissing her and telling her she was a natural sailor. She smiled brightly.

In the murk that could be called day, for there was no sunrise, only a lessening of the dark, the wind had not abated and the sea remained high. I told her to sleep for three hours and then I would try to rest.

She came to the cockpit with coffee so strong it strengthened me with a jolt. She leaned in and said, "This is how we drink coffee where I am from."

I smiled and took another sip and handed the cup back. I went below and was asleep in moments after I got the lee net in place to keep from being tossed out of bed. I woke after three hours refreshed and went to the galley and sliced the last of the bread and put great slabs of butter on it. I took it on deck along with more of the stiff coffee and took the helm from Jamila.

We carried on throughout the day and night. The spindrift at the crest of the waves made visibility near zero but we maintained our relationship to the wind. The sea was gray with great streaks of white torn through it.

In truth, I enjoyed these steady blows of the tropics. My mind had no time to wander and my focus was sharp as I tried to take in everything *Tirak* was telling me. Although this was Jamila's first big blow, she settled down quickly and I watched as she braced and balanced herself behind the wheel. This was a strong storm but not near what the ocean was capable of handing us. It came at a time when we needed help and it remained steady without the confusion that currents and wind can sometimes cause.

The next dawn was much the same as we were hitting fourteen knots at times. I checked the barometer and saw it had risen slightly and hoped the worst was over. By noon the wind had dropped to 50 knots but the sea was unchanged.

Near sundown, which I knew only by my watch, the wind had dropped even more and the sea had dropped to twenty-five-foot swells. We went back to two-hour watches and I spent most of the time sleeping in the cockpit near Jamila when I was off watch.

By midnight the wind had dropped to thirty knots and the sea, in the throes of exhaustion, began to be affected by the normal progression of the waves and current. They were confused but that only made the ride rougher, not harder.

The next dawn the sun graced us as it filled the night with the misty golden light that heralds a beautiful new day. Jamila took time to clean up the galley and salon of the many items we didn't batten down and then called me down for a large breakfast of Gouda cheese, eggs, steaks, fried potatoes and flatbread; a meal fit for a king!

I checked the sails for rents in the stitching but all was well. I shook out the reefs, set the staysail and we leaped along. We went to bed and slept to the sounds of water rushing past the hull and the humming of *Tirak*. Both of us were exhausted and had to rest.

When we awoke the sea looked as if it had never tested us and was a translucent, royal blue that relaxed the eyes. I checked our position and found we had been blown well off course but in the deep blue it was only a minor delay. I plotted a course to our next waypoint and we relaxed in the cockpit, letting *Tirak* do all the work.

We talked about the container ship and if it really had intended to crush us. I told Jamila that I saw a man on the bow giving directions and she asked how they could have found us in the middle of the ocean. I had wondered the same thing and we decided to check *Tirak* for any type of locator devices.

We spent the rest of the day going through all the equipment, lockers and cushions, and I finally began to examine the gear on deck. There were only a few places to hide an electronic device on deck so I started with the tender. It sat in a cradle mounted to the deck just forward of the main mast and had a canvas cover snugly tied down and secured at the mounts. I pulled the cover off the small outboard engine, exposed the fiberglass transom and found nothing out of order. I lay down to examine the cradle and in a recess for a mounting bolt I saw a small round object attached to the cutout. I gripped it and it came away from the cradle after a strong twist.

I recognized it as a military type beacon I had used years before, except it was much smaller and lighter. Jamila saw me bent over the tender and came to see what I had found. I told her it was how the container ship had found us and how our every move had been tracked. She asked what I was going to do with it and I simply tossed it into the deep. I told her that in order to trace it we would have to carry it with us and I didn't think it could be disabled without destroying it. I didn't want whoever was tracking us to know where we were going. I had no doubt that the man who took Mei was behind this. I only hoped that it meant I might be getting near a clue to where she was.

I continued my check of the deck area but found nothing that didn't belong. We moved back to the cockpit and Jamila asked why someone would want to kill us. I could only think that Mei's abductors wanted me out of the way but didn't want it to come to anyone's attention. Ships and boats were lost at sea with no explanations other than storms or hitting hidden reefs. If I didn't show up, a search might be launched but nothing would ever be found, except for perhaps a lifebuoy or other flotsam from *Tirak*. There would be no one to blame and in all likelihood would be thought of as an accident at sea.

I told her I saw the name of the ship, Flying Dragon, and we would get Moe to find out who it was registered to. She asked if I thought it might come back and I told her that it might head for our last fix or try to guess at our course but it was unbalanced now that it had lost so many containers off its forward deck. I thought it would be heading to its original destination or putting in at a big port to redistribute the cargo. I told her to be on the safe side I would alter course for a few days and then they would never find us.

She asked, "What if there is another one of those things onboard?"

"Then there is nothing we can do except keep watch and have someone check *Tirak* when we get to Fiji. I will send a message to Moe and ask him to have someone waiting to go over the ship."

She relaxed and I went to plot a course change and input it into the navigations equipment. I came on deck and altered course to the north and trimmed the sails to run close-hauled on a port tack. It would be more uncomfortable with a jarring movement and heeled over a bit more but we would only run for two days like that.

Jamila said that as long as she didn't see that ship again she wouldn't mind. We were bruised and a little battered from the storm but now the sea was gentle and *Tirak* leaped along in tune with the swells. I had missed the sunset but with a brandy, cigar and beautiful woman, I could wait for the next one.

I leaned over and kissed Jamila and she returned my kiss with urgency. I threw the cigar into the sea, sat the tumbler down and turned back to our present need. As I kissed her a thought popped into my head and I sat back.

"Tell me again how Mei knew how to get in touch with you."

She gave me an exasperated look but got up and pulled me to the cabin. She went to the bookshelf and pulled one of my novels down and handed it to me.

I opened the book and on a blank page in the front of the book was a handwritten letter:

Dear Douglas,

I hope by the time you find this you will have forgiven me for running away from you. I must go back to fulfill the agreement my father has made. I have no real choice in this.

Douglas, I want you to know that I have fallen in love with you and it hurts me so much to leave you. You will always be the one love in my heart and I hope that one day I can return to ask you for a second chance.

This past week has been something I never dreamed could have happened and it has been the best time of my life. You are so much more than you know right now but I know someone will help you find the answers that will free you from the burden you carry. I only wish it could be me.

I cannot believe I could be so brazen to come to you like I did. I was so embarrassed and frightened you would reject me. I have never done anything like that before. You are the first man I've been with and the only one I will love. Even though I go to do

*my duty for my family I will keep you in my heart and send my
dreams to you at night.*

*If you ever wish to contact me I have an email that no one,
except me, knows about. I will put it at the bottom in hopes that
someday I will hear from you.*

*You are a good, strong man and I pray you will find the
person to show you and guide you.*

I Love you, Douglas, with all of my heart. Please don't hate
me.

Jamila
jjjjj@cccc.com

I read the letter again. I couldn't believe it had been there
right in front of me all this time.

"I'm sorry I never looked at this before. I do love you,
Jamila, and have from the first time we met. I'm such a fool. I tried
to understand what you were going through and believe me,
please; you have only brought me joy and comfort in my dreams."
There was something knocking on the inside of my head, trying to
tell me there was more.

I took out my notes that I had written after talking to Mei on
the phone. What had she said? She had told me she was happy but
she used such broken English I knew she was saying what she
must. She only used the name Jing Wei and talked of her duty. I
was beginning to hate that word. Both times I had heard it from
the two people I love they were taken from me.

Then in a clear English sentence she told me not to forget
and sign the book and went on to use a very Southern expression
telling me to be calm and,

"Ya'll come a git yor rug rat ya heea!"
She was asking me to come and get her and I said I would. I spoke
to her in Thai and for the first time I told her I loved her and called
her my daughter. She responded by saying she loved her papa and
to come and get her.

I started going back over the whole incident but what was
it? What was it she said that was so important? Suddenly, like a
curtain pulled from a window on a bright morning, the light shone
through.

"Don't forget to sign the book."

I grabbed the book Jamila had handed me and went through it front to back but found only Jamila's letter to me. I jumped up and as I reached for the other books on the shelf I remembered Mei's hiding place under her bed. Jamila sat calmly, not wanting to break my train of thought, but when I dashed to Mei's cabin and began to rip the bunk apart she stood and watched nervously, hoping I wasn't having a breakdown.

I tore the mattress from the bunk and then ripped the wooden sheet which supported the mattress from the frame. There tucked into a corner was Mei's small bag where she had kept her treasures and not allowed me to see. I grabbed it and ran to the salon. I poured the contents out onto the chart table. There were only a few things there that were important to her; the doll my agent had sent her, trinkets she had bought, a few shells she had collected, the puka shell necklace I had made for her and one of my books she had bought and used to improve her English. She had told me that she would ask me to autograph it one day but then ran with it to her cabin.

I picked up the book with trembling hands and opened it to the first blank page and found a letter in her precise clear style. Anger filled me for being so inept and not thinking of it earlier. I felt Jamila's hand stroke my arm and she cooed to me to bring me back into control. I wiped the tears from my eyes and then began to read what Mei had written:

Dear Douglas,

I write this because I read letter from woman in your other book and I want you to see my words. I love you and want very much to call you Papa. I think one day I will and you will call me daughter. I think very much you love me. I love you very too much!

I worry about man come to find me and if he take me away, you must promise to come find me. I study and remember everything you teach me about our Home, Tirak. I look at maps and remember maps from the place he keep me. I study very hard for you. I want to speak perfect English like you do and make you proud of me. I find island on map where that man keep me before.

If someday I gone you must look for me there. I will do what I must and wait for you. If I must give my power I will. I don't need power because I have you. Look at end where the island is.

This woman who write the letter, I believe her words and I think you should too. I decide to write to her and tell her to come and help you. I watch you and see you lonely for someone and I think it is this woman, Jamila. You so strong I think I need help to take care you. She is a good woman I think and if you love her then I will love her too. I think she will be very good for you and for me. She give you same test I give you and you pass both test because you are strong and good man. Never forget that.

I promise to practice my English everyday and study hard to be a good daughter. I love you, Papa. You are only family I have now and only family I want. I know you love Mei Yue and I want very much to hear you say but never mind, because I can see when you look at me.

Papa, you were dangerous man before and I think you must be that man again for me. What you hold inside is hurting you and you must let it out so you can protect me. What happened before was not your fault. Look to your friend and look to your daughter, Mei Yue.

After you read this and tell me it is all right I will only call you Papa because you are my family now.

I love you
Mei Yue
N18 56 28 W175 16 40

I wiped the tears that flowed from my eyes and looked at Jamila. She too was crying and when our eyes touched she leaped into my arms and buried her head against my neck and sobbed. As I smoothed her hair I thought of how stupid I had been. All this time the answer to two questions lay within my grasp.

I still didn't know how two women, one a child and the other a woman I had loved and tried to put in my past, could love a man like me. I couldn't comprehend the love they offered me because I didn't deserve this chance at living a dream. I would clutch to their love in the hope that I would not perform my normal act and lose their love through my actions. I needed them both much more than they could ever need me but both had put no stipulations or limits to their professed love. My love was unbound in the words I had read.

I felt Jamila squeeze me and I looked down into her swimming eyes and said, "I love you."

She said, "I love you, Douglas. Now let's get our child back! I only know her through your words and her own but I am tied to her as if she came from me. If he hurts her he will pay dearly. Now get rid of the pity and get us there. You are a lucky man, Douglas. You have two women who have given you unconditional love and only expect your love in return. This is not something you can lose by being the man you were meant to be so stop all your thinking."

She was just like Mei. She was reading my thoughts. I wouldn't be able to hide from them and when they were both together I wouldn't be allowed time to look for my hole. I smiled at that thought. A new life had begun and I was required to do my part in making it good.

I went to the GPS and punched the latitude and longitude into it. I knew it was close to Fiji but the navigation screen gave me an exact spot. There was a small island with no name displayed. I enlarged the scale and saw it was only about one hundred miles east of Viti Levu, the largest island of Fiji and the island that our passage was taking us to. I brought out the chart for the area of the small island but it offered little. I would call Moe and ask him to provide information. We were still at least three weeks out of Fiji and even though *Tirak* raced close-hauled we only moved at around eleven knots.

Any other time I would relish her speed but just now I put it into context of how the rest of the world would view eleven knots. She could make this speed, with the right wind, day and night for as long as I asked it of her. I reset our course to take out the dogleg I had put in to avoid possibly meeting the giant ship again. The autopilot turned her heading and I went up to trim the sails.

I had no spinnaker. It was a sail I had never enjoyed using because it took constant monitoring, even though with the wind abaft the beam it would add to our speed. I was a cruising sailor and getting there was most of the fun. I would tweak her with the sails we had and only shorten sails if a squall or storm approached.

It would be a long passage now that I wanted to fly. Jamila saw my distress and comforted me with words that held me in check.

We continued our routine with round-the-clock watches. I would take the dog watch, from two in the morning until seven, and Jamila the day watch. We would share the evening watch, sleeping as we needed. I wanted to be with her all the time but I knew she needed time to herself also. As it worked out, we became closer, using the times we were together to talk about our life.

We came from such different worlds but while we talked and compared I saw that it was not as different as one might think. Growing up in a family environment, our value systems were enforced and taught though our parents. The biggest difference I could see was in our expectation and the importance of duty. Jamila was raised to accept her role as subservient to men but also how to move within these rules. Her father had allowed her to be educated and attend school in the West but held her tight to her family duty. I was taught to respect my parents and other adults, but once I finished high school I was released to the world to show my character and discipline to finish college.

Our religions, which I thought would be our hardest barrier to be climbed, became only an area for discussion. She knew of what I did in the military and who I was sent after, but she told me that they were bad men and not to think all Muslim thought as they did.

I had once talked to a Mullah, a teacher, as one who understood Islam, and he allowed me to compare some of the rules for life between Christians and Muslims. I asked him about sin and what a good Muslim thought about after he had sinned. He told me there were no good and bad Muslims, only Muslims, and that sin was an invitation for Allah to turn his head away from the sinner. Forgiveness was the choice of Allah, even for the righteous men. Salvation was also the choice of Allah. There were no standards but Allah's will.

I told him of the Christians' ability to speak directly to God and His Son and ask to be forgiven. In our Bible we were told it would be done. If we only believed and accepted Jesus as the only Son of God, then our salvation was assured. He laughed and said we were *naïve*. He said we would live and die and never see heaven.

Jamila had gained an open mind by rejecting the lesser role of a Muslim woman and studying the nature of Christian life. She said it was difficult to believe that a Christian could ask for forgiveness and fully expect that forgiveness to be given, not by good works but by belief alone and the grace of their God. She was unsure, but I assured her that whatever she believed, it would not interfere with our lives. I would respect her thoughts as I knew she would respect mine.

Chapter 17

As we moved through our passage her self-confidence became stronger and one morning I came on deck to do endurance exercises with her and found her waiting totally nude. Looking at her golden body, which had grown darker as she exposed more of herself to the tropical sun, was very pleasing to me. She had lost some of the roundness of her curves and her body was hard. She watched me staring at her and asked if I liked what I saw. I told her she was beautiful before and beautiful now.

I said, "Hard or soft, I love you." She laughed and said that this was her get Mei back body and once we had done that she would return to the softer woman that I liked.

I studied the charts, paper and electronic, and found the small unnamed island only one hundred miles from Viti Levu in the Fiji Islands. It was an atoll with three entry passes through the reef surrounding it. There was a small lagoon and no structures. It sat on a large coral reef with numerous small islets in the area. According to the charts, the giant shelf was only four feet deep at mean low tide, which meant *Tirak* would not be able to pass through this area on an even keel. She drew five feet sitting level.

We were seven days out of Fiji and I didn't want to pass within two hundred miles of this atoll in case there was radar surveillance watching the area around the island. I would use worst-case scenario to avoid detections before we set some sort of plan in motion.

Jamila was constantly looking over my shoulder, taking in everything I did. She was a comfort and strength, helping me to maintain my self-control. I found the closer we came to a resolution the calmer I became. Mei was always in the back of my mind, but I knew I would have to approach the execution of a plan from an analytical plane I had not been on for many years.

As more and more of my past came back to me I found the animal in me growing but I would not be the lone wolf of the past. I would use Jamila, just as I had used Moe in operations. I knew, deep inside, that this would be the only way to keep her safe, because I never went in with a team without putting the danger on my shoulders to protect others with me. I discussed all this with Jamila and even though I would have liked to leave her out of the equation, the look in her eyes told me it would be wasted breath so I held nothing back from her.

We were growing closer as we sailed *Tirak* and my soul began to fill in the emptiness inside. I began to teach her the dialect of the man who had Mei, with a plan forming in the back of my head. I knew that getting Mei back would be a beginning and not the final outcome. My family had to be protected.

The first time I had the thought of Mei and Jamila as being my family I had to stop and go to the bowsprit and let the wind and *Tirak* wrap me in a cocoon. *Tirak* hummed her love and the wind dried my tears. Even the dolphins were silent as they turned on their sides to watch me with big, clear eyes and permanent smiles.

Jamila waited for my return, took me in her arms, and in the full light of day we made love with slow, loving touches and kisses. Her taste and aroma were written into my brain in a place that could never be erased or locked away. She seemed to perform the same rites upon my body as she moved over me, stopping as if to lock me into her soul. Life was beginning again for both of us.

I watched her move on the foredeck in exercises of strength and balance. She was changing before my eyes into a dangerous woman bent on a cause that would protect her child. Even though she had never met or even seen a picture of Mei, there was no question of the maternal instincts which lay within her.

I was not sure of the exact moment in which it happened but we became one in a way only my daydreams had imagined. It enveloped me and my daydreams became a reality. She spoke of the same feelings and I could feel her relax, leaving questions of our future behind, or so I thought.

She spoke to me several times of the impact I had on her life. She told me that finding me on that island was something that was meant to be. Never in her dreams had she thought of being close to a Western man, much less taking one to her heart, but I had captured her and it was good. She would still laugh and blush at the wanton way she had come to me and how I had put *Tirak* before her body but in the end I had passed her test.

I laughed again at those words that came from Mei. Jamila had not thought of it as a test but thinking of Mei's letter showed her that it was exactly that. I told her I had never had anyone present themselves to me in that way and when she showed me her gift it had sent a heat and need through me I had never felt but it was much more than desire for her body. It was like she was offering me her being and I wanted it all.

In the heat of those thoughts we made frantic love and in the end we were panting from exertion and holding each other in a bond that would not die. There were things still to be said and it would take Jamila to draw them from me.

Three nights out of Fiji we sat in the cockpit watching a special performance of shooting stars and vivid quasars upon the night stage. The moon had not risen yet to dim the other characters. It would make its appearance as a waxing half-filled lady and perform as the main artist in that night's opera. Jamila cuddled close and began to speak of the fears she had brought with her.

She had previously told me she didn't know this woman who had emailed her. She had decided that even if she became the second woman it was her decision to be with me. Now she spoke of her fear that I would reject her after a period and would abandon her.

In the six days we were together she knew of my own fears and the lack of confidence I had in myself. Below all of my feelings of being inadequate, unworthy and my fear of rejection she saw the man I really was. She fell in love with two men and wanted to help me become whole.

When she left me it had crushed her in ways she did not understand for a long time. She had cried for weeks afterwards. She fulfilled her duty to her family and tried to be a dutiful wife in every way except sex. Each time her husband sent for her she felt she was being disloyal to me and could only let him perform without her participation. She knew she was committing a sin in the eyes of her upbringing but her love for me was locked in her heart. She kept it hidden from even her closest companions. She said she would have taken her love to her grave without guilt but after her parents died and she was able to divorce her duty she went on a mission to find me and to beg forgiveness.

I listened in silence and could not believe the words of love she spoke. Of all the people in the world to place her heart and soul with, I would have been my last choice. The acts of my life did not deserve that kind of love but in my daydreams it was exactly what I hoped for. I silently asked God to give me this chance to be a man good enough to deserve this love given to me.

She was in my arms and I pulled back to look in her glistening eyes and asked, "In your eyes I am the head of this family and whatever I command you must obey. Is that correct?"

She said, "I am yours to command, Douglas. I will defer to you in all things if that is your wish except one."

I asked her what the one thing she would not obey me was.

As I watched the lioness return to her eyes she said, "I will go with you to get our daughter!"

I smiled and nodded and then put on a serious face as I said, "As your man, I command you, Jamila Durian, to obey me in this always. You are to take your fears of me leaving you and cast them into the depths of the sea. I command you to comfort me and guide me as you have done in the past. I will not command but ask you to love me always as I will love you always. You will help me raise our child and others to come and give them your goodness, intelligence and strength. Will you do as I command?"

"I will, *effendi*. You are the light in my eyes and will always be so. Never will I fear for your love again. I am yours in every way you desire as you are mine in every way... Do you say we are to have more children?"

"That is my hope, my love. I have already seen the mother you will become and it pleases me. You make me want to be a father to our children."

She smiled back at me through tears of joy. After that night, even in the serious moments, we would look at one another and smile our pledges of fidelity and love.

I called Moe to give him our approximate arrival time and confirm our contact. He again told us not to put our commitment to each other on paper but to wait. He would not be with us on this mission but he was sending additional information on the island and the man who had Mei. He said there would be someone meeting us after we arrived. He did not wish us luck. As in previous times, we relied on skill, planning and faith.

I asked him what he was doing in Washington and he told me he had received the strangest email on his secure server. It was from a woman who insisted on meeting him and he was to see her tonight for drinks and dinner. With that I wished him luck and he laughed as we signed off. I told Jamila about Moe's upcoming date and she smiled her thin-lipped smile that told me she had a secret but refused to tell me what it was.

I spent too much time below deck trying to plan an operation on what little information I had. I knew we would spend at least several days in Fiji going over the information Moe was sending and no real plan could be put together until I could inventory equipment and information.

Foremost in my mind was keeping everyone safe during and after the operation. At no point was failure an option and it was taking some getting used to this new-found confidence.

Jamila would drag me on deck and insist I show her how to care for *Tirak* and generally redirect my attention. For her that was not hard. She would remove pieces of flimsy clothing as we worked and it took enormous effort on my part to concentrate on simple tasks. Her golden skin was darkening to a cocoa color in the sun and her body was hardening and losing much of her soft roundness as she worked and exercised.

She stood before me one day in a bikini bottom that was a wasted effort to wear and asked again if I liked her new body. I knew a trick question when I heard one, but the sight of her bare, glistening skin, long, silky, braided hair falling over her shoulder and those sultry eyes gazing on me took the answer from my lips. It lay in my eyes for her to see.

She simply smiled that secret thin-lipped smile and continued with her task of taking the port side number 1 winch apart.

At my request she helped me add refinement to the harsh, commanding Arabic I already knew. When spoken correctly it was a flowery language where each expression had a double meaning but also it was a language of love that leaves western romance languages far behind. I asked her how such a beautiful language could belong to people who put women so far below men. She said there was true love among the desert people but it was hidden from public view. She said she had seen the same conditions in America where men and sometimes women would dominate their mate but in the land of her people it had been a way of life for centuries.

Late one afternoon another sail appeared on the horizon and was making a course that would pass close to us. I could see it was not a chartered boat and from her setup I was sure I knew the people aboard. I altered course to pass close to the other boat and I had to smile at Jamila's dilemma about her state of dress. She was only wearing her bikini bottom. This would be a true test of her nerve. She became so agitated when the other boat was only a mile away that I laughed out loud, which caused her to turn on me with a blistering glare.

All I could say was, "I love you."

The fire of her look did not change but she straightened her back, lifted her chin and joined me to give passing honors. It was a beautiful ketch-rigged fifty-foot vessel, well-kept and shipshape. On board was a young man, an older man and two lovely white women with very nice tans and sleek lines. All were nude and waved without embarrassment.

The older man called from twenty feet away and said, "She's a beauty!"

I felt the heat pass through Jamila's body and I leaned down and said, "He's talking about *Tirak*."

Her elbow took the wind out of me and all I could do was point to his boat and give the thumbs-up.

He gave a hardy laugh and yelled as we separated, "You too are a beautiful lady," and gave Jamila a gracious bow.

She waved and with her right hand kissed her lips and touched her heart to him.

To ease my mind and take my thoughts off Mei, Jamila allowed me to do things I had never considered before in my state of fear but found such great pleasure in them. She would laugh at my concentrated smile as I worked.

One day as we were well into the passage I came on deck and found her sitting on the bowsprit rail with her left arm raised and her forearm resting on her head. She was looking at her left armpit and her right hand seemed to be manipulating her armpit in some way. I walked forward and she quickly lowered her arm and hid something in her hand. I gave her a questioning look and she blushed but held out a pair of tweezers to show me.

I sat beside her and asked what she was doing, and after a moment she raised her arm and began to pull tiny black hairs from her armpit, one at a time. I asked why she didn't use a razor and she told me she didn't like the feel of it and it was very relaxing for her to do it her way. I asked if I could try and we spent a few moments laughing at my ineptness and the fact that I had my face in her armpit with the look of a great hunter on safari.

We moved to the cockpit where she could lay down and relax while I continued stalking the herd. She tried to watch me but laughed so hard at my game face that she had to turn away. She made a soft sound of pleasure at each of my successes and the pleasure was returned to me in a way I never expected. It was a simple task that made me feel so much a part of her that it became a highlight for me to go on a *hunting trip*.

My next grooming experience was of even greater pleasure for us both. Jamila did not shave or pluck the cloud of hair above her flower, except at the outer fringes. She trimmed the smooth, thick hair to about a quarter inch long and I must say it was so much more erotic than the landing strips of the few western women I had seen.

I was granted permission to attempt this delicate operation and it was one of the most erotic experiences of my life. Once started, I was required to complete the procedure before we could move on to other pleasures. I would rest my head on her flat, strong belly to get the height uniform and then moved my head to her upper thighs to make critical judgments from that perspective. Her aroma sent a fire through me that took all of our efforts to delay the glorious conclusion. I was learning patience I didn't know I possessed. These small efforts were things I could never grow tired of.

Our last night at sea before reaching Fiji was fraught with tension and apprehension. My mind kept trying to find the hole I had so carefully dug over the years and Jamila was given the task, on her own, of keeping me above ground and quashing her own worries.

We sat in the cockpit and watched the moon rise in her half full and growing state. We were sailing east and sailed into her silver sparkling highway. The sea was black and faceted with thousands of small, broken jeweled reflections all around us. We consoled one another with love and knowledge that we would have Mei with us in a few days. I knew that it would be hard to approach the island in *Tirak* because the moon would be near full and even without radar she would be easily seen.

We practiced a few phrases in the dialect of the old man that Jamila would use and I practiced my Arabic. I wanted to instill fear in hopes we would not have to kill but I was willing to destroy anyone to protect Mei and Jamila. I desperately wanted to avoid Jamila killing anyone. Even with her protective need I knew that being a bringer of death would live with her for a long time, no matter the reason.

I asked Jamila if she would have a problem inflicting pain to discourage any attempts at retribution and she said she would prefer to ensure our safety in a more permanent way. She was quickly becoming a warrior and I hoped it wouldn't stay with her. She saw my concern and told me not to worry. She had never hurt anyone in her life but there were times when she had wanted to.

She promised she would abide by my decision no matter what the choices were as long as I was sure we would all come out of this safely. I would have to keep a strong hold on her during this. I knew from my missing past, which had begun to reappear, that death had consequences and one of us was more than enough to travel that hidden road of pain. Even as I thought of the possible effects I stopped to smile at the thought of being a family.

We even discussed how our sexual adventures would have to be modified with a young girl onboard. Jamila laughed at me and told me the frequency might have to be altered but the adventures had only begun.

Chapter 18

At dawn I brought out a new jib sail and old staysail. They were dark blue. We changed the foresails, hoping to give *Tirak* a different appearance. I put a single reef in the main and brought out the sail cover and attached it to the boom. It was blue as well. It would not fool someone who knew the rig of a sailboat but to a casual or untrained eye it might do the trick.

After stowing the original sails we settled in to arrive in Fiji just before sundown. The island of Viti Levu was a smudge with clouds sitting upon it like a bowler on the horizon. A few hours later I called on the marine band, without giving the ship's name, to order supplies and arrange for them to be waiting our arrival. An hour before we entered the harbor I called immigration and made arrangements to be met at the government dock along with customs on our arrival.

We entered the harbor at sixteen-thirty with the main furled and the blue jib and staysail in full view. There was a large marina full of sail and motor yachts but I had picked out a mooring buoy near the jetty, away from most prying eyes. We furled the staysail and flew in on the jib, with the motor idling, towards the government dock. I let fly the jib, turned into the wind and ghosted in. Jamila dressed very conservatively in white slacks, boat shoes and sleeved blue shirt, jumped to the dock and in a manner of a seasoned sailor threw a bowline over the dock bollards fore and aft. She returned to *Tirak* as the officials made their way down the dock.

I thanked them for their promptness and apologized for our last-minute arrival. I invited them onboard and had our paperwork laid out for them to review. Jamila opened all the cabin doors and waited quietly to allow them access to any part of *Tirak*. After stamping our passports, I presented them with a fine bottle of wine each and made an offer of a brand of whiskey from Palau. They turned their noses up at the whiskey and began a quick tour of the boat. Jamila, with those beautiful eyes, made the interlude pleasant for them and they returned to their office with dreamy smiles. Our supplies from the ship's chandler arrived and we stored them in the salon.

We quickly left the dock and motored to our mooring. As we were putting away the foodstuffs and dry goods I felt a bump against *Tirak*'s hull and a soft English voice with an Indian accent called out for permission to come aboard. I slipped my work knife with its sheath into the waistband on my shorts. Jamila grabbed a vicious looking butcher knife and stood ready to repel all boarders. I turned the spreader lights on and cautiously moved into the cockpit.

A dark-skinned man with smooth, black, wavy hair stood in a twelve-foot hard-bottomed inflatable with his hands held out to his side. He was smiling a friendly smile and waited until I had a good look at him and the tarp covering whatever he had in the boat. I asked him to slowly pull the tarp away and he complied. There were several boxes stacked neatly but no sign of weapons.

I asked if I could help him and he replied, "I am here to give you more justice than you had before you arrived here."

He said he was Walter Singh with a delivery from Team 5. I relaxed a little, turned off the spreader lights and invited him aboard. He reached down and picked up a valise and stepped aboard.

Walter said, "I have already scanned your boat and there are no locator devices onboard."

We went down to the salon and I introduced him to Jamila.

He spoke Arabic and said, "Your beauty has been foretold but Justice did not say you cool the winds of the desert and give sweet water to nourish me as I look upon you."

She smiled and offered her hand to him. He handed me the valise and we sat down. He told me the change of sails and late arrival was well done. He said there were several Chinese men who had watched the harbor for several weeks but they were not in view when we arrived.

I opened the valise and removed several satellite photos of an island with coordinates that Mei had left me. There were several written reports but I put them aside for later.

There were pictures of several Chinese men and a long lens shot of Mei Yue. I felt my heart tighten when I saw her picture. She was so small but held her head high as she looked out at the sea.

Three large Chinese men and one older Chinese woman stood close to her. I handed the photo to Jamila and heard her intake of breath as she saw Mei for the first time.

Her eyes glistened and she looked at Walter with lioness eyes and said, "Thank you for this picture."

He smiled and said, "You will have to control that look until you are ready to unleash your power. There will be people in town looking for just that look. This Mr. Wong has a few very good people around him. We have found out our first estimation of his organization was not correct. He is a dangerous man but he maintains his own organization and only has limited dealings with the Tongs out of Hong Kong. That is why we missed him in our original report but now he is a person of much interest to us."

I said, "Not much longer if I have anything to do with it."

Walter asked if I would help him unload his cargo and then he would leave and return midmorning tomorrow.

Once the boxes were unloaded and moved down into the cabin, Walter slowly steered his boat into the darkness of the harbor. I opened each box as Jamila looked over my shoulder. There were two Glock22's and a Walter PPK, which I handed to Jamila. The PPK was a small, light pistol and would be a good match for her. There were two M4 military rifles modified for sound suppression and optical scope. If one was hit with a high-velocity round from this weapon, one wouldn't be getting back up. There were a number of handheld explosives, remote charges and fighting knives. There was enough equipment for almost any type of operation.

I was up most of the night, inventorying, making a list of additional items and letting my body learn to cohabitate now that we were moored. I took a break and went on deck to smoke a cigar and sip a coke.

Suva was a bustling place. Fiji was a favorite tourist spot for Aussies, Kiwis and even Americans. Many private motor yachts and sailboats were docked at the marina and moored in the harbor. We were well hidden in the forest of mast. I didn't plan on being there long and after studying the target island's layout and surrounding reef I began to finalize a plan.

The smell of freshly brewed coffee brought me out of my sleep. Jamila stood over me and smiled. I apologized for not joining her in the cabin but she only kissed me in understanding. She handed me a list of things she would need and as I read the list of mostly clothing I wondered what she had planned. She told me she wanted to dress for the part she would play, and as I opened my mouth to protest, I saw the look in her eyes and remained silent.

Walter arrived at ten with a lovely woman. He introduced her as a member of his team and asked if we had additional requests. I handed him the two lists and he reviewed them. Jamila's list brought a smile to his face and he told us everything would be ready by sundown and delivered just after dark. He handed the lists to the young lady and she sped off toward the marina.

He joined us in the cockpit to discuss what we had planned and what part he could play in the operation. I asked about his background and he told us he was not a contractor but a member of Moe's group with a long leash. He proudly said he and his team member were American citizens and had very specific feelings about activities concerning child slavery and contracted abduction.

He leaned forward in a conspiratorial fashion and said Luang, the young lady, had been rescued from a fate much worse than what our child was involved in. I asked if he was responsible for her rescue and he smiled with pride and said she was now his wife after a long courtship.

Walter looked at us very seriously and said, "Moe is my friend and has given me background on you, Mr. Durian. I want you to know that Luang and I will be a part of your team and give direct assistance. You will go alone on the island but we will be offshore to give tactical assistance and cover fire if needed. We have a few nasties that would discourage a rogue elephant from pursuing."

I shook his hand and asked him to call me Doug. Jamila kissed him and spoke a phrase I did not understand. He beamed like the sun and looked at me with an understanding that I found gratifying but unsure why.

Luang returned just after sunset with all the items we had requested. Jamila prepared a meal of lamb chops, fried potatoes and a curry dish. We all sat down and had an enjoyable time.

Luang told of the time Walter and his team made a raid on a drug lord in northern Burma and he found her and ten other young women ready for shipment to be sold in a slave-trading business. They were to be sent to the Middle East and would probably never be heard from again.

Although it was not part of the operation, Walter made room for all the girls on their extraction helicopter. She said it was very crowded but the men would not leave anyone behind. They were hidden in Thailand for a few weeks and then all but her went on to the U.S. She stayed with Walter and, once she was granted U.S. citizenship, she went everywhere with him.

At first it was as a friend and companion but later it turned to love. Walter said for him it was love from almost the beginning but he didn't want to force his love on her. The happiest day of his life was the day she told him she wanted more than friendship. They were married a week later.

I asked her about going on field operations and she laughed, telling me if I had seen the life she lived before I would understand that helping the country that offered her so much was what she wanted and needed to do. Walter told us that she was a natural.

He looked at Jamila and said, "Luang has your eyes. She is deadly when it is necessary but leaves it in the field when we are home."

Luang said, "This will be our last operation. It is time to start a family and we have both agreed to find another way to serve our country." She stood, took Jamila's hand and went up on deck and I heard the boat pull away.

Walter gave me a critical look and asked if he could speak frankly to me.

I nodded and he began, "Douglas, I know what happened on your last operation. I also know you have suffered many years, not really understanding why, and you sought solitude. Moe sent me the file on you and I must say this because I may be putting my wife in danger. You must put what happened behind you and forgive yourself. You are going into this for two very good reasons and you will tenably be required to kill, not for your sake but for Mei and Jamila.

"This man is not someone who will forgive or forget. When you look at him you will see an old man, small and frail, but it is only a façade. He runs an organization of power in the underworld and has been so successful that even the agencies that were supposed to know about him have missed him for years. You are going to have to think of him as a high-value target who will hunt your family down if you fail. I have more information that I cannot share except to tell you there is only one course you have before you if you are to protect your new family. I would like to be the one to do this but I have been forbidden from going onto the island—unless you fail.

"If you let someone else do this for you, it will haunt you and take away the peace you have found in these women who have chosen you as their protector. You know what to do and you are the man Moe has told me you are. I can see it in you and in Jamila's eyes. As my father once told me, 'Don't fuck about! Do what you must and be a man.' I am sorry to be blunt, but what happened to that child in Afghanistan was an accident of war. Now it is time to live your life and to make life better for other children...your child!"

The heat that had risen in me suddenly died at Walter's last word. My child! As I stood Walter came up, not knowing what to expect from me, but I put my arms around him and hugged him.

I said, "Thank you, Walter. I have been thinking of every way I could to avoid killing, but I know I would give my life for Mei and Jamila and my life would not keep them safe. When the time comes I will remember your father's words."

We sat back down and I poured us a brandy and we began going over the plan I had put together. We spent most of the night refining it until all was ready except how to get in and out.

Walter suggested I move *Tirak* to the island of Ono, which was separated from Kadavu Island by a narrow channel. Both islands, south of Viti Levu, were remote. There were a number of dive resorts and the only way in was by boat or seaplane. We would make the approach to our objective by speedboat and return the same way. *Tirak* would be guarded and prepared for an instant departure once we had returned. If all went according to plan, we would return before sunrise.

We would put the plan into action in three days' time. Walter and Luang would meet us when we arrived at Ono and stay with us until the mission was over. Jamila and Luang returned around three in the morning and they were all smiles.

As Walter and Luang left for shore Jamila said, "I really like her. I hope we can stay in touch."

I told her after the operation was over we would share a bond but, depending on the outcome, it might not be one we would want to bring up too often, but I liked Walter as well.

We left before dawn and even though I was tired I was excited to get our plan underway. Jamila stayed close to me as we sailed for Ono. It would take only a half day but midway I dropped *Tirak*'s sails. The seas were calm and the current pushed us toward our destination.

I brought the pistols and rifles on deck along with several boxes of ammunition. I wanted to let Jamila hear the sound and use each weapon to become familiar with them. I didn't know if she had ever seen these kinds of weapons before, much less used them. She said she had taken shooting lessons in the U.S. but only with a small handgun. I went over the action of each type and had her handle and dry-fire them.

She loaded several clips and showed only mild nervousness at handling them. When she fired the Glock22 for the first time she jumped at the noise and recoil but after a few shots she was coming close to the oranges I had thrown off the stern. She liked the PPK much better. It was a lighter weapon with much less recoil.

When we moved to the M4, she couldn't believe how quiet it was and it had less recoil than the Glock. She switched to fully automatic and emptied the clip with a smile. She shot up the ocean but learned that with the three-shot selector she could hit what she aimed at. I fired each weapon to check the sights. We killed a lot of fruit.

We cleaned the weapons and I tried to explain the adrenaline rush of the real thing and once again went over her part. She was to trail me and only when we had Mei would she leave and move toward our pickup point with Mei. She wasn't happy to leave me behind but she agreed with what I told her. I explained that any change in plan would put us all in danger and would distract me.

I let *Tirak* drift and we made love. I could feel the tension in Jamila and her release was strong and loud. I had to smile at this woman warrior who had claimed me as her own. She had courage and strength that would see her through most anything that came her way.

I found a secluded bay to anchor in close to the little town of Vabea. Ono Island was forested and coconut trees lined the coral sand beaches. The water was so clear it looked as though we could reach out and touch the white sandy bottom.

Jamila wanted to swim but was afraid it was too shallow to dive into. I laughed and showed her the depth gauge. There was twenty-two feet of water under our keel. She still jumped in feet first just to be safe. I threw a life-ring out with thirty feet of line in case the current took her too far and then joined her. The water was cool as it came up from the drop-off outside the reef and it was good to take a moment to let my mind empty as we floated in the current. After we took a freshwater shower we lay on the bed and with her head on my chest I fell into a deep, cleansing sleep.

I awoke just before sunset and heard voices and felt a difference in the way *Tirak* came up on her anchor road. I quickly dressed in a pair of shorts and went on deck to find Walter, Luang and two dark-skinned men sitting with Jamila, enjoying some lemonade.

Lying astern of *Tirak* was a beautiful black speedboat with four 250-horsepower Yamaha outboard engines. The boat was powder-black and had no shine at all. One of the men invited me onboard and started all four engines and let them idle. I could feel the power and need of the boat to go fast.

He shut down the engines and led me into the small forward cabin. There were three handheld AT4-CS HEDP rockets, two SAM-7's and few things I didn't recognize.

I asked the range of the boat and he smiled and said, "Flat out, three hundred miles, but it has a cruising range of over five hundred miles."

I asked about the paint and he told me it was a special radar-absorbing material. I was duly impressed. When I moved back to *Tirak* he stayed onboard and the other man joined him. With two bright white smiles and waves they unhooked, started the engines and moved on to a plane in only twenty feet, then rocketed away out of sight toward Kadavu. Walter said they would return for the operation and guard *Tirak* while we were away.

I asked who was paying for all this equipment and he just smiled and said, "You have done us a great service by exposing this organization. We feel it's the least we can do. That's an official quote. Moe said, 'Whatever it takes!'"

We put the tender into the water and motored off to the little village. It was not fancy but clean and most of the houses had thatched palm frond roofs. The coconut palms with their large pinnate leaves and bunched fruit lined the packed coral streets. The bird life was surprising. On many islands the native populations had been wiped out by imported predators, but here on Ono the Fantails, Honeyeaters and Velvet Fruit Doves were everywhere, along with free-range chickens.

I was surprised to see the number of tourists among the natives but after hearing a few conversations found that this was a popular dive resort area. We enjoyed a night of dining, dancing and companionship. I too was growing to like Walter and Luang more and more. Luang was bright and happy with a sense of fun about her. I asked where she had grown up and she told me she was from a tiny village in China just north of the Burmese border. She offered no more and I dropped my questions of her past. She danced with me and I could feel her strength as her lithe body moved under my hands.

I put my lips next to her ear and said, "Walter is a lucky man and it is good to know you both are on our side."

She brushed her belly against mine and gave me such a seductive smile that it put me at a loss for words.

She laughed and said, "Jamila is a lucky woman as well, Douglas. That was only a thank-you for doing what you are doing.

There are too many people in this world who don't care about the suffering. You have made a difference in your life and it's time for you to stop looking for the end and start living again."

I gave her a quick kiss on the lips but my voice was caught in my throat.

We moved back to the table.

Jamila looked at me with those dark, beautiful eyes and said, "Luang, I may have to throw some ice water on him to take the heat out of his eyes."

I blushed and Luang said, "I think you can think of better ways than ice water."

Everyone laughed and Walter stood, took Luang's hand and said, "It is time to put some fire in my eyes, young lady." And they moved to the dance floor.

The next day we relaxed, swam and laughed at the stories Walter told of his upbringing. I knew that we had made close friends and would enjoy future times together. At one point Luang nodded to Jamila and they removed their tops and dove into the water. I looked at Walter and told him I couldn't believe how uninhibited Jamila was becoming.

He laughed and said, "If she stays around Luang for long, she will surprise you more. Luang was like a closed flower when I found her but when she realized that she loved me she opened up to a beautiful blossom. I never in my life thought I would find such a woman as her but I am thankful every day that I did. You will soon feel the joys of family, Douglas, and I hope you will let us be a part of that joy."

"Nothing would please me more, Walter! I look forward to a long friendship and watching your family grow. I just wish Moe would settle down. I saw a side of him I had never imagined when we were with the families in the Cooks."

Walter said, "He will have a surprise when next you see him but it is his surprise so I will say no more."

That night as we lay in bed Jamila clung to me and I could feel her body move in nervous quivers. I felt wetness on my chest from her tears and asked her what she was thinking of.

"I've never done anything like this before. Do you think I will be all right?"

"Yes, my love. I will watch over you."

She said, "Douglas, you have so much to be responsible for and I don't want to add to it."

"Jamila, if you want to wait in the boat, it will be all right."

She gripped my arm and even in the dark I could feel her eyes blaze at me as she said, "I am going to get Mei and don't ask me that again."

She softened her grip and kissed my lips.

"I love you more than I ever thought I could or would love a man but this child... our child, whom I've never seen except in a picture, will not meet me in the boat. I want us to be a family and if I don't do this I could never forgive myself. All I ask of you is to watch over us and do what must be done to protect us. When this is over Mei and I will watch over you and bring you such joy you won't have time to think of the past. You are the cool, sweet water that nourishes my soul and I will drink from that water every day, my love. Your strength will carry me through this and in two days it will be over. Do not let the sands of the past cloud your vision, Douglas, because your future lies with us. Do you understand what I am asking of you?"

This was another warning that was coming from the woman I love. It was entirely in my hands to keep them safe without the threat that could follow us if I failed to do what must be done.

"I understand."

She relaxed and I soon felt her even breathing as she slept in my arms.

As I drifted off to sleep, the green eyes were waiting on me. The child looked at me, not in hate but with an even, cool look. I tried to speak but could not. Tears filled my eyes and I felt her touch as she moved to sit in my lap. She took my hand and placed it on her chest. I could not feel the wound that I had inflicted on her. She sat with her head on my chest for a long while listening to my heart beat.

She then stood before me and put her head on my shoulder and said, "Protect them. You have nothing to fear from me. I am returning to my home and will leave you to care for your family. It was not of your doing and I am well."

I awoke to a cool cloth wiping the sweat from my body. Jamila looked at me with worried eyes but when she saw the peace on my face she smiled and kissed me.

I said, "I love you, my Desert Flower. Do not worry."
Her eyes glistened and she nodded and kissed me long and sweet.

The hour had come. The speedboat rested alongside *Tirak* and the two men transferred all the equipment from *Tirak* to the boat. It was eighteen hundred hours and we planned on reaching the island at around twenty-three hundred. Walter and Luang would hold the boat in position, giving us protection, and be ready for a high speed retreat when we had Mei with us.

The cabin was crammed with equipment so we all sat in the hydraulically cushioned chairs as we moved out at forty miles per hour. The sea was smooth for the first hour and then we got into the rollers that moved on their long passage to land. Walter handled the boat expertly and kept our speed constant.

Chapter 19

An hour before we arrived, Jamila and I went below to change into our combat clothing. I wore a standard pack with Kevlar inserts. I carried the two Glocks, M4, hand grenades and remote explosives, along with two combat knives. I applied grease paint to my face but just enough to take the shine away and then I pulled a small plastic bottle of scented corn powder from my small pack and applied it to my chest and neck. The scent was distinctive and Jamila gave me a questioning look but said nothing.

Jamila wore her Kevlar vest against her skin and covered it with a loose black covering with a distinctively Arab cut. She also wore a black head wrap that allowed only her eyes to show. Those eyes had a look that made me glad she would be with me. If she was nervous, she hid it well. She had the PPK tucked in her clothing with a vest holster and a wicked looking curved blade strapped to her leg. She would carry the M4 with a short strap to free her hands if needed.

I heard the engine noise change and felt the boat decelerate. I wanted to say something but she thumped me on the chest with the bottom of her right fist and then touched her heart and kissed her lips.

She said, "Tonight, I am your partner and I will watch your back. We will not fail!"

I returned her salutation and we moved out of the cabin.

We were only a mile offshore and the boat was easing toward the island. I heard the four huge outboards being raised vertically to allow for shallow water. Luang whispered that there was a radar tower two hundred yards to our left and only one man patrolling. He had gone back to the radar shack. Any more patrols along the beach would be taken out by them. I knew the layout by heart and said we would deal with the radar first and then move straight into the compound.

I didn't expect to find more than five men and one woman within the compound.

As the boat's hull touched the coral sand we went off the bow and up to the tree line. I made sure Jamila locked and loaded both her weapons, with safeties on, before we made our way to the radar room. We moved through soft sand, avoiding the hard-packed paths that crisscrossed the living area.

When we were twenty feet out from the radar shack the door opened. I raised my rifle but hesitated. I felt pressure on my back as Jamila moved closer. The man did not look back so I took the shot. The soft splat of the weapon followed by the body dropping straight down put me back into my mission mindset. That first shot cleared my resolve to protect my family at any cost. I moved quickly to the room, opened the door and stepped in. It was deserted. I set two remote charges, went back out and moved the body to the other side of the building.

There was no fence around the compound but something about the paths made me stop and search the ground. I found a buried wire bundle and traced a lead to a seam in the path. I used a covered flashlight and opened it just enough to see a narrow strip array arranged at three-inch intervals and two feet in length. They were pressure strips and would alert anyone watching if someone walked on them.

There were three buildings tied together by covered walkways. One was large and three stories high. It had windows all around and must be where Mr. Wong had his living quarters. The other two buildings were single story with sealed windows. I could hear the gas generator running some distance off and the hum of air-conditioners pumping cool air into all the buildings.

There was a larger building separated from the rest with two large sliding doors at its front. This was the helicopter hangar. The compound area was lit with small walkway lights. I guessed that if an alarm was sounded then lights would come on everywhere.

I wanted to find Mei and get her and Jamila away before I made a search for the man but had to choose which building. We moved to the one-story buildings and were making our way to the rear when Jamila put her hand on me.

From the other small building two guards stepped out, escorting a young girl along the path. I could feel Jamila tense and I put my hand on hers and shook my head no. I waited, hoping they would bring the girl back to the other small building, but they turned toward the large building.

I waited until I saw one of the men reach into his shirt pocket and remove a card. I stepped out and ran toward them. Just as the man reached out to swipe the keycard I put a bullet in his head, followed by the same to the other man. Without stopping I moved to the child and put my hand over her mouth, stopping her from crying out. I turned her away from the two dead men, lifted her and ran back to where Jamila waited. She took the girl in her arms and looked at her. The child was dressed in a pure white silk robe that was so sheer it did nothing to hide her small form.

Jamila whispered, "Who are you?"

The small Asian girl looked at her with terror.

"Do you know Mei Yue?"

She gave no answer and was shivering. I spoke to her in the dialect of the man and asked the same question. She looked at me but no words would come.

Jamila pulled her hood off so the child could see her face and again she said, "We are here to help you. We will not hurt you."

She kissed her cheek and smoothed her hair. I repeated my question and the child shook her head no. I felt a crush of defeat and looked back at the door. If Mei wasn't here, killing those men would put her life in jeopardy. I ran back to the bodies and dragged them to the side of the house and then returned to the child.

Jamila asked, "What was the name that the old man's people called Mei?"

I said, "Jing Wei."

The little girl's head snapped around at that and she pointed at the building closest to us.

I asked her, "Is Jing Wei in there?"

The child nodded yes.

"Is she alone?"

The child said, "She stay with bad lady. Door lock but they let us play every day."

I told Jamila to take the girl to the side of the building and wait. She gave me a look of anger but did as I told her. I moved to the door and just before I swiped the keycard I heard a movement to my left and then a spurt from a rifle. I moved at a run, making a quick circle with my weapon switched to fully automatic and brought it to bear.

I saw a body lying only a few feet behind me and Jamila squatting with her weapon pointed at him. I quickly looked around and saw no one else. I knelt down and saw three large holes in his chest and then looked back at Jamila, who had a look of disbelief.

I moved to her and took her in my arms and said, "You saved my life and this little girl's as well."

She said, "I've never shot anyone before."

"Jamila, you did it to protect me and Mei. It will be all right. Can you keep watching my back?"

I felt her body relax and she said, "I can."

I kissed her and then hurried toward the door that would lead to Mei. I swiped the card and heard the click of the lock. As I opened the door I looked back quickly and saw Jamila dragging the body to the side of the building.

I entered a hallway with nightlights built in the wall. There were three closed doors spaced down the hallway, two on the left and one on the right. I moved to the right side doorway and put my ear to the door. I was about to try the doorknob when I heard a voice call out in Chinese from inside the room.

"Where is Ying? I am ready for her now!"

Another voice said, "Chong and he took her away over five minutes ago. I will check on her."

"If he touches her, I will skin him alive. She is ready to give me her power and she must be untouched."

"Yes, Mr. Wong. I will attend you in a moment."

I stood to the side of the doorway and an older woman burst out and into my arms. I clamped my hand over her mouth and gripped her body to squeeze the air from her lungs. She sank to the floor and I relaxed my grip, pulled my knife and held it to her throat. She took a couple of quick breaths and said in the dialect.

"Who are you?"

I said, "It is not important who I am, and if you want to live, it is important that you answer my questions without delay."

I let her turn her head and she gaped at me and said, "You are a white man! How do you speak our language?"

I touched her neck with the blade and said, "Where is Jing Wei?"

"Get out of here or I will call the guards!"

I moved the blade an inch and blood began to flow from the light wound.

"If I ask you again and get no answer, you will be dead. Where is Jing Wei?" In her terror, real or false, she pointed to the last door on the left. I lifted her and moved to the doorway.

"If an alarm goes off, I will separate your head and give it to the crabs."

I knew that keeping a body whole was important to many cultures and a promise of separating it would bring cooperation.

She touched a spot on the door frame and then opened the door. I moved her into the small bedroom and saw a child sleeping with her back to us.

My heart leaped as I recognized Mei's form and called out softly, "Mei Yue. Wake up, Little Bit; it's Papa."

She spun on the bed but before she could yell she saw the woman and a man with a knife. Mei even in her sleep-tousled state was beautiful to my eyes and I wanted to take her in my arms. I pushed the woman toward the wall and went to Mei's bed but she looked at me with terror in her eyes. She only saw a man with many weapons standing over her.

Then I watched her nose twitch as she smelled the corn powder and as recognition came she leaped into my arms. I tried to put her down but she clung to me like a second skin. I knew I had made a mistake using her name, the one no one knew. I turned to the woman and she was already moving through the doorway.

I dropped my knife, took three steps to the hallway, lifting my M4 as I moved. I moved the selector to single shot and fired a round into the woman's back. She dropped and blood spread across the carpeted floor.

I stepped back into the room and put Mei down. She was staring at me, not in horror but with pride.

In English she said, "I knew you would come and bring the dangerous man with you. Don't you worry; she was a very bad lady. Are we going now?"

I kissed her again and said, "I have never told you this in English: I love you, Mei Yue, and want you to be my daughter. Will you?"

"Yes! Yes! Yes! I love you, too, Papa. Now can we leave?"

"Yes!"

I retrieved my knife, lifted her and walked out of the building. I went around the corner and saw Jamila and the child waiting. I smiled and put Mei down. She turned to look at the other child and she ran into her arms. Mei calmed her with a few words and then turned to look at Jamila.

She looked for a moment and asked, "Are you Jamila?"

Jamila couldn't speak and tears flowed down her cheeks as she nodded.

"Do you love my papa?"

She nodded again.

Then Mei leaped into her arms and kissed her and clung to her as she said, "I knew you would."

I said, "It is time to go. Jamila, take... wait. Mei, are there any more children here?"

Mei said, "No. After he took..." She stopped and looked down at the ground and tears came to her eyes. She continued. "He was to take Lei Wue's power tonight, and then he would find another one. He has kept me here until he thought it was safe to move me. That gave me hope, because I knew you were searching for me, Papa."

My mind came to a sharp point and the need to kill took me over as I said, "Jamila, take them to the boat and wait. I won't be long."

She saw the look in my eyes and then turned and moved off without a word. Mei looked at me with pride and she waved. I turned to finish what we had come for.

I walked to the door of the large building and put a fresh clip in my rifle, swiped the card and entered. It was a lavish house. The rooms were filled with expensive Chinese art. The furniture was antique, with Mother-of-Pearl and silver inlaid in every piece.

Incense burned in golden bowls and lights were on in every room. I checked the lower floor and found no one.

As I started up the stairway, a large man that I recognized from the bar came out of a room, turned, saw me and started to cry out. I put two rounds in him— one in the chest and one in the head. As he dropped I heard movement from the same room he had exited and two more men stepped out. They were dead before they had a chance to turn.

I continued up the stairway and stepped into the room. There was a Mahjong table with four groups of tiles set up for players. I scanned the room, switched to three shot, and put a burst into a door I assumed was a bedroom. I heard hurried movement and switched to automatic and emptied the clip. I had my pistol out as I dropped the rifle onto its sling.

A man burst through the door and fired wildly with a large caliber pistol at the point I had been standing. I was now next to the bedroom door and stepped up behind him, put the pistol in the small of his back and fired. The pistol bucked hard and I followed the man down as he dropped to the floor. I fired another round that took off the front of his face. I stepped into the room and found it empty. I holstered the pistol, put a fresh clip in the M4 and moved out into the hallway.

I checked each room and in what looked like a ceremonial room with a golden framed dais with a soft mat and silk covers I found a door that was hidden in the design of the wall, slightly ajar. I looked around at the erotic silk artwork and framed rice paper art that lined the walls depicting couples engaged in sex in various positions. I knew this was where Mei had been brought.

My mind darkened with a building rage but at the same time took on the crystal clarity of a hunting animal. I moved to the doorway and entered a dimly lit spiral staircase that led down to the ground floor. I heard shuffling and moved quickly to the sound. I rounded a corner and saw a door that lead outside swinging closed. I went to the door but it was locked. I tried the keycard and nothing happened.

I ran to the entrance I had used earlier and moved out to the path. I listened to the night and caught the sound of running and heavy breathing moving away towards the beach. I followed the sound and saw the old man entering the radar building. I ran to the door and threw it open and saw him grabbing for a microphone to a transmitter. I switched to automatic and let a burst destroy the radio.

He spun and fell into the seat by the radio.

He held up his hands and spoke, "Who are you? I will make you a very rich man. There is no need for violence. We can..."

"Shut your mouth, Mr. Wong. There will be no deals tonight. I am Jing Wei's guardian and I have come to make sure you don't do this to any more children."

"Her guardian...? You are the white man who found her on the ocean. I want to thank you for what you did. I will make you very rich."

"I don't want your money, Mr. Wong."

He laughed and said, "Money can buy anything... Mr. Durian... Yes, now I remember your name. You know you can go anywhere and I will find you. Even if you kill me my men will find you and the new woman you have. Yes, I know all of this. Walk away now and take the girl. I have no more use for her. Walk away and you will live."

I spoke to him in his own dialect, "You think you have taken her power but she did not give it to you. Your men are all dead and no one will ever find you. You will die and I will scatter your body over the sea so that you will never have peace."

"How... How do you know my language?"

I heard a noise behind me and spun with the M4 ready. Jamila stepped through the door with her face wrapped and only those deadly eyes were showing. She walked over to the old man and slapped him, drawing blood from his lips.

She spoke one of the phrases I had taught her in the dialect. "You have harmed my daughter and you will never find peace. You name will be wiped from the book along with all of your family."

He tried to stand but she slapped him back into the chair.

She turned to me and said, "*Effendi*, I am here to serve if you require me."

"I need no help in this but you may have his family. Leave us."

With her right hand she kissed her lips and touched her heart and left.

The old man began to cry saying, "You can't do this. I only deflowered the girl, like I have done many times before. They all left here alive. You don't know who I am, how much power I have. This is a mistake."

I said, "Your power over children is gone."

I switched to single shot and fired three rounds, two in the chest and one in the head, and then I turned and walked out. Jamila was waiting with Mei. Mei ran to the building and looked in and then ran back and jumped into my arms.

She kissed me and said, "Papa, can we go home now? I want to get to know my new mama."

"Yes, my love, we will go home and be a family."

Walter pulled the boat one hundred yards offshore and nodded to me. I remote detonated the radar room and we watched a huge ball of flames rise up and consume the building. Walter fired one of the AT4-CS rockets and the house went up in flames. Luang used the second one to destroy the other buildings and then the third to destroy the large fuel tank, used for the generator and fuel for the helicopter. A great ball of fire rose up and engulfed the hangar.

We strapped in and Walter showed us what the boat was capable of. We ran for two hours at 80 mph and then he brought the boat to a stop. I helped him throw all the ordnance and containers over the side except the pistols.

He said, "It is twelve thousand feet deep here. The pistols are unregistered and are yours to keep. We will soon give you the paperwork necessary to carry them anywhere in the world. Now, let's have a bite to eat."

We spent the early morning drifting and letting Mei and Lei Wue get to know everyone. Luang held Lei the whole time and spoke to her quietly. I watched as Lei relaxed in her arms and just as the sun was rising she fell asleep but Luang would not put her down.

As the new day rose in triumph over the night, the sea reflected its rosy golden light in millions of faceted sparkles and the few puffy clouds in the west turned to bright pink banners that seemed to proclaim this special moment as one that would not be forgotten.

I sat with my arm around Jamila and Mei sat on each of our legs and looked from one to the other, making sure that this was real. We did not move until the heat of the sun told Walter it was time for us to return.

As we pulled alongside of *Tirak*, Mei jumped out and ran to her mast and hugged her as part of our family. Walter and Luang kissed and hugged us as they prepared to leave.

Walter said, "Will you return to the Cooks?"

"Yes. We have more friends to visit. Will you join us?"

He smiled and said, "I think we would enjoy that very much but we will have to see. You can be sure that we will meet again, my friend. The child will go with us and I...we will see that she is safe."

Mei spoke to Lei and she smiled and hugged Mei. She then ran and jumped into the arms of Luang. I thanked the two men who had watched over *Tirak* and they jumped in the boat with Walter, Luang and Lei.

Before Walter sped away he said, "Do not check in with the authorities in Hondo. Find an island to wait for someone to meet you."

"I know just the place. Tell Moe we will be with our friends. He will know." Walter opened up the speedboat and was out of sight in only a few moments.

I laughed and said, "I don't know if Walter could take life on a sailboat but I think we will see them in a month or so."

I stripped to my shorts and dove into the clear ocean water and was soon joined by two beautiful women. After our swim we went below and all fell into our bed in the aft cabin and were asleep in moments.

Chapter 20

Three hours later I raised the anchor, set the sails and moved out into the blue. Next stop, the Cook Islands. It was late afternoon and I hoisted the blue foresails and the reefed main and we sailed out the pass to the west of Ono. Once we were out of sight of land I called Mei and Jamila to help change the foresails. I trimmed the sails and *Tirak* jumped forward on a port tack with the wind abeam. She shivered in delight as the rollers passed under her.

I sat in the cockpit alone. The sun set and tall thunderheads far to the north lost the light at their base but the anvil and mist of clouds that flowed out from it turned a bright orange and held the color long after the sea darkened around us.

Jamila and Mei came on deck laden with a glorious meal of macaroni and cheese, with a bottle of hot sauce and beer and fruit juice.

Jamila said, "Mei made this as her welcome home dinner."

I smiled at my favorite simple fare and hugged Mei for knowing just what I wanted. We sat in the cockpit and ate, with little talk. I could see that there were things to be said so I just enjoyed the feeling of being with my family. I would not think of them as new because this was a daydream I had lived with for many years.

After the meal was cleared and they took their seats close to me, Mei began.

"Douglas, I have things to tell you about what happened while I was gone."

I held my hand up to stop her and reached for her, pulling her to my lap. I kissed her lips and said, "Mei, I want you to tell me anything you wish but before you do I want you to know something."

I looked into her face and could see apprehension and I looked at Jamila and saw only love for us both.

"I want you to always call me Papa because since I passed your test that is what I've been. You are my daughter and no one or anything can change that. You saved me, Mei, more than Jamila saved me. I love you, Little Bit, and if you ever doubt that, all you have to do is look in my eyes. When they took you away and before Jamila came I behaved very badly. I gave up hope. You came to me in a dream and told me to wake up and come for you but I only crawled back into my hole, feeling sorry for myself. Jamila and Moe changed that and made me see what I was missing in my life. I was missing you, Mei, and I couldn't go on without you. So whatever you have to tell me, know that it does not matter. You are mine and I am yours. I have a family and I need and want you both to watch over me. Will you do that?"

With glistening eyes Mei looked up at me and said, "Yes, Papa. I want that more than anything in the world. I will take care of you with Mama's help."

Jamila rushed to us and began to cry tears of joy. She looked at me and said, "Mei called me Mama."

Mei straightened up and began to tell us what had been done to her and, as much as I wanted to stop her, I knew I had to let her say the words to cleanse them from her.

She talked for an hour and in the end she said, "I have always dreamed of having a family that would let me be a part of them and help them. I dreamed that but never thought it would happen until I woke up on *Tirak* and Papa washed me and took care of me. Then I read the letter Mama wrote to you and I knew she was important and I wanted her to come and help me. You were a mess, Papa, but even then I could see the goodness that you tried to hide. I promise I will make you proud of me and make you happy. I love you, Papa, and I love you, Mama."

The tears started again and all I could say was, "You already make me happy and proud."

We spent the month's passage learning to be the family I had always dreamed of. Jamila and Mei entertained me and we all told stories of our lives before we became one. Jamila told Mei everything about how she met me and told her secrets of her life. They became mother and daughter with a mission to cover the hole I had lived in, forever. They allowed me my moments of solitude but the times grew shorter and shorter because I needed to have them close so I could reach out and touch them. *Tirak* was included in our time of discovery and she pranced and sang in tune with Mei's voice.

To my delight, Mei began to teach Jamila how to speak with a southern drawl. I would laugh at some of the expressions that came out of their mouths. They both spoke of a desire to go to the land I was raised in so they could try out their new dialect. I told them there would be many surprised folks when they heard them speak.

I don't know the exact time it happened but my feelings of depression and inadequacy left me and my daydreams found little time to come into my mind. I was in the place I had been waiting for as I sat by the door, waiting for someone to knock and open it. When it did open there were Mei and Jamila with their arms outstretched to me.

We sailed into the small lagoon on the island where our friends lived. They had many of their belongings packed but the houses were still in good shape. Mei wore her special Puka shell necklace and raced up the beach into the arms of others who loved her. That night the men told us they were ready to leave for a new island but everyone refused to leave until I had returned with my daughter and wife. They had been waiting for two weeks.

Jamila wore the mother's necklace that the women and girls had spent so much time making in preparation of our return. We had no gifts for them and the food supply was dismal after a month at sea but it did not take away from our happiness. We danced and talked into the night and then slept in one of the houses while the families slept in the other.

The next morning a sixty-foot motor yacht blasted into the lagoon and I was disappointed that our little paradise was to be spoiled by others. As I looked gloomily at the huge boat, it cut its engine and dropped anchor all in one motion. I thought this guy was a speed demon.

A great blast of the boat's horn brought everyone to the beach and then Walter's head popped up from the upper cockpit and he yelled, "I was hoping we wouldn't miss you, my friends."

The boat swung on its anchor until its stern was pointed at us and Luang and Lei Wue ran to the transom and waved. Mei Yue became so excited she ran into the water and started to swim towards the boat. I quickly jumped in the tender and picked her up and then sped toward the boat named *Hondo's Best*.

As we came alongside Mei leaped onto the yacht and flew into Lei's arms and then to Luang's. I tied the tender and climbed aboard just as Walter reached the afterdeck. We hugged and laughed. I was facing out towards the beach and Walter motioned with his head to turn around.

I turned and watched a dark-skinned woman ascending from below. She had a multicolored cloth wrapped neatly around her hair and it rose like an angled tower above her head and then she turned her eyes on me. I froze and then I felt Mei take my hand and stand as still as I was.

The woman had a face that spoke of royalty; high forehead and cheekbones, thin nose, pink lips upon a wide mouth and eyes that would stop anyone, man or woman, in their tracks and demand respect. Her skin was black as the darkest night but with a shine and texture of silk that looked so inviting.

She continued to ascend and I saw that her body was wrapped in a tribal sarong. She had full breasts and a thin, lithe, willowy body with long, shapely legs. I wanted to look at her body but her face drew me back and told me that I shouldn't stare.

I didn't know whether to bow, speak or just stand in awe and Mei was speechless as well. She stood before us looking with not unkind eyes and held her hand out for Mei to come to her. Mei took her hand and the woman, or should I say lady, bent down and kissed her cheek and whispered something to her. She then straightened up and stepped toward me. I stood frozen in her presence. She stood before me, looking me evenly in the eyes. She slowly wrapped her arms around me and kissed my lips and slowly opened her mouth to mine. It was such a shock as electricity ran through me, I didn't know what to do except return her kiss.

Just then a great bellow came from below, "Get your hands off my woman, infidel!"

I think I jumped three feet back and turned to see Moe standing there with the biggest grin I had ever seen.

I turned back to the woman and she too was smiling a warm, friendly smile as she unwrapped her turban and stepped towards me and said, "I'm sorry, Douglas. Moe made me do this. I think he wanted to impress you with his new toy."

"New toy...?"

"That would be me, but I am no toy and he is so sweet I have to indulge him in his games with his best friend."

"Best friend...?"

She laughed, making a sound as sweet as an angel and then kissed me once more before moving into Moe's waiting arms.

Moe said, "Hey, I said kiss him one time, baby."

"I couldn't stop myself, honey. Could I take him downstairs for a while?"

Moe spun to the smile of this beautiful woman and his anger flew from him.

He smiled and said, "Under no circumstances can you take him down below!" Moe turned to me and asked, "What do you think, Dougy?"

"Where did you find her and why is she with you?"

"Now, that's a question I ask myself every day, but she loves me...what can I say? She found me. Remember the strange email I told you about? Well, Sharika is the woman that insisted on meeting me. After our third date, we've been together every day since. I am one lucky man, Dougy, and I have Jamila to thank!"

He then turned to Mei and knelt down and said, "I was saving the best for last, sweetness. Come here and meet your Godfather."

Mei ran to him and he lifted her in his arms and kissed her and I could see his eyes glistening.

He said, "I never had a doubt about your papa getting you back, and to be here with you and all my friends is one of the most important days of my life. Dougy, go get everyone and bring them onboard."

"Not until I kiss these other beautiful women."

I turned to Luang and Lei and they rushed to me. It was as if we hadn't seen each other for years but it had only been a month.

I spoke to Lei in the dialect saying, "You are a beautiful child, Lei. Are you happy?"

She answered, "Yes, Uncle. I have been rescued and have a new family and it is truly like a dream. Thank you for rescuing me."

I kissed her again and nodded.

Mei, still in Moe's arms, asked, "Are you really gonna be my godfather?"

Moe laughed so hard I thought he would fall over.

He said, "Where did you learn to talk like that? You sound like you just got off a boat from Georgia."

"My Papa taught me to speak Southern. Do you like it?"

Moe said, "You're gonna be the hit of the parade, little darling. Yes, I like it very much!"

Everyone sat in the large salon, including the native families, and we waited for Moe to begin. He came from the stern stateroom with Sharika on his arm but she went to sit with Jamila and put Mei on her lap. Jamila and she were old friends from childhood. Sharika had left for her education very early and never returned but stayed in constant touch with Jamila. They had met and renewed their friendship when Jamila went to America to attend university and again after she left her duty behind.

Moe had a large valise that he placed on the table and he began. "This is a proud day in my life. I am to give gifts to my best friends that will ensure that they will be safe and protected by the greatest country in the world. Mei Yue, step forward."

Mei jumped up and moved to Moe. He presented her with a leather binder with documents inside.

He said, "Jamila, step forward."

Jamila came to him and she too was given a leather binder.

Moe said in a proud voice, "These documents are citizenship papers, passports, and birth registration for Mei."

Jamila and Mei opened their packets and held up the blue passports they found inside. Mei looked at the paperwork, suddenly began to cry and then ran to me. She showed me the birth certificate that named me as her father and Jamila as her mother. Her passport had the name Mei Yue Durian. Tears sprang to my eyes as I looked into the smiling face of Moe.

Everyone was excited and laughing but Moe stopped them with a shout and said, "We're not finished! Douglas and Jamila, step forward."

Jamila took my hand and we approached Moe. He handed me a gold-bound leather binder with a hug and kiss for us both. Jamila and I opened it together and looked at the certificate of marriage.

We looked into each other's eyes and I said, "I have waited for you all my life and I will love you every day of my life. You are the sweet water that gives me life and the sweet smell of Jasmine that fills my soul, Jamila Durian."

Jamila said, "I will love you and strive every day of my life to make you happy and at peace. You are the desert air that wraps me in your heat and the cool ocean water that soothes my soul, Douglas John Durian."

Moe reached in his pocket and handed two small boxes to me and one to Jamila. We opened them and found two gold wedding bands and an engagement ring. My hands shook as I placed the two rings on the woman of my dreams' left hand. Before everyone could rush in to congratulate us, Moe shouted once again.

"One last important thing and then we will have a party to remember. Lei Wue, step forward and bring Walter and Luang as well."

Walter and Luang each took one of Lei's hands and moved to Moe.

He stooped down and said in a soft voice but so everyone could hear, "Lei Wue, would you like to be a part of a family again, to have a mother and father to love you and take care of you?"

Lei looked up at Walter and Luang and then said to Moe, "I no want to leave Walter and Luang. I will stay and work for them. They will take care of me."

Moe gave her a stern look and said, "No. You must have parents. Take this and see who we have picked out as your parents. Go on now, open it."

Hesitantly Lei opened the leather-bound folder and to her great surprise she found a picture of her standing with Walter and Luang. She looked up at them and Luang lifted her.

Walter took them both in his arms and asked, "Lei, Luang and I want you to be our little girl and we promise to take care of you and make you happy. Will you be our daughter?"

Lei Wue cried and could only nod as we all rushed in to start the celebration.

Chapter 21

That night after the men unloaded supplies from the large yacht there was a party like that island had never seen. A large transom hatchway was opened and great slabs of the finest boat-building woods were offloaded, along with all the supplies. Moe explained that the motor and fittings would be delivered in a few days. This was only one of the many gifts he had brought for the islanders. They had no words of gratitude and Moe made it clear he would accept none. He also made it clear that they were our friends and we had gained much more from them than they had received.

We had eaten as much as we could and then the dancing and singing began. After Sharika's initial display of haunting beauty, she threw off her façade and showed her happiness at having found Moe and her new friends. She learned the foot dance quickly and several times the native women slapped their husbands playfully to break their eye contact. We all joined in and in the resilience of youth, Lei was bubbling as she and Mei showed us a traditional dance from China, where they had lived their old life.

During the evening Mei would often return to Jamila's and my side and cuddle. My joy was complete and as I felt the ethereal tendrils of my former self try to creep in, they would vanish when I saw my two women looking to me.

We spent two weeks on the island and we helped the men lay the keel and complete the basic hull of our friends' new boat. The mounts for the engine were set and we all helped lift the small diesel into its cradles and set the shaft. I watched Walter place a long-life tracking device into the boat and he said it was only to know how to find them when we returned. The women and children shared secrets and a constant laughter flowed among them.

The night before we were to leave there was another celebration. The families outdid themselves in the preparation of the expansive meal; seafood of seemly endless varieties and even a coconut tree was sacrificed to cut out the pulp from the heart of the tree to be used as a hearty vegetable. This was sometimes called *million dollar cabbage* since the tree had to be cut down to gather the tender fibers.

The women had planned the entertainment in the two weeks the men and boys worked constructing the boat and it began with all the women dressed in native sarongs performing the foot dance. Even those of us who still didn't grasp the intricacies felt the allure of the motionless bodies and the slow movement of the feet and the looks on their faces.

Each of the cultures represented put on a display of singing and dancing. Our native hosts sang several songs in their high-pitched melody that rose and fell in happiness and sadness. Then Mei and Lei complete with handmade costumes, danced and sang in the eastern style that left us wanting more. They strutted off to change back into their island wear to the applause of us all.

Jamila and Sharika, veiled, sang songs of the desert and life of their old world. It was at first a little unpleasant to our ears, but then as I listened I found myself captured by the hard desert life of olden times and made me want to know more of that world.

Moe got up and with the accompaniment of Walter's entertainment system on the boat, he sang 'Down on the Boardwalk'. His deep bass voice had us swaying to the tune. Next up Walter and Luang stood and put on a performance of Indian and Eastern Chinese songs and dance. The two types blended together in a lovely ballad of lost and found love. As they sat down, all eyes turned to me in expectation.

I felt the panic rise at the embarrassment I felt standing before a crowd but as I looked into the faces that surrounded me I had an epiphany. Until that very moment I had made minor attempts to stay on the outside edge of the camaraderie that had formed a bond between us. I suddenly had no fear of these friends. No matter how poor my singing would be, it would be enough for them. The word friend had taken on a new meaning for me.

I stood, moved to the center and sang one of the few songs I knew completely, 'Seven Bridges Road'. I had a tenor voice when I could bring it forth and tonight it came with a flutter and I put my heart into the song.

At the end there was silence but before I could turn to run Jamila said in a loud voice, "That shore was purty," in a perfect southern drawl.

Then everyone was clapping and laughing and Moe said, "Dougy, what have you done to these two beautiful exotic women?"

Mei jumped up and proudly said, "I taught Mama how to talk like that. When we go to the place Papa grew up we are gonna turn some heads!"

Moe laughed and said, "No doubt about that, Little Bit! Next thing you'll be screaming and yelling at a NASCAR race."

I could see the wheels turning and leaned down to Mei and said, "We'll be sure to see at least one of them, daughter."

I held my hand up for quiet and prepared myself for a speech that I needed to express to all of these wonderful people.

"I have to say that I am the luckiest, most blessed person that I know right now. Over these past few months I have come to see what a pitiful person I have been for all of my life. I have used very poor excuses to live my life outside the crowd, but there are people here that would not let go of me.

"These last two weeks, living here and working with old and new friends, I've realized that this is the life I will have from now on. I have thrown my self-pity into the sea and my soul is full and happy. I have an old friend who never lost hope in me. I have new friends that I know will always be so no matter the distances we travel. I have a daughter who saved my life and demanded things of me I didn't think I could deal with, but she was there to lend me her power, warmth and confidence. I love you, Mei Yue Durian.

"The woman I have loved for years has returned to me with a love that she stored up for all the time we were apart. She too saved my life. I love you, Jamila Durian. I have this to say to you both."

I put on my best Chinese accent, trying to imitate Mei, and said, "You must be very much big fool to save this life. In China, when you save a life, you are responsible for that life. Now I belong to you and you must protect me!"

Everyone laughed and I held up my hands to quiet them.

"I truly cannot understand why all of you had faith in me when I had none in myself but I love you all and there is a new

Douglas John Durian that stands before you and he is the happiest man in the world."

There was not a dry eye in the group that rushed me, lifted me up and ran to the water to throw me in and then join me. This was a good day!

The hour came when it was time to leave. We would sail to Hondo Island and take on supplies but this time Mei would arrive as our daughter and not hidden under her bunk. Sharika insisted on her and Moe sailing with us and we made room in the small starboard berth for them. As we sailed the calm sea *Tirak* clinked, jingled and hummed in contentment and she sliced the blue water, carrying her family towards a new home.

I sat with Jamila on the dog watch and enjoyed the night's stage above. The silver trail of the moon shown like it was embedded with diamonds as it pointed the way west. I kissed her and called her Mrs. Durian with complete satisfaction and she nestled close. I was beginning to caress her in a way that would lead to more when Mei joined us. She could see the heated glint in our eyes and only smiled.

She said, "Mama and Papa, I won't stay long but I have a question. Where are we going next?"

"Where do you want to go, Little Bit?"

"I would like to see America and where you grew up but only for a little while. I don't think I could be away from *Tirak* too long; I wouldn't want that."

"Then that is where we'll go! Afterwards, we will either find a home by the sea or just head out to see the world before you have to go to college."

Jamila said, "That's a wonderful idea but, Mei, wherever you go to school, it will be near the sea and we will be close by if you want us to be."

Mei kissed us and told us goodnight and sleepily went below.

Jamila removed her sarong and said, "I think it is time to work on that addition to our family, my love."

#

Another book for your reading pleasure by Dannie Hill.

Tyler Hill's Decision

A young adult adventure that everyone will enjoy reading!

On his first camping trip to the Appalachian Mountains Tyler is attacked by bears and he becomes hopelessly lost deep in the mountains.

He meets an old Cherokee man who helps him find his way home and at the same time teaches Tyler about the mountains and the Cherokee people.

This is a story of a young man's search for answers about his heritage and the decisions he makes.

An unbiased look at Native Americans and the Cherokee people!

Read about author Dannie C Hill and all his upcoming novels at:
http://smallmountainpub.com

Coming Soon

Outer World- Prairie

A Fantasy/Adventure

Two people meet out on the great expanse of the prairie. One is from Prairie and the other from another outer world. They fall in love and go on an adventure to help save their world and fight for their lives and their freedom.

They are pursued by an ancient enemy who wants to enslave or kill all the people of Prairie. They meet others and band together to fight and if necessary die for their world.

The enemy finds that their technology is useless on the outer worlds and they are forced to use weapons from their past. They are on Prairie, the most distant of the outer worlds, to find a mineral that will devastate their old foes and to enslave or exterminate the inferior people of these distant worlds.

The people of Prairie will fight and die before they give up their freedom and their home.

Note from the author:
I invite you to make a review of the books I have written at the site where you made your purchase. I would further invite you to let me know what you think of my books or any comments you wish to make at my website.
Thank you for reading.

Dannie C Hill